"It appears I am forced to employ other methods to exact payment."

Bethany's stomach gave a violent lurch as she realized, terror stricken, what this repugnant man meant. "You—you'll never get away with this," she stammered, less than convinced of the claim herself.

"We shall soon see what happens when Paulo learns that his latest lover is at my mercy. And if he doesn't consider your life worth nine million cruzeiros, you had better hope that your aunt does."

She felt the cold steel of the knife at her throat. "Where are you taking me?" she rasped.

"Do not trouble yourself about details. If fortune smiles, you need not stay away long. Otherwise, in time I am sure you will grow accustomed to perpetual darkness...."

ABOUT THE AUTHOR

Elaine Stirling has been a voracious reader for as long as she can remember, books being her refuge during frequent moves as a child. She lived in various parts of the United States, Mexico and South America, and grew up to find that wanderlust was as incurable as her passion to write. Elaine now lives in Toronto, Canada, with her two young sons and looks forward to the day when they can share her travel adventures.

UNSUSPECTED CONDUCT

ELAINE K. STIRLING

Harlequin Books

TORONTO • NEW YORK • LONDON
AMSTERDAM • PARIS • SYDNEY • HAMBURG
STOCKHOLM • ATHENS • TOKYO • MILAN

To David,
who, through it all,
never stopped believing

———————◆———————

Harlequin Intrigue edition published October 1985

ISBN 0-373-22028-6

Chapter One

Half an hour after Bethany had slogged through Boston's first blizzard of the season, her nose was still numb. She tapped the tip of it gingerly while thawing out at her desk and was relieved to feel a responding tingle. With any luck, the appendage wouldn't turn black and drop off during her breakfast meeting on the dumping of toxic wastes. The clients had been miffed enough to learn that their case was being handled by Burgess Grey's daughter instead of the noted senior attorney himself.

Added to the threat of frostbite were the brand-new, frightfully expensive leather boots lying in a heap by her desk, one heel askew from a nasty confrontation with cobblestones.

With a sigh, Bethany propped her elbows on the desk, chin in hands, and drummed her fingers on her cheekbones. Here she was, at thirty years of age, a tall, reasonably attractive blonde and a successful corporate attorney; yet all she had to look forward to that day was her edification on some vile bubbling green acid, the potential loss of her nose and a long limp home. Whatever happened to the glamour?

But Bethany's glum train of thought was interrupted by a buzz on the intercom. Hoping for a cancellation of the breakfast meeting, she pounded on the receiver. "Yes, Sarah?"

"Person-to-person call, Bethany, from Rio de Janeiro." Her secretary's attempt to sound blasé was far from successful.

"Rio?" Bethany repeated, her blue eyes widening as a series of thoughts ran through her mind. The only person she knew in Brazil was her aunt Zoe but she'd never known her aunt to call before, so it had to be something serious. However, one did not sit and ponder while the caller, footing the bill, waited, so Bethany depressed the flashing button. "Ms. Grey speaking."

"Bethany, darling! How terribly important you sound!"

There was no mistaking that wonderful, effusive voice. "Aunt Zoe, hello! What a surprise!" The connection was terrible, and Bethany had to shout. "Is everything all right? How are you? How's Uncle Sebastian?"

Instead of the response she anticipated—"We're fine, dear"—there was a crackling silence. Instinctively, Bethany tensed.

"But surely you knew?" came her aunt's puzzled voice.

"Knew? Knew what?"

"Sebastian died two weeks ago."

"Oh, my God, no," Bethany said, in those age-old words of denial that death always inspired. "I'm...I didn't...I'm so sorry, Aunt Zoe. I had no idea." Her mind grappled for explanations. How could she not have known? Zoe was her father's only sister.... That was it, of course—her father! But she would deal with that later. "Was it sudden?"

"Quite sudden, dear. His heart." A pause. "How odd; your name was included on the flowers—well, never mind. That's not why I'm calling."

"Is there anything I can do, Aunt Zoe?" Bethany asked, realizing as she uttered the words that people always asked this question but seldom meant it.

"Yes, darling, there is. You're the only one in the family I can trust—apart from my stepson, of course—and you have the expertise I require most desperately."

"You'd like legal advice?"

"Of sorts, and a shoulder to cry on."

"But how—"

"I'd like you to come to Rio." Aunt Zoe's flatly issued statement left little doubt that an immediate reply was expected.

"I see." Bethany riffled through the pages of her desk calendar, mentally fumbling with ways to rearrange her schedule over the next few weeks. Perhaps after Christmas...

"The tickets have been wired to the American Express office in Boston, dear; the flight leaves tomorrow night. I'm sorry it's such short notice, but—"

"Tomorrow night?" Bethany echoed in disbelief, even though everything she'd ever known about her impulsive aunt should have prepared her for this. "I'm not sure," she began, then stopped herself. Dammit! Here she was, one minute sanctimoniously offering her assistance and, in the very next breath, making excuses why it wouldn't be convenient. A death in the family was never convenient. All the more reason to help out if she could. "All right, Aunt Zoe, I'll be there. But I think I should warn you that what I know about Brazilian jurisprudence wouldn't fill a teaspoon, and legally I have no authority to advise you.''

''I understand perfectly, and don't worry. I shan't do anything to put your wonderful career in jeopardy. As for Brazilian law, there's nothing special to know. Sebastian's is just one large corporation, like any other large corporation.''

Bethany smiled. There was no point in expounding on the intricacies of the corporate world. Anything that wasn't made of clay or painted or soldered from scraps of metal was quite beyond Zoe's realm of interest. ''How long can I expect to be there, so I can juggle my schedule accordingly?''

''I should think two weeks will be plenty of time. That will give you a chance to get some sun. Now don't forget, darling, it's hotter than blazes down here right now, so people dress in practically nothing at all. Now I must run. Thanks a million, and we'll see you the day after tomorrow.'' The line was dead before Bethany could utter the second syllable of goodbye, but then, that was typical of her aunt Zoe.

Alone in the silence of her office, Bethany shed tears for Sebastian Andrade, the man who had made Zoe happy in her adopted Brazilian homeland. Bethany had met him only once, when he and Zoe visited Boston shortly after their honeymoon. They had brought along Sebastian's nine-year-old son from a previous marriage, but Bethany hadn't paid much attention to the skinny, doe-eyed boy. She had been much too enthralled, as twelve-year-old girls were wont to do, with Aunt Zoe's dashing, dark-haired husband, whose accent she found positively dreamy. She remembered gaping at Zoe's diamond—it had seemed as big as an ice cube—and wishing that she, too, could grow up and marry an international gem merchant as her aunt had done.

Zoe and Bethany shared the same birth date, so over the years it had become customary for Bethany's birthday gifts from her aunt to be a little more elaborate than those for her two older brothers. Her parents had often made known their disapproval of Zoe for her overindulgence, but such protestations had only served to fuel a little girl's imagination. Bethany used to dream that she had been kidnapped as an infant by the people now posing as her parents and that Zoe was really her mother. Not that she didn't love her mother and father; it was just that, by comparison, they seemed so...dull.

Forcing herself back to the present, Bethany swiveled her chair around and gazed out at the snow and ice that rode a bitter wind past the office window, nearly obliterating the grasshopper weathervane of Faneuil Hall and the dome of nearby Quincy Market. "Hotter than blazes" was sounding better by the minute; and come to think of it, she decided as she tugged the collar of her white silk blouse into place over a charcoal jacket, she wouldn't miss itchy woolen business suits, either. Not one little bit.

But there was still that matter of dumping toxic wastes, Bethany recalled with a shudder. She stood up, crammed a stack of files in a burgundy attaché case and left her office, shutting the door firmly behind her.

"I ASSUME you are now going to accuse me of buying up every available copy of the Boston *Globe* that day, not to mention *The Wall Street Journal.*"

Distinguished-looking, silver-haired Burgess Grey was responding to his daughter's suggestion that he had deliberately withheld the news of Uncle Sebastian's death.

"It was in the *Globe*?" Bethany asked, sinking a little farther into the oxblood Chippendale wing chair in her father's office. She had to hand it to him; he was an absolute master at deflecting blame.

"Of course, it was in the *Globe*," he muttered, peering over the half glasses he used for reading and for instilling fear into the hearts of his adversaries. "Your aunt was a Grey, and lest you forget, we are a fairly prominent family in this city. And then, of course," he added as an afterthought, "Sebastian Andrade owned the seventh-largest gemstone business in the world." Burgess Grey shook his head in the universal gesture of parental disappointment—the one that made Bethany feel like a six-year-old all over again. "How many times have your mother and I tried to impress upon you the importance of reading obituaries? One of these days, you're going to humiliate all of us by phoning a client—"

"I know, I know, and finding out he's been dead for five years," Bethany said, concluding one of the many lectures her father bestowed on her regularly. Just her luck to have missed the death notices that day. It was like those insidious dustballs that would pop up in her apartment whenever her mother visited, despite a solid week of intensive housecleaning beforehand. "Okay, so I missed reading about it. That still doesn't explain why neither you nor Mother mentioned it. I've been home for dinner twice in the past two weeks.

"Now, Bethany. Sebastian was Zoe's third husband. You can't expect us to make a big fuss when—

ever she outlives another one. The way she operates, I daresay she'll snatch up and survive two or three more hapless husbands before she's through." He made an appropriate cluck of the tongue. "The first one was the worst, that consumptive French poet—"

"Yes, Dad, I've heard her life story before." At least, she'd heard her father's jaded version of it. Bethany straightened up in her chair and gripped the armrests, bracing herself for the fireworks yet to come. "All I'm asking, Dad, is that next time there's a death or a divorce or anything remotely newsworthy, let me know, all right? In exchange, I promise to keep up on my obituaries." She gave him a smile meant to clear the field for the next battle.

Her father leveled steel-blue eyes at her for what seemed like hours. "Agreed. Now, why don't you tell me why the sudden interest in Sebastian."

She should have known he'd pick up on that. "Aunt Zoe called me this morning."

"What?" Crimson crept up his neck like mercury in a thermometer.

"She wants me to go down to Rio for a couple of weeks." Bethany had to struggle against an urge to dive beneath the chair. Her father's temper, at times, would explode and soon to descend on her like fallout.

"And pray tell, why?"

"She just. . . she needs someone from the family to be with her right now." It didn't seem wise to elaborate just yet.

Her father rose to his imposing height, his eyes burning with anger. "And how did you come to be chosen?"

Bethany swallowed hard. Maybe he already suspected ulterior motives. "Well, you know Zoe," she said a breezily as she could. "She's always thought of me as her . . . well, favorite." She nearly winced at how egotistical that sounded.

Burgess Grey snorted in disgust. "You foolish girl, you're still harboring childish, starry-eyed notions about that woman. By now you should realize that your only basis for having them is because of those tawdry gifts she always showered on you." He leaned over, planting one large hand on his desk and pointing at Bethany with the other. "Let me tell you something about your aunt. She tossed aside her family's good name years ago, and she's been trying to buy it back ever since. Well, money does not buy respectability, young lady. It never will!"

Bethany was willing to admit to the starry-eyed notions; maturity hadn't changed her opinion of Aunt Zoe a jot. She was less than convinced, however, that her aunt was trying to buy her way back into the Grey family's good graces. She suspected Zoe couldn't give two hoots about her fancy Beacon Hill heritage.

"I appreciate your opinion, Dad, but I'm still going to Rio."

"No, you're not."

"I already promised her I would."

Her father's jaw was working furiously. "Then write and tell her you've changed your mind."

"I can't do that, either." Defiance, even at thirty, still did not come easily; the words were sticking to her tongue like flypaper. "I'm flying out tomorrow evening."

"It's out of the question! I forbid it!"

Bethany blew out a long, slow breath, hoping her voice would not betray her. In case it did, she spoke softly.

"Look, Dad, I've been practicing law for six years now, and I haven't taken any time off except for a long weekend here and there. Are you forbidding me as a daughter . . . or as an employee?"

Burgess Grey's shoulders slumped a little, and the fire in his eyes receded. Bethany longed to shut her own eyes to the pain she had unwittingly caused him, but she knew she couldn't. There were some issues one simply could not back down on.

"What about the Daggart acquisition?" he asked. "Have you drawn up the documents?"

"I have."

"And the amalgamation you were working on?" She detected a thread of defeat in his words.

"The paperwork is done, and Steve has agreed to handle the closing," she answered, referring to another of the firm's junior partners. "You know how quiet it's been lately. I have nothing urgent coming up."

"Yes . . . well, it's that time of year," her father muttered, sitting down heavily. "What about Christmas? You know how your mother counts on everyone being home."

"Christmas is three weeks away. I'll be back by then." Bethany went around to the other side of her father's desk, leaned over and planted a kiss on his cheek. "Dad, don't go making too much of this trip. I can use the change of climate right now, and I promise to take Aunt Zoe with a grain of salt."

He looked up at his daughter. "Then promise me you won't be playing lady lawyer while you're down there. Sebastian's is probably in one hell of an uproar right now, and it wouldn't surprise me if Zoe were looking for some free legal advice."

Startled by her father's insightful remark, Bethany had to work at keeping her expression noncommittal. "Don't worry. I've already warned her about that." She gave him a reassuring smile as she walked toward the door. "By the time Christmas rolls around, we can both forget we ever had this conversation."

Burgess Grey stared long and hard at his daughter and sighed heavily. "I hope so, Bethany. I sincerely hope so."

THE BEST WAY to reclaim one's bearings, Bethany always found, was to seek out places where life was stripped to its basest elements—Filene's Basement, for example, where hundreds of women could be found hunting and gathering, engaged in the same survival ritual they had been performing for tens of thousands of years; except that nowadays they went in search of discount designer labels instead of roots and berries.

Bethany spent the next morning elbow-deep in bunks of clothing—winnowing summer tops, bathing suits, silk dresses and lingerie. When she emerged four hours later, exhausted but wonderfully renewed, she carried with her two shopping bags full of what she thought would fit Zoe's description of practically nothing at all. True, she had a closetful of perfectly acceptable summer clothing, but the ever-practical cutoffs and terry cloth were meant for Hyannis, not for exotic, sultry Rio de Janeiro. At least, that was how it seemed to Bethany.

With a bit of luck, she was able to wangle a last-minute appointment with her hairdresser to trim her short, swingy hair. She wore her thick, straight blond hair tapered, with bangs to soften the effect of her strong cheekbones and enhance her wide-set eyes, which she considered her best feature. Bethany had long ago become accustomed to having a face considered unique, not beautiful. Kinder people called her striking.

As for her figure, she was tall and leggy enough to get away with a few extra pounds, a decided disadvantage when it came to disciplining herself to diet or exercise. Nevertheless, with the right kind of bathing suit, she hardly had to suck in her tummy at all. Not bad for thirty.

By the time Bethany boarded the shuttle flight from Logan to Kennedy, the uncomfortable scene with her father was all but forgotten. It was only natural that, being the youngest child and only daughter, she would have to endure a more lingering growing-up period; there was nothing to do but squeak through.

The cabin of the 747 destined for Rio de Janeiro resembled the proverbial can of tightly packed sardines, although the jet's occupants had considerably more movement. There were Brazilian families with nannies, and more children than Bethany could count. All of them were talking at once and jamming the overhead racks with the latest appliances, until the harried flight attendants managed to impress upon them the consequences of transporting videocassette recorders above their heads. There were dozens of North American tourists, all of them with New Jersey accents and not one of them under age sixty. Bethany felt sorry for the businessmen who already looked exhausted as they tried to block out the bedlam by jamming their heads into postage-stamp-sized pillows and dreaming of double Scotches.

She looked down and made a swift assessment of her green linen slacks, camisole and loose silk jacket.

Feeling wonderfully relaxed and casual, she decided no one would ever mistake her for an attorney—and that suited her just fine.

So far, Bethany had been lucky. The plane was backing away from the passenger tunnel, and she still had the whole row of seats to herself. For a while, she had entertained the fantasy of some gorgeous prototype of Brazilian male sitting beside her, but then she quashed that idea in favor of a good night's sleep. On moving vehicles she had a tendency to nod off with her mouth hanging open, not one of her more appealing qualities.

The plane was moving slowly to the runway when Bethany noticed an overweight man in his late thirties bumbling down the aisle, a motley collection of photographic gear hanging every which way from his neck. Her amused curiosity turned to dismay when she realized he still hadn't taken a seat and was approaching her row. Sure enough, he stopped directly across from her, pulled out his boarding pass and checked it against the number above her head three times before he was satisfied. Then he peered at Bethany, showed her a mouthful of huge front teeth and said, "Hullo, there."

"Hi." Bethany had to duck quickly to avoid being hit in the head by the man's camera, which swung wildly as he lowered his girth into the narrow seat. When he did manage to sit down, he filled up a third of the empty seat between them.

"Cold enough for ya?" was his opening line.

Bethany gritted her teeth and smiled. "Sure is." She could easily throttle whoever coined that insipid phrase and its summer counterpart, "Hot enough for ya?'' but she doubted this man could appreciate her sentiments, so she looked out the window instead.

"What's a pretty little thing like you doing in a place like this?''

Bethany squeezed her eyes shut. *Why me?* "I'm going to visit relatives."

"Ya don't say. Well, I'll be darned. Great way to see the country, and it'll save you a pretty penny, know what I mean?'' Bethany turned to stare at him with something like awe; she'd never met a walking cliché before. Undeterred, the man held out a pudgy hand. "Elmer Fletcher, Poughkeepsie."

Oh, what the hell. Her curiosity was getting the better of her. "How do you do?'' she asked, shaking his hand. "I'm Bethany Grey, Boston. What brings you to Rio, Mr. Fletcher?''

"I'm a bird watcher."

"Really? How fascinating." Those three innocent words turned out to be Bethany's undoing. Elmer Fletcher mistook them as an invitation to launch into a detailed, animated soliloquy of his life. By the time a Brazilian sunrise appeared outside the window many, many hours later, Bethany knew more than she ever cared to know about Amazonian winged life. Now all she wanted—craved, in fact—was sleep.

AN ATTRACTIVE WOMAN wearing a flowing buttercup-yellow sundress stood waiting in the reception area of Rio's Galeão Airport. Her thick auburn hair was pulled back in a chignon, and her marvelous bone structure gave her the look of a woman in her early forties, instead of her actual age of nearly sixty.

"Aunt Zoe!" Bethany cried when she spotted her aunt. Having emerged from the Customs inspection with merely a cursory nod at her luggage but a long ogle at her body, Bethany was relieved to find a familiar face.

"Bethany darling!" Zoe's face lit up, and they rushed into each other's arms. "Just call me Zoe," her aunt whispered in the middle of their hug. "Otherwise people might think I'm older than you."

Bethany stepped back and held her aunt at arm's length. "Not by looking at you, they wouldn't. You're ravishing!"

"And you, dear, are a marvelous liar! But look at you...." Zoe exclaimed with initial exuberance until she moved in for a closer look. "You're so pale. You look as though you haven't slept in days. And what happened to your hair? You used to be so blond!"

Bethany broke into a laugh that, in her present state, bordered on giddiness. "It's wintertime in Boston, Zoe. Everyone looks like this." She hoisted one suitcase in each hand and left the carry-on bags for her aunt. "Although I will admit I'm a little behind on sleep. You would not believe the man I sat next to on the plane."

"You must tell me all about him," Zoe insisted as she led her staggering niece through the front doors of the terminal. "Don't worry, darling. By the time you go back home, you'll have an absolutely smashing tan, and that dishwater hair of yours will be spun gold." Zoe was nothing if not completely honest.

As she stepped outside, the force of the tropics hit Bethany like a full sponge. Steaming, scented, the air seemed to be of an altogether different composition from the thin, brittle atmosphere of Boston; it was like the difference between a raw potato and a luscious, juicy papaya. Bethany took a deep lungful of the fragrant air, and her whole body responded with a delicious tingle.

Zoe drove like a native, conquering mountain switchbacks in nothing lower than fourth gear, attempting to be the first car out of an intersection regardless of how much rubber she left behind, with frequent and prolonged use of the horn. All this she accomplished while regaling Bethany with anecdotes about life as an American in Brazil.

The city of Rio flowed like lava between the mountains, filling every crevice and niche with skyscrapers, monuments and spiraling highways. The mountains themselves seemed frozen in a geologic instant of upheaval. Monoliths of bare, thrusting granite, they rose harsh and unyielding and were, in a primeval way, beautiful. In places, time had softened their contours with a carpet of rich green forest but still had not conquered them. On the crest of one rugged mountain stood a statue of Christ the Redeemer, his arms outstretched above the city, his gaze eternally benevolent.

"I'm so pleased your flight arrived on time," Zoe said as they drove past what had to be the yacht club, with dozens of graceful ships moored in the bay. "It means you'll be able to see Paulo before he leaves for work."

"Paulo?" Bethany asked, vaguely recalling the name of Sebastian's son. "Your little stepson is working already?"

Zoe tossed her niece a bewildered look, narrowly avoiding a jaywalking fruit vendor in the process. "My dear, Paulo is six feet three and has charm that would melt an iceberg."

She parked the car in front of an elegant high rise on Copacabana Beach. Inside, the elevator whisked them to the penthouse apartment on the top floor. Zoe opened the door, inviting Bethany to step inside first, and there, passing by on his way to the kitchen, was the gorgeous prototype of Brazilian male that had failed to materialize on the plane.

Except, Bethany realized, when he stopped and turned to look at her that the fantasy had not done justice to the flashing dark eyes, the ready smile and the low rumble of a voice that could have been preceded by lightning when he said, "So this is Bethany."

The suitcase she held in each hand fell to the floor with an embarrassing thunk. "So you're Paulo," she returned lamely, trying desperately to match her memory to a skinny, doe-eyed nine-year-old with this tall, broad-shouldered, fully grown man. It was no use; there was little resemblance.

He had just come out of the shower, judging by his wet, springy, cocoa-brown curls and fresh, soapy scent. An amulet hung from a gold chain around his neck, nestling in the thick mat of dark hair on his chest. He wore nothing but a pair of navy soccer shorts, which amply displayed his long, lean and muscular body. Bethany forced herself to blink so as to sever the current of attraction that was making her stare as if she'd never seen a naked, or nearly naked, man in her life.

"I seem to remember you had eyes that were too large and too far apart, and you had a square face," Paulo said with a spontaneous, good-natured laugh.

Bethany gave him a rueful grin. "If you look closely, you'll see nothing has changed."

Although Paulo, on the other hand, had changed a great deal, his captivating features, now perfectly suited to a man in the prime of his youth, were the same ones that had overpowered his face as a child. His long-lashed, sable-brown eyes danced over her, self-assured, vibrant. The structure of his sun-bronzed face was firm, free of crags and worry lines, radiating the healthy glow of an athlete.

Bethany had never been attracted to a man's mouth—the men she knew usually had thin, grim-looking lips—but Paulo's mouth was worth noticing. It was broad and sensuous but totally manly, with a full lower lip that seemed made for slow, unhurried, languorous kisses.

"Perhaps you are right," Paulo said, jolting Bethany's frenzied mind back to more decent thoughts. "But now everything has come together in a most appealing way."

"What?" She couldn't remember what they'd been talking about.

"Your face."

"Oh, that," she replied, and blushed.

"There, you see?" Zoe exclaimed. "Didn't I tell you he was a charmer?" She went up to her stepson and perked up his curls with her fingers.

"Aren't you forgetting, Zoe? It's part of my job," he said with a grin, while Bethany's medium-sized ego deflated just a little. "Now if you ladies will excuse me," he said, nabbing a peach from a fruit bowl on the counter, "I have to get to work." He disappeared down the hall for a moment, then reappeared, wearing a striped soccer shirt over his shorts and holding a pair of running shoes in his hand. "Be sure to get plenty of rest today, Bethany."

"I beg your pardon?" Did she really look that bad?

"I am taking you tonight on a tour of Rio, and night tours can be exhausting." With a peck on the cheek for Zoe and a wink at Bethany, Paulo was out the door. His invitation, issued in a soft, rolling accent, lingered in Bethany's mind.

Convincing herself she had imagined his suggestive tones, Bethany decided to take stock of her surroundings. The living room was large, one wall made entirely of glass, with a balcony beyond, overlooking the white sandy arc of Copacabana. The walls were vanilla, the floors parqueted in exotic light woods. The painting, carvings and furniture were contemporary and so abstract in design that Bethany wasn't sure which chunk of carved brazilwood was meant for sitting. She finally opted for a low sofa of champagne leather, but as soon as she sat down, she realized it was a poor choice. The piece of furniture seemed to be wrapping itself insolently around her derriere, almost forcing her into a reclining position.

Passion pit, she sniffed, glancing about the room derisively.

"You must excuse the furnishings," Zoe told her, crossing the room with a swish of her dress. "As you may have noticed, the place reflects the predilections of its owner."

"This isn't your apartment?"

"Heavens, no," Zoe answered, reaching into a kitchen cupboard for a pair of ceramic coffee mugs. "Paulo bought this condominium himself last year. Sebastian and I—that is, I—live about three hundred miles north of here at our country home in Ouro Prêto." She stopped what she was doing, and her eyes took on a faraway look. "The house is near the emerald mines where Sebastian had gotten his start. He used to love taking walks in the early evening, reminiscing about the early days—on the rare occasions he could get away from the city, of course.''

"It sounds like a lovely, peaceful place," Bethany said.

Zoe wiped away a tear with a quietly indignant huff. "Yes. I'm sorry, I was rambling there for a moment. Have you had breakfast yet?"

Bethany shook her head. Actually, she was too exhausted to eat, but she was also too hungry to go straight to sleep. Wrestling herself from the clutches of the seductive sofa, Bethany got up and went to join her aunt at the kitchen counter.

"Does Paulo always dress like that for work?" It wasn't a particularly relevant question, but Bethany hoped Zoe would make allowances for her weariness after the long flight.

Her aunt was slicing crusty bread, and she smiled at the mention of her stepson. "You mean the soccer uniform? Paulo spends his mornings coaching kids, then work at Sebastian's in the afternoons and evenings. He earns enough in commissions to take a month or two off every winter."

"Commissions? Isn't he being groomed for management?"

"Not Paulo." Zoe stuck her head deep into the refrigerator, emerging a moment later clutching a carton of eggs. "He's never had any interest in taking over his father's business, much to Sebastian's dismay. The boy is perfectly happy selling gemstones to tourists, which is understandable when you get to know his personality."

Bethany enjoyed her breakfast of scrambled eggs, toast and coffee, despite the fact that her eyelids seemed to stay closed a little longer every time she blinked. Zoe sat across from her, drinking coffee, and watched in silence as Bethany ate.

"Would you prefer to rest before I tell you why I wanted you to come to Rio?" Zoe asked suddenly.

Bethany glanced up from her plate and saw how the morning sun emphasized the worry lines on Zoe's face. "You can tell me now," she replied gently.

Zoe looked immensely relieved. "Last week, Sebastian's will was read. I inherited the entire business—mines, showroom, everything."

"Nothing went to Paulo?"

"No, but that had been agreed upon between them years ago. Paulo was the beneficiary of a large insurance policy that was paid to him in full a few days ago."

"I see. Do you intend to run Sebastian's yourself?" Bethany asked, hoping her aunt wasn't looking for a few tidy tips on how to run a corporation.

Zoe raised an open hand to her chest in consternation. "Me? What on earth do I know about running a business? I can't balance a checkbook. Besides, Vlad left me enough money to get by quite nicely, and Sebastian never let me touch a cent of it." Vladimir had been Zoe's second husband.

"Then why did he leave the business to you?"

"I don't know...for me to sell it, I suppose. What else could he have done? I mean, it's not as though he expected to die."

"So you do plan to sell?"

"Yes, that's where you come in."

Perhaps, Bethany thought, it would have been better to wait until after she'd had some sleep. She was in no state to deal with such a delicate, almost impossible request. "Zoe, you know I have no competence in Brazilian law to advise you on a matter like this—"

"I realize that, dear, but do hear me out." Zoe drummed her fingers on the countertop in a sudden display of nervousness. "For the past year or so, there have been some rumors—nothing substantial, mind you—that my husband had dealings with some... unsavory characters.

A shiver skittered along Bethany's spine. "You don't mean...the mob...loan sharks?"

"No, no, nothing that serious, I'm sure," Zoe said, sounding anything but sure. "More likely, it was only the fringe element—hustlers, the people who grease bureaucratic palms, that sort of thing. It's not really so serious when you think about it, but—"

"Zoe, tell me exactly what it is you want me to do."

She gave an offhand wave. "All I want is for you to take a look at Sebastian's records—financial statements, contracts, agreements, whatever is on paper—and tell me if there's anything suspicious. You do that sort of thing all the time, don't you?"

Bethany gave a tired smile. "Not all the time. I've done company audits, of course, for a number of clients, but what you're asking is a job that should be done by a team of local accountants, not by a junior attorney from a foreign country."

"Yes, it must sound as if I'm hopelessly ill-informed, but you must understand that here a person can pay to obtain whatever results he wants. I'm not saying that most local professionals aren't honest—I'm sure they are—but as a particularly thickheaded American, I'm totally at their mercy. And I'm terrified of casting the slightest shadow on Sebastian's memory, if it turns out he did nothing wrong. You can't imagine the scandal there'd be. That's why I need someone I can trust implicitly, who can tell me what I'm up against before I proceed with the sale."

The tone of desperation in Zoe's voice weakened Bethany's resistance. "What about the language barrier?" she asked. "I don't know a word of Portuguese."

"Paulo will be helping you, and he knows a great deal about the business."

Bethany slid off the bar stool, swaying slightly. "All right, Zoe. I'll do what I can, but I'm not sure it'll be of any help."

Zoe reached across the counter and squeezed her niece's hand. "Thank you, darling. You've already been a help, just by being here." She turned and looked out the window above the sink. "There's just one more thing," she said, her voice oddly strained.

"What's that?" Bethany asked.

"You mustn't breathe a word about why you've come to Rio."

Chapter Two

Bethany regarded her aunt with confusion, and a disquieting feeling tugged at her. "Of course I won't, but why would you even worry about such a thing? I can't speak the language, I don't know a soul—"

"I'm not talking about while you're here," Zoe replied, arching an eyebrow.

"Oh, you mean Dad."

Zoe spread out her hands. "I'm not out to mislead anyone, darling, but I do feel that Sebastian's memory ought to be protected among the family as well. You understand, don't you?"

The unnamed sensation emerged with disturbing clarity from Bethany's sluggish mind. She felt like the rope in a long-standing tug-of-war. But since she was in no shape to weigh the consequences, it seemed wiser to placate Zoe. At this point, what harm could it do? She reached out and patted her aunt's arm. "Don't worry. It won't be the first secret I've kept from Dad for his own good."

Bethany was vaguely aware of having started her own little stockpile of lies: first, telling her father she wouldn't get involved with Sebastian's, then promising Zoe she'd stay quiet before she even knew what she was up against. But she wasn't really lying. She was just protecting people's feelings, trying to keep the waters calm, if only on the surface. That was the tried-and-true Grey method of doing things, wasn't it?

Besides, Zoe's request to keep her brother in the dark was not unreasonable, and Bethany had no intention of involving herself or anyone else in the family with the gemstone company's problems after her two weeks were up. Whatever she found—if she found anything—would be left for Zoe's attorneys and accountants to sort out. And if there were significant repercussions in the business world, her father could always read about it in the *Globe*, couldn't he? Quid pro quo.

Suddenly, Bethany wasn't feeling very well, and it must have shown on her face, for Zoe came around the counter, exclaiming, "Forgive me! Here I've been filling your head with dire reports, while you're about to collapse." She strode across the room and scooped up Bethany's bags. "Come on, let me show you to your room."

Grateful to be rescued from her melancholy thoughts, Bethany followed her aunt down the corridor to the guest room, where Zoe deposited the bags and gave her niece a firm hug.

"I can't thank you enough for coming to help Paulo and me out," Zoe said. "Just your being here makes me feel that everything will turn out right after all."

Bethany tried to ignore the churning feeling in her stomach and gave her aunt a weak grin. "Funny, that's not what Dad's clients say when they see me."

"Somehow, darling, that doesn't surprise me," Zoe answered with a grimace. "Now sleep well, and shout if you need anything." With that, she left the room, shutting the door behind her.

It felt good to be alone, if only for a little while. All she needed was sleep and she'd be able to see things more clearly after she had some rest. She looked around at the large, comfortable bedroom and peeked into the walk-in closet and the en suite bath. The furnishings were much more traditional than those in the living room—the rosewood bed, bureau and writing table were immediately recognizable as such—except for the abstract oil paintings, whose subject matter she couldn't identify. A huge potted palm occupied one entire corner of the bedroom, and the bedspread and drapes were of a crisp batik in vibrant purples and yellows, so that there was a primitive aura of the jungle in the room that somehow managed to put Bethany at ease.

Heaving the larger of the two suitcases onto the bed, she rummaged through her clothes and pulled out a mint-green lace nightgown and robe. She slipped out of her rumpled travel clothes and hung them up. Upon reflection, she decided that she had been letting her imagination get out of hand; Zoe was the kind of person who could wrest melodrama from a grocery list. Her entire life was one long *coup de théâtre*; in fact, Bethany suspected her aunt would be miserable if things simply went along in a humdrum, predictable manner. It was one of the reasons Zoe had never made a very good Grey—she was much too dramatic. This whole business about her late husband would probably just turn out to be one huge wild-goose chase.

As she donned her nightgown and crawled under the purple-and-white-striped sheets, Bethany mused that her own life was sadly overdue for a bit of adventure.

And there were certainly worse ways to find it than to be in Rio poking through the records of a near-legendary gemstone business, alongside the tall, dark and handsome Paulo Andrade. Yes, indeed...much worse ways. With that final scintillating thought, she fell fast asleep.

THE ROOM WAS DARK when Bethany awoke, and for a moment she couldn't remember where she was. But she quickly recognized her surroundings as she heard Aunt Zoe's slightly off-key contralto belting out an aria from *Carmen*. Bethany chuckled a little as she stretched her arms above her head and rotated her ankles, for she found her aunt's singing amusing; not so the discordant creaks and snaps emanating from her own tired body.

"Okay, that's it," Bethany muttered to herself, flicking on the bedside lamp and climbing out of bed. "No more excuses."

She pulled the drapes shut and launched into arm circles, the first warm-up in her sadly neglected exercise routine. In a few weeks, she'd have announced her annual New Year's shape-up resolution, anyway. Ignoring the reaction of her sluggish metabolism to this sudden upset in schedule, she gritted her teeth and resolutely began jogging in place.

By the time Bethany stepped out of the shower half an hour later, her nausea had passed. Why was it, she wondered, that everyone else in the world who exercised experienced runner's highs, developed increased stamina and acquired better eating and sleeping habits? Not she. She'd just as soon have gone back to bed for a week, or attack a batch of fudge. Maybe she actually had an allergy to physical exertion and would be forever doomed to lug around five extra pounds.

With a shrug of defeat, Bethany stepped into her new turquoise jumpsuit; it had narrow straps, a softly gathered waist and slim-fitting legs that ended just below the knee. Looking into the full-length mirror, she was thrilled by her transformation. The image that stared back at her seemed taller, slimmer, blonder and more bright-eyed than she was accustomed to seeing; apparently the feminine look suited her better than the tailored clothing she usually wore. She even found herself wondering whether Paulo would like it, but immediately dismissed the thought.

Paulo wasn't there when Bethany entered the living room, and she deliberately ignored her prickle of disappointment—a far cry from the time she had tried to lose him in the park near her home in Boston so she could play with her girlfriends.

Zoe was at the dining-room table arranging a mass of bright tropical blooms in a ceramic vase. "Sleep well, dear?" she asked.

"Like a log, thanks," Bethany answered, and went over to sniff the flowers. "Mmm, they're lovely."

"Aren't they, though? They're from a wonderful little flower stall just around the corner. I adore living in a place where one can buy flowers outdoors all year round." Zoe wrinkled her aristocratic nose. "Was it dreadfully snowy in Boston when you left?"

Bethany tapped her own nose protectively. "Don't remind me, please." She went to the balcony doors, slid them open and stepped out into the balmy night air. "Is Paulo still working?" she asked casually, wondering why she was dwelling on him so much. He was a sweet fellow, but nearly a decade younger than anyone she'd even spoken to in years. Her business associations rarely brought her into contact with someone close to her own age.

"No, he's doing something or other at the soccer club. He called earlier to say he'd be home around ten and to go ahead and eat without him."

Bethany came back inside. "Did he mention our...tour?" she asked, brushing nonexistent crumbs from the table.

"No, but I'm sure it's still on. Paulo wouldn't forget a thing like that."

"Where do you think we'll go?" Only seventeen more questions to make it an even twenty, Bethany thought with acute self-annoyance.

"I have no idea, dear, but it won't be cathedrals or museums. *Cariocas* aren't much for dried bones and Byzantine arches." Zoe stepped back to assess the arrangement and nodded her tacit approval. "Would you mind terribly if we ate out this evening? I didn't get a chance to stock Paulo's refrigerator, and I can't think of a thing to make with wheat germ, yogurt and limp celery."

Bethany couldn't think of a thing she'd rather do.

THE RESTAURANT ZOE CHOSE was one of many sidewalk cafés along the Avenida Atlantica, directly across from the beach. The place was buzzing with activity. Some people were dining and others were nursing their drinks while engaged in highly animated discussions. A street vendor hawked gaudily painted marionettes, and at a nearby table a couple of guitarists and a flute player were holding an impromptu jam session.

After the waiter had taken their order, Bethany sipped her beer and watched the constant parade of people passing by their table. Young lovers strolled by in a sort of arm-and-hip lock that Bethany imagined required no small amount of coordination, stopping midpace, without concern, to engage in fairly passionate kissing every once in a while. Even more remarkable were the old men, most of whom looked American or European, with shiny freckled pates, knobby knees and hollow chests, linked arm in arm with the most gorgeous café au lait Brazilian women, none of whom could have been a day over twenty-five.

"So this is where old millionaires come to die," Bethany said in an aside to Zoe.

"Or to live," her aunt replied with a laugh. "Depends on how you look at it." She ran a finger around the rim of her glass, and her expression grew wistful. "I wonder whether Sebastian would have done something like that if he'd outlived me. Or do Brazilian men find Miami Beach more alluring?"

Bethany touched her aunt's arm. "I'm sorry, Zoe. I didn't mean to resurrect painful memories."

"Nonsense. I love talking about Sebastian. It makes me feel closer to him."

Just then, their waiter arrived with the largest pizza Bethany had ever seen, smothered with every topping known to man. She whispered to Zoe, "Are we inviting all the good-looking, unattached guys at the other tables to our party? Is that why you ordered this monstrosity?"

"I hope not," a deep, familiar voice answered from behind. "There's barely enough for the three of us."

Bethany spun around and focused on a pair of lean, long legs encased in black rugby pants. Her glance ran up the male torso, past an open-collared white knit shirt to a warm smile and even warmer eyes. "Paulo! I didn't hear you come up behind me."

He flicked a strand of hair playfully from her cheek. "You were too busy eyeing the other men." With one hand, he swung a chair around from another table and placed it between the two women. "Besides," he added with a wink at his stepmother, "soccer players are light on their feet, aren't they, Zoe?"

"You weren't always that way, my dear," Zoe answered with a laugh. "I thought you'd track us down in time for dinner. Have some pizza."

Paulo held out his hand in Zoe's direction. "See this woman, Bethany? My guardian angel." He dove into the pizza, while Zoe groaned in mock embarrassment, though she was clearly delighted by the praise.

As they ate, Bethany realized that although she had been having a perfectly lovely time with her aunt, Paulo's arrival had added an extra sparkle to the evening. She could see it in Zoe's eyes, and she felt the change in her own mood. He had a natural way with people, and she wondered whether it was his engaging, easygoing manner or, perhaps, some inner facet of his personality that was responsible for his charm.

That he was naturally gregarious there was little doubt, but judging from the festive atmosphere around them, that seemed to be a national trait. And while Paulo obviously enjoyed an advantaged position in life, he seemed totally unaffected by it. There was nothing world-weary in the set of his shoulders, no lines of tension marred his face, no gleam of cynicism was reflected in his dark eyes. His outlook seemed as candid and as trusting as that of a child.

Bethany tried to think back to her law school days when her male friends had been Paulo's age. All of them, it seemed, had either been zealously committed to hopeless causes, or were the type who drove themselves relentlessly to become stolid professionals, with ulcers and broken marriages. But then, she'd never associated much with athletic men and had no idea whether the "all brawn, no brain" cliché had merit. Perhaps it did. Hadn't Zoe hinted that Bethany would understand Paulo's lack of ambition once she got to know him better? That was it, of course! Paulo was happy because he was just a simple kind of guy.

Immensely pleased with her astute deduction, Bethany sat back while Paulo recounted details of the morning's soccer match with the kids. Men like Paulo were comfortably nonthreatening. A woman could accept her natural physical attraction as a simple bio logical response, without worrying about entering any complicated psychological entanglements—a feeling comparable, she supposed, to men's fascination with centerfolds.

When only a limp pepper and a cold mushroom were left on the pizza platter, Paulo turned to Bethany and said, "Are you ready for your tour?"

"Sure," she said breezily, preparing herself for a nocturnal view of the stadium or a visit to the locker where he stored his equipment.

"What about you, Zoe?" Paulo asked. "Are you sure you don't want to come with us?"

Zoe threw her stepson a droll look, and Bethany was shocked to find herself hoping her aunt wouldn't accept. What an ungrateful reaction—just as unforgivable as the sense of relief she felt when Zoe declined. "I'm going to stay right here, finish my coffee, then go straight to bed. I have a long drive ahead of me tomorrow." Zoe waved them away. "Now be off with you, and have fun!"

"My car is parked a few blocks from here," Paulo told Bethany as they left the café. "You don't mind a little walk, do you?"

Paulo's little walk, Bethany soon discovered, was more like a seven-league stride, further complicated by the fact that the beautiful mosaic sidewalks, so scrupulously washed, were slippery when wet and, in some places, had pieces missing. After Bethany executed a particularly ungraceful stumble, Paulo realized her predicament and slowed his pace. He also took her hand, which not only put her at ease but made her feel all warm and trembly. *It's all right,* she told herself, *nothing to fret about.* Just a little chemistry caused, no doubt, by the way he had taken her hand—not by overlapping palms, but with his fingers linked between hers. Bethany thought of changing the position or letting go altogether, but she didn't want Paulo to think his touch was having some special effect on her. Besides, she rather liked holding hands with him.

"Is Zoe driving to her country home tomorrow?" Bethany asked, anxious to divert him with a bit of chatter.

"Yes, right after lunch."

"I thought she'd want to stay around while I did the audit."

He looked down at her with an unreadable expression. "We have telephones. If you find something, you can call her."

Was Bethany imagining the derisive tone in his voice? It was hard to tell because his English, though impeccable, bore the sliding cadences of Portuguese, with inflections that could not easily be interpreted.

Suddenly they turned off the main boulevard to a narrow side street illuminated only by the security lights from small shops. As they passed by a clothing store, Bethany noticed a linen cloth spread on the sidewalk as if for a picnic. She slowed her pace for a closer look. Arranged on the cloth were a full bottle of rum, two unsmoked cigars, a bowl of popcorn and a pair of flickering candles. Meager fare for a picnic, she thought, and less than ideal surroundings. "Look at that, Paulo. What is it?"

He gave it barely a passing glance. "It's an offering to Exú," he said, pulling her reluctantly behind him.

"Really? Who's Exú?" she asked brightly, imagining a harmless custom akin to setting out jack-o'-lanterns.

"The devil."

A cold chill ran down her spine. If he had said, "Some god," or, "An evil spirit," she might not have given it another thought. But...*the devil*! Somehow that sounded to her like a reference to a tangible incarnation. "Who put it there?" asked Bethany, craning her neck to get one final glimpse of the offering, but it was already gone from sight.

"How the hell do I know who put it there?" Paulo snapped. "There are thousands in this city who practice *umbanda*. Whoever did it wants a change in fortune or a cure for a sick relative, and he will probably also attend Sunday mass just to make sure all the forces will be working in his behalf."

They came to Paulo's red vintage TR-7, and he opened the door to let Bethany in. He walked around to the other side, opened his door and slid in beside her. Bethany waited until he had turned the key in the ignition. "Do you believe in it?" she asked.

"In what?" He was looking over his shoulder and backing the car slowly.

"Umbanda," she said, nearly cringing at the feel of the strange word on her tongue.

It seemed that Paulo's jaw tightened a little. "No, Bethany, I do not believe in *umbanda*." Then with a quick, efficient twist of the wheel, he pulled the car out of the impossibly tight spot and drove out onto the road.

Much to Bethany's surprise, they did not drive to the soccer stadium or the locker rooms, but to the adjacent beach of Ipanema. Here, as in Copacabana, the sand and water were taken over by the clubs and restaurants at night.

Paulo brought her to a place just off the beachfront avenue. It looked like a private villa, whitewashed, with a red tile roof and high, vine-covered walls. The street itself was quiet, but music and laughter drifted from behind the walls of the club.

"This isn't a cathedral or museum, is it?" Bethany teased as they went through an iron gate and along a flagstone path.

"Not exactly," Paulo admitted, his mood visibly lightened. "But I think you'll like it."

The front door of the club, which had no name visibly posted, was guarded by two fierce-looking giants. Inside, the small rooms were steamy and densely packed with a young, well-dressed and obviously affluent crowd. From the profusion of red-and-black-striped shirts, Bethany surmised that this was the private domain of a particular soccer club.

At one end of the first room was a bar manned by a tall, lanky fellow with a gold earring and bandanna. Where there was room to stand, people were lined up shoulder to shoulder, four deep; the tables, built to accommodate two, somehow managed to seat six apiece.

All the women, nearly without exception, were beautiful, displaying varying degrees of bare shoulder, back and cleavage. The ambience was at once overwhelming, hypnotic and utterly seductive. Bethany felt herself meld into the mood as if she'd simply left her inhibitions at the front door.

Everyone was touching someone, somewhere—not in overt seduction, but as a seemingly natural extension of human communication, the gestures picking up where words left off. As Paulo and Bethany moved through the crowd, they were caught up in it like in a current. People greeted Paulo as though they hadn't seen him for months, and Bethany was not regarded as a stranger, but welcomed as a friend. Women kissed her cheek and men took her hand while murmuring charming greetings in Portuguese. Actually, for all she knew, they might have been insulting her, but they did it beautifully. Bethany felt marvelous being cast into this totally alien culture. She glanced up at Paulo, and his face seemed to radiate a certain pride. When his arm slipped around her waist, she leaned into him comfortably.

They came to a table where two empty chairs were miraculously conjured up, and they sat down. Paulo knew everyone at the table, and the greetings, as usual, were hearty.

"Would you like me to order for you?" he asked Bethany, speaking close to her ear over the din. She nodded, and he placed an order with a waiter who had materialized from the crowd.

Two particularly handsome soccer players—one dark and bearded, the other blond and rugged—from a nearby table managed to engage Paulo in what had to be a replay of their latest scrimmage. Their rapid-fire Portuguese was punctuated by wide sweeps of the arm, with the ball of one hand smashing into the palm of the other, and they even demonstrated their footwork, despite the fact that there was little enough room to stand, let alone pretend to play ball. When the drinks arrived, Paulo excused himself from the conversation and turned his attention to Bethany. He handed her a glass with a lovely-looking fruity concoction and took the beer for himself.

"It looks delicious," said Bethany, holding up her glass. "What is it?"

"*Batida*. It's full of vitamin C."

"Really? And what else?" she asked.

She had already taken a sip by the time Paulo said, "Cane liquor."

It was too late. Bethany's mouth was filled with a fiery vapor that curled its way into every crest and hollow, then coiled down her throat like a phantom serpent. An instant later, the sensation was gone, replaced by a pleasant feeling of lethargy and a lingering taste of fruit. "Ooh," she remarked, a little breathless, "that's nice."

"Glad you like it," Paulo replied, and sipped his beer.

"Tell me, Paulo," Bethany said, propping an elbow on the table and leaning her chin against her hand, "how can someone play soccer, coach soccer and talk soccer every day of the year and not go crazy?"

Paulo treated her to an engaging grin. "Isn't there anything in the world you love doing so much that you would gladly do it all day, every day?"

"Not that I can think of." Bethany picked up her glass and brought it to her lips. If he'd been more complex, he'd have anticipated her answer to that one.

"How about making love?" he asked.

Bethany's glass clunked against her lower teeth, a gaffe mercifully unnoticed by anyone else. After a stunned moment or two, she realized Paulo had merely been making an analogy, not issuing an invitation. "Uh...I don't think I'd care to..." she managed to gasp. "Where I come from, we do everything in moderation, not like...in some other places."

"Now, Bethany, you must not generalize about people. Brazil is a large country, just as yours is, and there are only two groups of Brazilians who are known to do things to excess."

Bethany stared at him, wide-eyed. If she hadn't known better, she'd have sworn he was about to launch into a sociological discussion, and jocks weren't supposed to be able to do that. "Who are they?" she muttered, feeling the foundations of her theory start to crumble.

Paulo took a long drink from his mug and leaned across the table. Their knees were touching, which had nothing to do with anything, Bethany tried to convince herself.

"First, there are the *paulistas*," he said, "from São Paulo. They are addicted to work."

"I see," Bethany answered. That wasn't so profound. "And the other group?"

"The *cariocas* of Rio; we dedicate ourselves to the pursuit of pleasure."

Bethany sat up and folded her arms, moving her leg out of reach at the same time. Physical contact tended to distract her, and she felt that he was not taking their conversation seriously—proof that Paulo, though cute, was not much of an intellectual. "Sounds counterproductive to me," she said with a sniff.

"Not at all. You see, the *carioca* actually works very hard, because he knows work is unavoidable, but all the time his heart is elsewhere."

Bethany studied him hard. No, he wasn't waxing philosophical; he was just spouting clichés. She issued a soft challenge. "How does a *carioca* do that?"

Paulo lifted his hands, palms up. "Simple. Imagine for a moment that you sew buttons in a small shop in Rio. Rather than waste time complaining about your job, you think about the attractive man you saw on the beach. You imagine yourself meeting him. He rubs coconut oil on your body." Paulo leaned forward and gestured to emphasize his words. "You spend the day together, the evening dining and dancing at La Tour, and the night making rapturous love in his bed. You see? You have put in a full day's work with a smile on your face, while your heart was elsewhere."

Bethany was unusually slow with a retort; her imagination was still grappling with Paulo's beach fantasy. So he had a clever way with words; he was obviously a salesman. Finally an appropriate rejoinder limped across her mind. "Yes, Paulo, but with an attitude like that, I would be destined to sew buttons for the rest of my life."

"Instead of what?" he countered.

"Well, uh, aspiring to own the shop, for example."

"Or perhaps a chain of shops, and then an international franchise?"

Bethany shrugged. "Sure, I guess so. What's wrong with that?"

Paulo stiffened, and his eyes grew wary. The hand that gripped his beer mug turned white with tension. "My father started thirty years ago with nothing but a single overworked emerald mine. When he died, Sebastian's was the seventh-largest jewelry business in the world. But he would not rest until he surpassed H. Stern, and even DeBeers. He killed himself trying. Tell me," he said bitterly, "what is the sense in that?"

Paulo's pain slashed through her, and Bethany realized how totally mistaken she'd been about him. He was intelligent, he was perceptive...and he was hurting. They were no longer just matching wits in this conversation. "You win," she said quietly. "There is no sense in that."

Paulo ordered another beer; then he said, "Give me your hand."

"I beg your pardon?"

"Your hand," he repeated, taking hold of Bethany's in his own. With head bent, he examined her fingers, tracing each one with an unhurried fingertip. His touch was featherlight, gossamer, yet Bethany felt every cell of her skin come alive.

"What are you doing?" she rasped.

"What I do every day. I know how to look at a woman and tell her what kind of gemstone will bring out the sparkle in her eyes, or warm her skin tone, or make her feel young and beautiful again."

Bethany gazed, dumbfounded, at her captive hand. "You can do all that just by looking at a woman?"

The glance he gave her was tinged with irony. "I must talk to her as well, but of course, you and I have already been talking."

A flood of self-consciousness turned her face tomato-red. Had he really been sizing her up all the time she was evaluating him? She must have come across like an idiot, she thought helplessly. Well, then, she'd have to use a little levity to throw him off. "I'll bet I'm just right for a whopping twenty-five-karat emerald, right?"

"Never," Paulo said without the slightest hesitation. "Even if you were to lay the cash on the table, I would do everything in my power to dissuade you."

"Why?"

He looked up. "Because an emerald would compete with your coloring, instead of enhance it. And you are not the kind of woman who wears jewelry to impress others with its cost."

"All right, then," she said, amazed. "What would you suggest?"

Paulo took his time and didn't let go of her hand. "Your fingers are long and slender; you would wear a marquise cut well. For your fair skin, an aquamarine in a simple gold setting, and because you're tall, the stone should be no smaller than eight karats."

He was quite remarkable. Bethany felt herself being drawn by his charm like a fly to a web. And although he wasn't holding her fingers tightly, she felt powerless to pull away. "What color aquamarine?" she managed to ask.

"Ah, yes, a very special shade." His eyes caressed her face. "Can you picture the color of a whitecap on the crest of a wave?"

Bethany thought hard, but her abysmal lack of imagination defeated her. "White?" she offered weakly.

The wilting look Paulo gave her was probably not one he used on real clients. "It's neither white nor blue, but something in between."

"Oh, I guess you're right."

"Now, imagine that same color at night, with moonlight reflecting off it."

All of this personal attention was turning Bethany to jelly. Paulo's customers didn't have a chance. "Okay, I think I'm beginning to see what you mean."

"An iridescent silver blue." He reached out and slid the back of his finger along her cheek. "It's the same color as the flecks in your eyes when you smile."

Bethany's heart slammed against her chest and then began to race madly. Her eyes were forged to Paulo's fathomless brown pair, and her mouth was rendered hopelessly bereft of speech. She didn't care if he never let go of her hand.

But then a small part of her mind detached itself, reminding her that while he was very good at his job, that's all it had been: a demonstration of his professional capabilities. Bethany pulled her hand away and imposed a coy smile on her numb face. "Paulo, if you always put that much effort and dedication into your job, there's no way you could be fantasizing about women on the beach. You're just as addicted to work as the *paulistas*."

He stared at her a moment, then threw his head back and laughed heartily. "Excellent, Bethany! You have succeeded, as a well-trained attorney should, in turning my words around and using them against me."

Bethany breathed a ragged sigh, inclining her head in a mock bow. "I'm glad you're impressed," she said, relieved that a shred or two of her dignity had been salvaged, yet feeling guilty about having harbored such outrageously condescending thoughts about him earlier.

"You are absolutely right, Bethany," Paulo acceded, holding up his drink in a toast. "I am especially fortunate in that I have three things I would gladly do every day, all day."

Bethany looked at him, puzzled. "Play soccer, sell gemstones... What's the third?"

"Make love," he teased, his dark eyes flashing triumphantly. "Come on, let's dance."

Bethany allowed herself to be led away to the dance floor, stunned by the sudden verbal parry. How could she have let herself walk into that one so blindly? Hadn't she been the debating champion for three years straight in high school? And English wasn't even Paulo's mother tongue....

She was brought back to the present by the rock-samba beat of a live band pulsating through the floorboards. No fewer than thirty couples were moving in a sensous, undulating rhythm in what had to be the most densely populated spot on earth. Panic-stricken, Bethany pointed at the couples and muttered, "I couldn't possibly dance like that," but her body didn't even put up a struggle when Paulo pulled her to him.

If he had heard her comment—and she wasn't sure he had—her latent puritan misgivings probably wouldn't have fazed him in the least. To her, all of this seemed somewhat bacchanalian, but everyone else was enjoying the music, doing what came naturally. She could either make herself look like a fool by resisting, or she could try to relax, move with the flow and pretend she was a *carioca*.

Paulo had his arms linked casually, but most effectively, around her waist, one hand splayed against the small of her back. He had caught her off guard, with her arms jackknifed against his chest; the awkward angle of her body was making it difficult for her to follow the rhythm of his steps, and she felt her arms going to sleep. So she took the only viable alternative: she leaned back slightly, lifted her arms and draped them around his neck—a greatly miscalculated strategy. Their lower bodies came together with startling intimacy at the precise moment that their eyes locked, and a circuit of visual and physical intensity seemed to flow between them.

Diving for cover into the relative safely of Paulo's broad chest, Bethany shut her eyes and tried to lose herself in the music, but everything seemed to be conspiring against her. The lead singer was caressing a ballad in a sugar-and-cinnamon voice, the pulse of its lyrics fluid and sensual. The rhythmic *carioca*-colored language flowed through Bethany's mind with images of open palms on a skin-covered drum. Whoever had said French was the language of love should have been there on a night like this.

The room was filled with the essence of body heat, musky and pungent. Bethany could feel dampness spring out on her arms, her thighs and her face. Paulo's body was like a slow-burning kiln, his cotton knit shirt simmering against her cheek, his iron-hard thighs incandescent. But none of these sensations could compare to the cascading sensuality of the pelvis-to-pelvis dancing. That Paulo was aroused was blatantly evident, and Bethany felt as though her lower body had somehow become forged to his. It might have been the music, or the insidious beat but something had transformed her into a quivering mass of tactile nerves and tissue.

Unconsciously, she must have squirmed, for suddenly Paulo's arms brought her closer yet—if such a thing were possible—and while the singer poured out the climax of his heart-searing ballad, Bethany's body reacted in the strangest way, as though a lion had roared in the pit of her stomach.

"Whoa," she murmured when the sensation had passed, leaving her giddy and light-headed.

"Did you say something?" Paulo asked, nuzzling her ear.

Summoning unknown reserves of self-control Bethany nailed her feet to the floor and tersely announced, "This has got to stop," an instant before the song ended and the singer left the stage.

Paulo looked down at Bethany's rigid form. "I know what you mean. I hated to see it stop myself," he said, his grin guileless. Bethany didn't bother to correct him. For all she knew, her body might have sabotaged her vocal cords and muddled the message.

Fortunately, Paulo did not notice that Bethany's knees kept buckling as he led her back to their table— a result, no doubt, of the outrageous chemistry experiments they'd been conducting on the dance floor. Then and there, Bethany decided that any future tours with Paulo would be conducted in the full light of day, in the company of scads of noisy, pushy tourists. She didn't know what had come over her, but she had no business fooling around with this...this excessively virile man-child who was practically her cousin!

When they got to their table, Bethany felt Paulo's hand tighten round hers. A moment later she saw for herself the cause of his tension. A small, wiry man was waiting for them, his mottled skin the color of tobacco juice, his hair slicked back and his small eyes hooded by one thick eyebrow that grew uninterrupted across his forehead. His greeting to Paulo was effusive.

"Deixe-nós, Choco," Paulo growled, as he helped Bethany to her seat. *"Não tenho nada que dizer."* Bethany could see that Paulo wanted to be rid of the intruder.

The man he'd called Choco gave a shallow laugh and turned his odious eyes to Bethany. "Perhaps, my dear friend, we should conduct our business in English so as not to seem rude in front of your new *garota*. I must say, you outdo yourself this time. *Americana*, no?" He spoke with a metallic hiss; the sound, Bethany supposed, a serpent would make if it could speak.

Paulo reached in front of Choco and picked up his beer mug, but as he brought it to his lips, his eyes met the older man's, and he returned the mug to the table untasted. "We have no business to discuss," he told Choco, "and I am not your friend."

"Aah, but how greatly you are mistaken," the little man sneered. "Your father and I were friends and business associates, and so should we be...in his memory." He leered at Bethany. "Would that not seem right to you, my lovely?"

Paulo dug his fingers into Choco's skinny arm. "Leave her out of this!"

Choco's reaction was just as swift. His free arm reached for the opposite sleeve, but the quick reflexes of one of Paulo's friends prevented Choco from carrying out his intentions. He tried to pull away, but the two younger men held him fast. "You insult my honor, Paulo Andrade," Choco uttered in low warning. "I will not stand for it."

"Honor?" Paulo gave a harsh laugh. "You call reaching for your switchblade honorable? Try it again, Choco, and this entire room will be down your throat."

Choco's shoulders sagged a fraction. "Then let us simply discuss the matter of payment like gentlemen."

Disgust turned Paulo's eyes to chips of flint. "If you did provide services to my father—legitimate ones, that is—the accounting office staff will ensure that you are paid. We have had other *despachantes* on the payroll, and they have always been remunerated satisfactorily."

"But this time it was a gentleman's agreement," Choco protested. "A handshake between friends, nothing more."

"And you expect me to believe that? I am young; I am not a fool. Good night, Choco. Why don't you stay and finish our drinks for us?" Paulo gestured Bethany to her feet, and they walked away.

"You will regret this!" Choco called out after them. "Nobody dares to cheat Choco!" Paulo ignored him.

"What if he tries to follow us?" Bethany asked, her icy hands gripping Paulo's arm.

"He won't. My friends will keep him entertained for a while." Paulo nodded good-night to the bouncers and brought Bethany outside to the car.

"But he obviously knows how to find you," she pointed out. "What are they going to do with him?"

Paulo's shadowed face was infuriatingly compla-cent as he opened the door for her. "I don't know. I suppose they'll just have to let him go." Bethany could have sworn that Paulo was smiling as he walked around to his side of the car.

Chapter Three

The measured exhalation of air from Paulo's lungs ran in counterpoint to the slap of rubber soles against pavement. Right, left, right, left, right—exhale... exhale...exhale.... Only the sweat poured freely, unchecked by the disciplined rhythms of Paulo's body as he coursed the distance from Leme Beach to the far tip of Copacabana.

Rio de Janeiro came closest to perfection in the quiet moments before daybreak. Buses and taxis were still too few to foul the fresh morning air; the streets were free of drunken revelers, prostitutes and pickpockets. For all too short a time, the universal sins of city life were absent.

On the beach, old men bent and stretched their wiry limbs, their weathered faces turned to the near-nascent sun. Groggy vendors stocked their kiosks while street sweepers whisked away the refuse of the night. And there were runners like Paulo, who silently counted off the measured distances along the beachfront, disavowing pain, ignoring exhaustion and nausea, pressing on relentlessly until the requisite miles were run.

Three more to go, Paulo thought, then cursed himself. It was only halfway—much too soon to think about the end of the run. He needed to clear his mind completely, dismissing even the gentle sounds of lapping waves, the ripple of ocean breezes across his body, the lure of ivory sand a scant arm's length away. Most days, Paulo found the tranquillity of dawn conducive to a good run, but this morning everything seemed to taunt him, chipping away at the borders of his resistance, beckoning him to collapse on the quiet beach...and to think.

Perhaps if he ran a little harder. Responding to his brain's signal, Paulo's legs lengthened and quickened their stride. He had to do something to make the gnawing in his gut go away, to stop wondering, to stop worrying....

He had never intended to frighten Bethany. The evening had been progressing so well, precisely according to plan. Another dance, a moonlight walk, some more conscientiously applied charm, and he would have had Bethany right in the palm of his hand. And even though he had no desire to hurt her, someone had to look out for Zoe; and Paulo was willing to do whatever had to be done.

His real mother had been a mere shadow of a woman, frightened by the prospect of raising a son, fearful of being a wife, terrified of life. Not so Zoe. And when she took over the role of Mrs. Sebastian Andrade, she hadn't tried to fit herself into Paulo's confused image of what a mother should be. She became his confidante, his mentor; she became his friend. She hadn't demanded Paulo's love and devotion; she earned it. While his father had been away building his gemstone empire, Zoe had always been there when Paulo needed her and absent when he needed the space. If there was any decency, any resilience and strength in Paulo Andrade, he owed much of it to Zoe, a debt he could never sufficiently repay.

And now that his father was gone, the task of protecting her fell on Paulo's shoulders. She was a woman who, despite her outward displays of confidence and flamboyance, had a desperate need for love and approval. Sebastian and Paulo had given all they could, but they knew it was the estrangement from her family in Boston that was hardest for Zoe to bear.

She had been so thrilled to learn her favorite niece was coming down, Paulo hadn't had the heart to point out the obvious. As predictably as mice come to cheese, Zoe's family was now crawling out of the woodwork to console the recently bereaved and extremely wealthy widow. Bethany, despite whatever admirable qualities she might have possessed, was still only an emissary, and he could just imagine the instructions that had been issued to her: *Humor the crazy old woman; she won't live forever. Let her know how much we care.* People like the Greys, with more pedigree than money, were infinitely patient. They would be perfectly content to circle endlessly, like vultures, waiting for the moment they could swoop down for the feast.

Paulo still cringed whenever he recalled their one and only visit to the illustrious Greys of Boston. Nine years old, he had wandered quietly around the house, too young to be included in conversations, too old to be chucked under the chin and cooed over; but he'd observed a great deal. Bethany at the time was silly and boring—but Paulo hadn't liked girls in general then. Her teenaged brothers were arrogant. Their iceberg of a mother made a point of enunciating every word she spoke with a raised voice as if the visiting foreigners were both deaf and stupid. The only hospitable person was Bethany's father, but Paulo distrusted him from the start. Looking back on it, Paulo considered Burgess Grey to be the kind of man who was only nice to people for a reason, and judging from Bethany's now pleasant personality, Burgess had obviously taught his daughter well.

A sharp pain bit into Paulo's side, warning him that he was overdoing it. He never should have picked up his pace. He still had a mile and a half to go, and he wasn't sure he could make it. His face a study in concentration, Paulo tried to take rapid, shallow breaths, knowing how crucial it was to relax the knotting muscles quickly before he cramped up altogether. The pain was excruciating, but he was determined to keep his mind on the running. Left, right, left, right...

Dammit! If only Choco hadn't shown up when he did last night, things would still be right on schedule; but then, that lowlife was famous for showing up where he wasn't wanted. His name meant "The Squid," and with his grasping tentacles, a self-proclaimed conjurer of anything with ink, he earned the name well. His job of *despachante*, a cutter of red tape, was the by-product of a government hopelessly snarled by its own bureaucracy. No self-respecting business could hope to survive in Brazil without the services of these middlemen. But Choco would have tainted whatever profession he had chosen. He was a sniveling sneak, the worst kind of coward. Not even the criminals would have anything to do with him. Everyone knew the only dangerous thing about Choco was his own ineptitude, yet Paulo had deliberately misled Bethany to believe otherwise. What a stupid thing to have done! It wasn't like him at all.

Another cramp, so strong he could scarcely breathe, seized Paulo's side. He knew he should stop, but if he didn't have a good run, he'd never get through the day; and it would be that much harder to get his miles in tomorrow. He couldn't let Bethany's presence disrupt his life like this. He had to get back in control....

God, she was so much like Zoe! Their coloring was different, but the bone structure, the eyes, even the ways they gestured—a subtle tip of the head, an offhand wave—were nearly identical. Their personalities, too, were similar, although he suspected neither woman was consciously aware of it.

Zoe lived her life like a wild bird, trusting her instincts and following the pull of her heart, contrary to all reason and logic. Bethany, on the other hand, was like that same bird raised in a cage. The instinct was there to spread her wings and fly; but since she'd never tasted freedom, she couldn't identify the restless longing for what it was. Paulo had recognized it, though, almost from the instant she had arrived. He could see it in her eyes, beyond the professional smile and the outward calm. The inner reflections mirrored there were as multifaceted as a diamond, their brilliance burning twice as bright. Bethany...with the softly curving body, strongly defined face and faintly amused tilt of her chin. She seemed to think of herself as unattractive; but like the ugly duckling in the classic tale, she was a swan—every bit as lovely, every bit as regal.

A pity, thought Paulo. In different circumstances, he would have gladly shown Bethany how to spread her wings and fly. But fascinating as she was, taking her to his bed was out of the question. She was still a

Grey, and he couldn't let his physical urges distract him from what had to be done.

Tonight, Bethany was to begin the needless task Zoe had requested of her, and Paulo intended to be at her side for every single minute of it. First, he would make up to her for the incident with Choco. It might take some time, but eventually he would put her at ease once more, bring her guard down, then expose her for what she really was.

With an agonizing moan, Paulo crumpled onto the nearby sand, doubled over, the tortured muscles wrenching his body. There was still a half mile to go.... *Dammit! Why did Father have to die anyway?*

THE HEAD OFFICE AND SHOWROOM of Sebastian's, in its propitious location atop a downtown high rise, commanded a dazzling view of Sugarloaf Mountain and Guanabara Bay. Inside, the blue-and-gold *Belle Epoque* decor of the reception area called to mind a gilded, opulent era when extravagant finery was the norm and Brazilian society claimed to rival the cream of Europe. The walls boasted turn-of-the-century portraits of the emperor and his family, as well as depictions of Rio as a young city of *palácios* and promenades, horse-drawn carriages and aqueducts.

Bethany had already examined each of the paintings and was doing her utmost to show some interest in an incredibly ostentatious display of imperial jewels, with limited success. Paulo was still tied up. Not that it was his fault. In the twenty minutes that had passed since their arrival, he'd been cornered by no fewer than half a dozen employees of various ranks as they entered the building to begin their workday. At the moment, he was conferring with the pretty, olive-skinned receptionist, his bottom planted on a corner of her desk as he pored over the appointment book.

Bethany had to hand it to him., Paulo, dressed in what appeared to be standard *carioca* business attire of black slacks and white shirt, with its sleeves folded to the elbows, had a lithe, easy way about him, which, despite his advantaged position as son of the founder, had earned him the genuine affection of his coworkers. There were no elements of the spoiled rich kid in Paulo Andrade.

It wasn't that she minded the wait; it was just that her reasons for being there were making her distinctly uncomfortable. She felt as though she was a hanging judge, lurking around the corridors of a courthouse, scanning her potential victims and wondering whose days were numbered. She knew the sentiment was ridiculous; no matter what she found out through the audit, it would not be her responsibility to bring the offenders to justice. As a corporate attorney, she'd sooner quit than dabble in criminal law. Still, she couldn't help wondering which of these contented employees might be an embezzler, a forger or a thief. Only when she came face-to-face with one well-dressed executive who gave her a scathing look did she realize she was being terribly obvious. She made a conscious effort to look bored.

The unfortunate thing was that it hadn't even been necessary for her to be there that morning; everything could have been done satisfactorily after hours. It was Paulo's idea that she take the tour offered to all Sebastian's clients, claiming it would give her a better idea of their marketing strategies and production methods. Perhaps he was right, she thought halfheartedly, shifting her weight from one foot to the other.

Unconsciously her eyes focused on Paulo, so that when he lifted his head and caught her staring, she started as if he had read her thoughts from across the room. She even imagined a dark look of scorn in his eyes, but in the next instant he gave her a tight, tired smile.

It was hard to know what to make of him after last night. There were obviously more layers to him than she had at first suspected, but which of them figured predominantly in his personality she couldn't quite determine. She was willing to admit she might have imagined his sinister smile outside the club. The street was dark, and she'd been spooked by that awful Choco character. Afterward, Paulo had driven her home, apologized for being tired and gone straight to bed. Hardly the makings of a murder plot, she decided in retrospect.

At breakfast, the entire matter seemed so trite that Bethany hadn't bothered to bring it up. Besides, Paulo looked terrible. There were shadowed crescents under his eyes and lines of tension between his eyebrows, and he looked as if he hadn't slept a wink. Even now, he didn't seem a whole lot better.

Just then Paulo got up from the desk, touched the receptionist's shoulder lightly, said something that made her laugh and then crossed the room. "I'm sorry I kept you waiting so long," he said.

"It's all right. I didn't mind," Bethany lied.

"There's only one tour bus scheduled for this afternoon, so you and I can spend the day at the beach."

"The beach?" gasped Bethany. *So what was wrong with the beach?* This was Rio; Rio was synonymous with beaches. There'd be plenty of people around; surely she had nothing to worry about. "Okay," she agreed after a long lapse. "It sounds like fun."

Paulo gave her a curious look. "So shall we get started?"

Bethany followed Paulo down a mahogany-paneled corridor lined with backlit showcases displaying an astounding variety of Brazilian gemstones in the rough. There were clusters of magenta tourmaline, rock-candy crystals of deep purple amethyst, smoky imperial topazes, diamonds, rainbow-hued aquamarines and, of course, emeralds, which, in size and quality, bore little resemblance to the grass-green chips Bethany had seen in jewelry stores at home. The corridor led to a bright, white room in which smocked men and women were working at huge tables full of glistening gems.

"There is where the uncut stones are sorted and graded," explained Paulo.

Bethany moved closer to examine the tables, and it seemed to her that every stone looked alike, yet the jewelers were able to separate them as nimbly as if they'd been labeled *A*, *B* and *C*. She turned to Paulo. "They don't come out of the mine looking this uniform, do they?"

"No, they don't. We have workshops near the mines where the extraneous material is removed and an initial sorting is done. A great number of the stones we mine don't meet our standards, and they're culled at the source."

Automatically assuming the role of corporate attorny on a plant tour, Bethany asked, "What becomes of the inferior stones?"

"They're sold at wholesale prices to the neighboring jewelry stores. We make virtually no profit on the transaction, but it does help to keep the small businesses afloat."

In the next room, where the gems were cut, faceted and polished, Paulo introduced Bethany to an English-speaking lapidarist who was pleased to explain his work to her. His project that morning happened to be an exquisite pink topaz the size of his thumbnail.

His first step had been to determine how to enhance the area of the stone with the deepest shade of pink and then cut away the surplus with a small hammer. Next, he pressed the stone against a vertical grinding wheel to create the facets of a brilliant cut. At this stage, the gem was already beginning to assume its final shape. Then he would make the facets more precise in a procedure called lapping, one too delicate to trust to the human hand. He would attach the topaz to a dop stick, insert it into the hole of a jamb peg, and apply each facet in turn to a horizontally rotating wheel. The final step of polishing, he said, was in some ways the riskiest part of the entire operation. Superheated by friction, the stone could easily fracture, but if the procedure was done properly, the surface of the gem actually melted and spread over the stone to give it a lustrous and uniform shine.

Caught up by the fascinating intricacies of the business, Bethany forgot her initial reluctance to take the tour and thanked the jeweler profusely. She could have stayed and watched him all day. But she did allow Paulo to bring her to the final, and most impres-

sive, display. Huge murals and three-dimensional
reproductions illustrated the titanic forces that had
shaped the earth millions of years earlier, when the
planet was nothing but a grinding, spewing ball of
unleashed energy. To think that such catastrophic
chaos could produce orderly prisms of light and color
in the form of gemstones was mind-boggling and gave
one a new and healthy respect for the forces of the
planet Earth.

By the time they reached the retail showroom,
Bethany felt like a lump of clay on a potter's wheel. A
salesman would never find a more pliant customer; in
fact, it was all she could do to keep from pulling out
her credit cards on the spot and giving in to the gemstone fever that had gripped her with a fury. But since
she hadn't come there as a potential buyer, she was
forced to content herself with sitting in a corner of the
showroom to observe how the sales transactions were
conducted.

The comfortable paneled and carpeted room was set
up with small linen-covered tables, most of which were
already occupied by salesmen and their clients. Coffee was served in silver demitasses to the visitors while
they pored over velvet-lined boxes of jewelry and un-
set stones. Conversation, though hushed, held an element of anticipatory excitement, as though the
decisions centered on not whether to buy, but how to
choose from the vast array of gems available.

Located beside the showroom was Sebastian's pièce
de résistance. Whether or not a purchase was made,
patrons were invited at the end of their visit to Sebastian's exclusive gift shop to choose a memento of their
tour, *gratis*. Bethany looked the items over and found
not a single tacky trinket among them. There were

souvenir sets of gemstones in the rough, glossy photo books about the gemstone industry, delicate Brazilian lace and color prints of Rio's spectacular mountains and beaches.

One retail outlet had been strategically placed near the exit to give the tour taker a final chance to buy a pair of emerald earrings or a bracelet. Warmed by the hospitality of the lapidarists and salespeople, the visitors, it was expected, would find it difficult to walk out of Sebastian's with only a free gift and no purchases. Bethany was amused to see several people who had withstood the temptations of the showroom enter the retail outlet on their way out. It took her great strength of will not to follow their example.

Paulo was in much better humor by the time they left the building and stepped out into the dazzling midday sun. He still looked tired, but the lines of tension on his brow had eased, and he seemed relaxed. "So what do you think of my father's creation?" he asked.

Bethany smiled. "You should be very proud. But I do have one suggestion to make."

Paulo seemed to know she was teasing. "Let's hear it."

"There ought to be a sign posted at the entrance saying: 'Browser Beware.'"

Paulo's response was a good-natured laugh. "I'm pleased to learn you are impressed with our marketing techniques."

"Impressed? I'd say they were lethal," she countered, enjoying the sparkle in his eyes and gladly taking the arm that he offered. The prelunchtime crowds of downtown Rio had turned the sidewalks into a teeming sea of humanity, so Bethany was grateful for Paulo's guiding her to his car.

They were both silent during the drive home. Bethany rolled the window down on her side, and the summer breeze blew silken strands of her hair across her face, which she didn't even bother to push away. Elbow propped on the door, she drummed out the rock 'n' roll beat of the song playing on the radio. Even a routine drive gave Bethany a sense of exhilaration and an appreciation of Rio's upbeat pace: cars darted from lane to lane, and men hung on recklessly to the sides of trucks, as if life for them was one giant dare.

"You ought to wear red more often," Paulo said suddenly.

Bethany turned to him, a flutter of pleasure rippling through her, for she had not even been aware that he'd noticed her dress. "Thank you. Red's my favorite color, but I seldom have the nerve to wear it." She looked down at the silk dress; it had a wide boat neckline that slipped down a little over one shoulder. She enjoyed wearing it; she felt casual, comfortable...and a little daring.

"Why are you afraid to wear your favorite color?" Paulo asked as they drove through the Botafogo tunnel.

"I don't know," Bethany admitted, grateful for the darkness that hid her embarrassment. Why couldn't she have kept her mouth shut? "I don't wear clothes that detract from my...well, professional image."

They emerged from the tunnel, and Paulo looked her over when they stopped at a traffic light. "But professionalism comes from the way you conduct yourself, not how you dress. What's wrong with looking desirable, the way you do now? Your clients won't mind, and your adversaries might even be tempted to underestimate you.''

Bethany toyed with the ends of her sash. Did she really look desirable? ''I-I never looked at it that way before,'' she stammered and fell silent. Whatever had possessed her to go on that impetuous shopping spree in Filene's, anyway? The reasons didn't seem clear to her now. It couldn't have been to please Paulo, whom she had still thought of as a gawky kid. Nor was she one to bother experimenting with new looks. That was the kind of thing she'd done at sixteen, when decades of adulthood stretched out ahead of her and the choices seemed endless. But at thirty, one did not tamper with an image that worked.

Okay, so she was willing to admit that this new look was fun for a change, and the beige, charcoal or navy-attired attorney of Grey & Associates seemed a little stuffy in comparison. But that was why people took vacations, wasn't it? To let their hair down, to go a little crazy. It didn't mean she was going to be like this for the rest of her life. No, that would be absurd. Maybe she'd look back on all this as mere post-adolescent rebellion.

The condominium's softly illuminated elevator was empty when they stepped inside, yet Bethany found herself looking twice at the wind-tousled woman in scarlet with the flushed cheeks and the sparkling eyes before she recognized her own reflection in the mirrored walls.

''Anyone you know?'' Paulo laughed, easily zeroing in on her confusion.

''I'm not sure,'' she admitted with a wry grin.

The doors closed and Bethany automatically moved to the rear of the elevator, leaning against the brass railing and looking up to watch the numbers go by. Paulo came to her side and slid his arm behind her, so that it brushed the back of her waist lightly. He, too, watched the passing numbers, and it suddenly struck Bethany as to what a ludicrous habit that was. They were the only people on the elevator, so they would hardly miss their floor even if he did look away long enough to kiss her. Just as Bethany was about to dismiss the thought, Paulo looked down at her with scorching dark eyes. Suddenly Bethany was aware of how the length of his body aligned with hers, and through the fabric of her dress she could feel the hard contours of his hip and torso. As if the two of them formed the covers of an open book that ought rightly to be closed, Bethany longed to turn and face him, to bring her body to his. She knew her overly bright eyes were revealing her fevered thoughts as clearly as if she had been speaking aloud, yet she felt totally powerless, unable to block out the magnetic intensity of Paulo's nearness. Fortunately, at that moment the doors opened. Bethany realized that Paulo hadn't made even a single advance; he had merely moved his arm across the railing and stood there, waiting. So why was it that as she left the elevator, Bethany felt as though a virtual tempest of activity had occurred within its confines?

Zoe was setting the table for lunch.

"There you are, darlings," she said. "I hope you don't mind a cold plate. I wasn't sure when you'd be back."

"Sounds great," Paulo replied, crossing the living room to kiss his stepmother on the cheek and to nab a carrot stick from a platter of raw vegetables.

"How did you like the tour?" Zoe asked her niece.

"It was absolutely fascinating," Bethany replied, baffled that the elevator ride had had more of an effect on her than the entire tour.

When Zoe looked up, her expression turned to one of concern. "Are you all right, dear? You look a little flushed."

Bethany tossed Paulo an I-told-you-so glance. "It happens when I wear red," she muttered dryly. "It makes me look feverish."

"Maybe you really have a fever," Paulo suggested from far enough away so that Bethany couldn't punch him in the ribs, the wretch.

"Do you have to go back to Ouro Prêto so soon?" Bethany asked her aunt when they'd sat down for lunch. The thought of staying alone with Paulo in the condominium was more than a little unnerving. Not that she couldn't handle him, but it hadn't been part of the understanding when she'd agreed to come to Rio. Then again, Zoe hadn't said much of anything on the phone; perhaps she'd never intended to spend much time with her niece.

"I'm afraid so, darling. Ovidia, our housekeeper, hasn't been herself since Sebastian's death, and I don't dare leave her alone any longer than I have to. She's been with us for so long, we all feel quite responsible for her." She reached out and took Paulo's and Bethany's hands in each of hers. "Besides, I know I can trust the two of you to straighten things out for me, and my presence would be of absolutely no use anyway."

"I will see you again before I leave, won't I?" Bethany asked, trying to suppress her childish feelings of abandonment.

"Of course you will. If I don't get back here by next week, Paulo can drive you up to Ouro Prêto when you're finished with what you're doing here. Won't you, Paulo?"

"I'd be more than happy to," Paulo replied, giving Bethany the distinct impression there were at least a thousand other things he'd rather do. But Zoe didn't seem to notice.

"Good. It's settled, then," Zoe declared as she got up from the table. "Now I really must run. Mesbla is having a wonderful sale, and I intend to buy out their entire art supplies section. I've neglected my sketching for much too long."

"Don't shop too late," Paulo admonished, getting up to clear the table. "You know how we—how Father used to feel about your driving alone after dark."

"Yes, I do, dear, and as I used to tell your father, that's the reason cars have headlights, so they can be driven in the dark. Marvelous invention, really."

"And what if you have car trouble?" Paulo countered, with Bethany in silent agreement.

Zoe held out her hands. "I shall light the flares, lock all the doors and clutch a can of Mace to my breast until help arrives. Now stop worrying about me! Sometimes I wonder which of us is the old woman."

Her theatrical retort nudged a reluctant smile from Paulo's lips. "It will never be you, Zoe," he admitted.

Zoe snatched up her shawl and an oversized purse from the sofa, then turned and wagged a finger at her stepson. "Now you remember to take good care of my niece!"

"Promise," he said, nodding curtly.

"And you, young lady," Zoe added, whirling around to Bethany, "pay attention to what Paulo tells you. Underneath that charming exterior is a very responsible young man, and he knows this city!"

"I'll remember that," Bethany replied dutifully, feeling for all the world like a twelve-year-old being left by herself for the first time. She wondered if Paulo felt the same way.

"One more thing," Zoe added, and for a very brief instant she looked her age. "If you find something—anything—let me know right away." Bethany and Paulo echoed their assurances to Zoe in unison, hugged her and saw her out the door.

COPACABANA BEACH was practically in Paulo's front yard. A short walk across the Avenida Atlantica and there it was, in all its hedonistic glory. The sun was out in full force, blinding the unprotected eye with dazzling reflections off the sand and water, melting ice cream and Popsicles the instant they were bought, and driving all but the hardiest sun worshipers to the nearest refuge of shade or air-conditioning. Only a few tourists could be found, recognizable by their tomato complexions and noses smeared thick with zinc oxide. For the most part, however, those who were lounging on towels, playing volleyball, splashing in the cerulean water or strutting their stuff—depending on their age and proclivity—were the people who were born to the climate, their skin accustomed to the tropical sun's relentless rays.

Bethany, plodding through the sand behind Paulo and trying not to kick it into people's faces, felt like a marshmallow among walnuts. There was something inherently stultifying about being transplanted from one's native habitat to a region in an opposite season. If she were in Boston right now, she could step out into a raging snowstorm on Newbury Street and feel nary a hint of self-consciousness; but having been culti-vated in a zone with four distinct seasons, her metab-olism did not know how to cope with instant summer.

"Is this spot okay?" a low rumble of a voice cut in.

Bethany blinked. "What?" Paulo was indicating a place on the sand to spread out the blanket, but since it seemed to be the only space left on the whole beach, she couldn't imagine why he bothered asking. "Sure, it looks fine," she replied, and watched while he bat-tled a breeze that kept tossing the blanket back in his face.

Paulo looked up. "Do you think you could help me with this, or do you prefer to stand there and clutch your robe all day?"

"Oh, sorry. Guess I was daydreaming." Bethany bent down and took two corners of the blanket, trying not to notice that her feet were whiter than the sur-rounding sand.

"Are you cold?" Paulo asked, puzzled, since it was almost as hot as in a blazing furnace.

"No. Was I shivering?"

"I believe that's what you were doing."

She gave him a wry grin. "I was thinking about winter."

"Do you miss it?"

"Not in the least."

With the blanket in place, Bethany dropped to her knees and deposited her beach bag beside her. When she looked up, Paulo was lifting his T-shirt over his head, and it was all she could do not to gasp out loud.

Too tight and much too skimpy, were the first thoughts that came to her stunned mind when she saw Paulo's burgundy swimming trunks. Not that they didn't do him justice—in fact, they dramatically called attention to his physical attributes—but Bethany, more accustomed to seeing men in track shorts or cutoffs, which provided a baggy anonymity, was unprepared for his unembarrassed display. And while she'd never cared for men who wore precious metal around their necks, the gold chain and amulet nestled in the dark hair on Paulo's chest looked just right, somehow. Funny how one's perceptions and prejudices seemed to lose their meaning away from home, Bethany mused as she drew in a deep but rather erratic breath.

"Don't you think you're a little overdressed?" Paulo asked, stretching out beside her.

Bethany cleared her throat and gave a rueful glance to a group of beach beauties a few feet away. Like most of the other females on the beach under forty, they wore swimsuits consisting of little more than cords and tiny scraps of cloth. "I think I'll still be overdressed when I take off my robe," Bethany remarked with a sigh.

Paulo dismissed the infinitestimal binikis with a grimace and a wave. "Don't worry about them. The fascination wears off quickly, believe me."

Knowing the moment could hardly be postponed any longer, Bethany finally let the striped robe slip from her shoulders, trying not to notice how Paulo's eyes followed her every movement. From the corners of her eyes, she could see her orange maillot with the rainbow splashed across the front explode into view, and she wondered again what had come over her to buy such a suit—cut high at the hips, low at the front, with no back to speak of. And the color! It was a gorgeous shade of tangerine, but hardly appropriate for someone accustomed to basic black. Oh, well, she could always save it for vacations abroad. Bethany offered Paulo a weak smile and made a great production of rolling up her robe for a pillow.

"That's a very attractive bathing suit," Paulo said softly, staring at the parts that weren't there.

Bethany had to bite her tongue not to intercept with, "Ah, you're just saying that" and to say, instead, in a fairly convincing tone, "Thank you." There. It hadn't been so difficult to accept a compliment... even though she knew he was just trying to make her feel better.

Paulo smiled, looking as though he was about to say something else; then he seemed to change his mind. He reclined on the blanket, arms folded behind his head.

Bethany lay down beside him and closed her eyes. Within seconds, she was reveling in the sensation of golden rays on her skin, the tingle of the saltwater breeze, the wafting scent of coconut oil and the resonant hum of conversation and laughter nearby. She must have even dozed for a minute or two—there could have been no other explanation for the abrupt change in her from relaxed tranquillity to an acute awareness of Paulo's body were inches from hers. That they were lying side by side among hundreds of other people seemed to make no difference. Somehow she felt disturbingly close to him, intimate. Intimate and yet...comfortable.

"Paulo," Bethany said, ignoring the stirrings within her that had no place in their relationship. "What happened to your real mother?"

"She died when I was four."

"Oh, I'm sorry. Do you remember much about her?"

He didn't answer right away. "No, I don't. Most of my recollections come from what people tell me about her. She was a proper, old-fashioned Brazilian wife who seldom went out and never spoke unless she was spoken to. And she was forever at confession, though I cannot imagine why." The tone of Paulo's voice wasn't critical, but sympathetic, as if by looking back on his mother's life, he sensed the loss, the lack of fulfillment, she must have suffered.

"Zoe's entry into your life must have come as quite a shock," Bethany said lightly, preferring to steer the course of the conversation away from painful reflections.

He rolled onto his side and propped himself up on one elbow. "I think I had an easier time of it than my father did," he said with a chuckle. "I used to think Zoe was my—how do you say it?—fairy godmother."

Bethany turned to Paulo in surprise. "You're kidding! So did I! And all along I thought it was just me."

Paulo gave her a strange look, as if she'd said something quite impossible for him to believe. Then he shrugged it off. "Zoe probably strikes many people that way. She's not like those of us whose feet are set firmly in reality. It is as though she simply refuses to grow up."

Bethany thought for a moment. "That's not such a bad thing, is it?"

"No," Paulo admitted, turning away to scan the ocean's horizon, "that probably is not such a bad thing." He was silent for a minute or two, then sat up and looked at Bethany. "You should see your face. It could use some sunscreen."

She touched her cheeks. "I think you're right." She sat up and dug through her beach bag till she found the plastic bottle. Then she poured the lotion into her hand and slathered it over her face, neck and chest. Paulo watched her as if they were the only two people on the beach and, oddly enough, Bethany found herself enjoying the attention.

"Let me do your back," he offered.

"Uh...no, I don't think so."

He looked hurt. "Why not?"

What was she supposed to say? *Because if you touch me, I won't be held responsible!* Bethany had gradually become accustomed to the sight of Paulo with next to nothing on, but skin-to-skin contact was another matter altogether. All she needed was some physical reminder of their little dance sequence the other night and...well, it simply wasn't worth the risk.

She realized, however, that she'd look like an utter fool if she tried to put the lotion on herself. After all, this was a public beach, and there were many couples applying lotion to each other's backs. It didn't mean anything!

Bethany slapped the bottle into Paulo's hand. "It's all yours." Feeling as if she'd just relinquished control of something irretrievable, she pivoted on her bottom toward Paulo and turned her back back to him.

A frigid squirt of lotion on her skin made Bethany bolt upright and gasp, but soon the sensation was replaced by the warmth of Paulo's palms as he spread the thick, slippery liquid in a gentle massage. Heat penetrated Bethany's body in relaxing waves, not only soothing her skin but also easing the stiffness in her muscles from her newly reinstated exercise routine. Paulo certainly couldn't be faulted for a lack of technique, and he took to his task with obvious dedication. Each stroke of his palms seemed to melt away another fragment of her trepidation, and the pressure of his fingers worked to loosen her reserve.

Bethany wasn't consciously aware of the direction in which Paulo's hands were moving until they reached her waist and, gliding upward, touched her between the ribs. "Paulo, that tickles!" she wailed and tried to wriggle away.

"Sorry. But you shouldn't bounce around like that. It's distracting."

Bethany tossed an indignant look over her shoulder. "You think I'm distracting! What about you?"

Paulo's dark eyes were half hidden by thick lashes, his head tipped back in a look of deep contentment, as if he knew precisely what he was up to, and why. "I'm only trying to be thorough," he murmured. "You wouldn't want me to leave any places exposed, would you?"

Bethany groaned and whirled her head around toward the turquoise water, hoping to muster some self-discipline. She shouldn't allow Paulo to affect her this way. She shouldn't let him interpret this innocent interlude as an invitation to more intimate contact. After all, she had been around a few years longer than Paulo, and she was well aware that some men were obsessed with sex. She knew how to avoid unwelcome advances in the boardroom as well as on the beach.

As Bethany indulged in such mental moralizing, Paulo resumed his ministrations. He kneaded her shoulders until they relaxed and became supple; then he allowed his fingertips to run along the ridge of her spine in a wonderful, indescribably delectable course. Bethany gave a cry of surprise, turned around and glared at him. "What was that you just did?"

"Feels nice, doesn't it?" he returned, grinning, looking about as guileless as a tiger cub. "Now why don't you lie down on your stomach, and I'll do the back of your legs."

Bethany's mouth fell open. "You must be joking!"

"Why? Don't your legs burn?"

"Whether or not my legs burn is not the issue here, as you very well know!"

Paulo held out his hands, palms up. "What is the issue?"

Bethany rolled her eyes. "Oh, please, spare me."

Reaching out, he took her chin between his thumb and forefinger, steering her face to his. "I'm having difficulty understanding this attitude of yours. If I happen to enjoy the feel of your skin while I'm preventing you from getting second-degree burns, what harm is done?"

Paulo's damnable *carioca* logic didn't impress her for a minute. She hadn't been out in the sun that long! "I'll tell you what the harm is!" she shot back. "You and I have ended up alone in that condominium of yours, as if I needed to remind you."

"Yes, so?"

"What do you mean, 'so?' You're my cousin, for goodness' sake, and you're way too young!" The words jumped off Bethany's tongue as if they couldn't wait to get out, and now they seemed to hang in the air like scandalous headlines. She wished she could crawl away and hide.

Paulo was doing a poor job of swallowing a smirk. "Are you attracted to me, Bethany?"

"Let's just say you are very different from the three-piece suits I deal with every day," she replied in classic understatement. She could have sworn Paulo was waiting for her to continue. "I, uh, I shouldn't have to tell you that you're a...good-looking guy," she added reluctantly.

"But I'm too young," he said, echoing her earlier statement.

Why did it suddenly occur to Bethany that she wouldn't want him any older? Was she some kind of cradle snatcher? "It doesn't matter," she replied. "You're still my cousin."

Paulo leaned back on his hands and stretched his long legs in front of him. "What about the relatives from Zoe's first and second marriages? Do you consider them your relatives?"

Bethany shrugged. "I have no idea who they are, or if there are any."

"That's precisely my point. I was nine years old when your aunt married my father. You and I were raised on opposite ends of the globe. There would be nothing incestuous about a relationship between us."

Bethany's head jerked up. "We are *not* going to have a relationship!"

"Fine!" Paulo countered just as emphatically. "Then you might as well let me put lotion on the back of your legs."

Bethany stared at him in astonishment. He'd done it to her again—turned her words completely around—and she was supposed to be the lawyer. Wordlessly, she handed him the bottle.

A COOL EVENING BREEZE drifted in through the kitchen window as Bethany tossed a salad for dinner and Paulo put steaks on to broil. The knock on the door was so faint that neither of them was sure they'd heard it at first.

"Were you expecting someone?" Bethany asked.

"No," Paulo said, turning off the oven. "But whoever it is got past security." He crossed the room and opened the door. "Antonio!" he said in surprise.

Antonio was about ten years old, skinny and saucer-eyed, wearing a torn T-shirt and rubber thongs. Hopping from one foot to another, the child launched at once into breathless Portuguese, in obvious agitation. Paulo knelt down, grasped the boy's shoulders and urged him to slow down. In the next moment, Paulo let out a low, agonizing moan.

"What is it?" cried Bethany, fear ripping through her as she rushed to his side.

Paulo looked up, his face chalk-white. "It's Zoe—there's been an accident!"

Chapter Four

"Oh, my God, no!" Bethany groaned. "What happened? How bad was it?"

Paulo stood up and snatched his wallet and car keys from the hall closet. "There's no time to explain. I have to go—"

"Wait, Paulo!" she called out to the tall form stalking toward the elevator, with Antonio scampering alongside. Hurriedly, Bethany snapped the lock in place and slammed the door shut behind her. "I'm coming with you!" she cried, in case the elevator arrived before she did.

But the elevator took an eternity to come. Paulo, cursing, slammed the ball of his hand futilely against the lighted arrow pointing downward and actually seemed to consider descending thirty-two flights of stairs; at last, however, the elevator arrived. Although Paulo had voiced no objection to Bethany's presence, neither did he so much as glance her way on the ride down.

"Zoe is alive, isn't she?" Bethany demanded, furious with Paulo for being too bullheaded to realize that her anguish and her need to know were just as real as his.

"Do you think I'd be in such a hurry if she weren't?" he snapped, running his fingers through his curls and pacing the elevator until it rocked. "The accident happened on the highway to Ouro Prêto. I warned her about driving after dark..."

As soon as the elevator doors opened onto the basement parking level, they all raced in silence to Paulo's car. Antonio climbed into the tiny space in the back, and Bethany took the passenger seat. Its tires squealing, the car sped out of the parking space, up the ramp and into the flow of nighttime traffic.

Bethany tried to stay calm and remain silent, while Antonio, gesturing at intersections, apparently was giving Paulo directions. She suddenly realized that if Zoe were in the hospital, Paulo would hardly need a ten-year-old boy to tell him how to get there. "Where is Zoe?" she asked Paulo.

"At Antonio's house," he answered, as simply as if Zoe were there for a visit.

"What on earth is she doing there?"

Paulo ignored Bethany's indignant tone of voice, but his fingers gripped the wheel a little more tightly. "Antonio's father and uncle recognized her car at the side of the road, and brought her to the city in the back of the truck they were riding."

"They put an accident victim in the back of a truck?" Bethany said in stunned disbelief. "Why did they do an asinine thing like that?"

Paulo took his eyes off the road long enough to slide her a scathing look. "They were trying to keep her from being robbed and left for dead before help arrived," he ground out in a voice dangerously devoid of patience.

"Oh, great," Bethany fumed, throwing up her hands. "And they probably broke a few more of her bones in the process!"

"Shut up, Bethany! I'm in no mood to listen to your bigoted opinions right now!"

"So why couldn't one of them have waited with her while someone called for help?" She just couldn't sit by quietly while her aunt was lying injured, somewhere at the mercy of total strangers who didn't even know that an accident victim is never supposed to be moved. And to have Paulo defend their irresponsible actions!

"If it had been their truck, and if they'd had the money to make a phone call, they probably would have done just that." Paulo said, with exasperation in his voice. "Not everyone enjoys the luxury of carrying around money." He sighed deeply. "Anyway, it doesn't matter now. They did what they thought was best."

Bethany sat back and put her head down, pressing her temples with her fingertips. Paulo was right. It was too late to argue about a fait accompli, and she would only risk antagonizing everyone. She prayed that Zoe would be all right. At least she was in the care of Paulo's friends...

Then she saw where the car was heading, and anger, despair and fear seized her. They were climbing one of the hills that jutted up behind Rio, a hill covered with teeming slums, known as *favelas*. Seen from the city in daylight—crooked little houses built of scraps and painted in riotous carnival colors, with roofs of corrugated tin—they looked almost picturesque, like colorful collages. But now, as they followed a lateral access road that was little more than a rutted lane, Bethany realized what a distorted view that was. The doorless hovels, only occasionally illuminated by a single bare bulb, revealed pitiful conditions, and the stench of raw sewage and rotting fruit pervaded the air. Bethany clamped her hand to her mouth and swallowed hard, not knowing whether she wanted to cry or be sick. What chance for recovery could Zoe possibly have in this fly-infested hellhole?

Paulo parked the car in as unobtrusive a spot as possible and locked it securely after they had stepped out. Not that it would do much good, Bethany thought as she scanned the dark, curious faces in every doorway staring openly at them. They'd be lucky if the car had tires when they got back.

Too distraught to utter the slightest protest, Bethany followed Paulo and Antonio along a steep, twisting path that snaked its way around mud walls and heaps of trash. Occasionally crude drainage ditches, bridged over with worm-eaten planks, cut across the path. At one point, where it was too dark to see and they had to depend on Antonio's voice to guide them, Bethany stumbled and let out an involuntary cry.

She heard Paulo stop in his tracks and curse. He came back and reached out to take her hand, saying, "You never should have come. This, no doubt, offends your North American sensibilities."

Much to Bethany's dismay, it did; but it rankled her to admit it. "Don't worry about me," she said, taking his hand only long enough to recover her balance. "Let's just keep moving." At last they reached Antonio's house, a gaudily painted patchwork much like all the rest. It consisted of two rooms, with a light bulb burning in each one. Obviously, Bethany observed, they were one of the luckier ones. The front room was crammed with people; the head of the household, a swarthy middle-aged man, pushed his way through the crowd to greet the new arrivals. After a few words with Paulo, he motioned them to follow him.

Zoe was lying in the back on a sagging double bed, covered with blankets that looked fairly clean, if tattered. Her eyes were closed, her face was a sickly gray and a makeshift bandage on her forehead was stained with dried blood. At her bedside, a wizened old woman, holding a basin of water and a rag, kept watch.

"Oh, God, Paulo, look at her!" Bethany cried and moved quickly toward the bed.

"Don't jostle her," he warned.

Bethany turned and glared at him. "She was dragged all the way up here on a bouncing truck, for heaven's sake! Don't talk to me about jostling her!" She glanced up, askance, at the old woman who had obviously not understood a word and, Bethany hoped, no doubt thought that Bethany's raised voice was only an expression of concern. Which it was, in a way, although she vowed to herself to curb her temper from now on.

Paulo knelt beside the bed and gently lifted Zoe's wrist. "We're here, Zoe. Can you hear us?" There was no response, and a knot of panic rose in Bethany's throat. "Her pulse is strong," Paulo said and stood up. "I'll go call an ambulance. I know where there's a phone tapped in near the access road."

"You're not going to leave me here!" Bethany blurted out before she could stop herself.

Paulo's mouth hardened and his eyes flickered with impatience. "Surely you don't want to leave your aunt alone with all these people. Think what they might do to her," he said sarcastically.

Bethany looked away, recoiling from the sharpness, however justified, of Paulo's retort. "Go ahead," she mumbled. "I'll be fine." She looked up, but he was already gone.

A feeling of unease fluttered briefly in Bethany's stomach but faded when she looked at her aunt. Zoe looked almost peaceful lying there, as if she somehow knew she was being well cared for. Bethany heard movement behind her and turned around to find the people from the other room politely filtering in, curious about their American guests.

Bethany smiled nervously. "Does anyone speak English?" she asked, her eyes flitting across the crowd of people. There was an elderly man, no doubt the husband of Zoe's nurse; two middle-aged men she guessed to be Antonio's father and uncle; and a woman with four children around her, one of whom was Antonio. Surely they didn't all live in this house together, mused Bethany, yet she had seen narrow triple bunks in the other room, and there was a pile of bedrolls beside her.

The man who seemed to be the patriarch shoved a reluctant Antonio to the forefront of the group. "I speak a little English," the boy said shyly, and Bethany's face flooded with shame. How much of her unmindful ravings had he understood while they were in the car, she wondered.

"Come here, Antonio," she said gently, holding out her hand. Wide-eyed, the child came to her and slipped his skinny palm into hers. "Thank you for coming to tell us about Zoe," she told him. "And please thank your family for everything they've done.''

Antonio nodded and turned to translate the message. The reaction was one of embarrassment—the shuffling of feet and a few mumbled phrases that Bethany took to mean, ''It was nothing.'' Then the head of the family snapped his fingers and issued a terse order to the woman, who scurried out and came back with a chair for Bethany. The only other person with a place to sit was the old woman at Zoe's bedside.

There was an awkward silence and little by little the people began to drift back to the other room, leaving Bethany alone with her aunt. Holding Zoe's hand in hers, she looked around the small room. Its walls were made of ill-fitting planks of bare wood, adorned by pinups of Tom Selleck, Linda Evans and a few Brazilian movie stars. Above the bed was a crucifix and some religious icon Bethany didn't recognize. Suddenly, inexplicably, she felt like crying, and she wasn't sure whether it was out of concern for Zoe or for the desperate bleakness of these good people's home. It had been a long time since anything had stirred her conscience so profoundly.

Just then, a young woman Bethany hadn't seen before came in with a cup of coffee on a saucer and two vanilla wafers. A toddler clung to her skirt, eyeing the refreshment as the woman handed it to Bethany. She thanked the woman and considered giving the child a cookie, but there were all those other children, and she didn't have enough to share with them. So she sipped the coffee and left the cookies discreetly on the saucer, certain she couldn't eat a bite anyway. The hot coffee was strong but delicious, and actually seemed to fortify her, despite the room's insufferable heat.

The wait was beginning to seem like hours, and Bethany began to worry that something might have happened to Paulo. What on earth would she do? The old woman must have sensed her guest's feelings of helplessness, for she rose slowly and came around the bed to bring her the basin. There was some kind of herbal poultice floating in the water, Bethany noticed as she took the basin on her lap. The woman showed her how to sponge Zoe's forehead with the rag and presumably described the curative effects of the herbs, of which Bethany understood not a word; but somehow the woman's calm words and soothing demeanor were comforting.

Paulo finally did arrive, with two ambulance attendants and a stretcher in tow. The men made a cursory inspection of Zoe's injuries, determined she was fit to travel and deftly transferred her to the stretcher. Paulo went outside first to direct the attendants down the path, but Bethany lingered at the front door. She felt she had to do something to show her appreciation, and then remembered that she always carried some emergency cash stashed somewhere. She checked through the pockets of her jeans and, sure enough, found some folded American bills. She took them out and went back to the bedroom. The old woman was standing on a chair and carefully unscrewing the light bulb from the ceiling. A lump filled Bethany's throat as the woman stepped down and smiled at her.

"For the children," Bethany said, pressing the bills into the woman's palm and indicating with gestures what she meant.

The woman's leathery face split into a knowing grin, and she nodded vigorously. *"As crianças!"* she declared, pointing through the doorway at the children.

"That's right, yes," Bethany answered, giving the woman a quick hug before she hurried off to catch up with Paulo and the others.

THE DOCTOR in the hospital's emergency ward said Zoe had been extremely lucky, for it looked as though she had suffered only a mild concussion, a few cracked ribs and some minor lacerations. Paulo and Bethany were assured that Zoe was resting comfortably and told that they could see her in the morning.

The police and a tow truck followed them to the outskirts of Rio, to the site of the accident. Despite the rugged terrain, the highway was in good condition. They had expected to find Zoe's car near some blind corner or switchback, but instead, they discovered it had plowed into the sheer rock face of a mountain along a straight stretch of road. All that was left of the car was a crushed hulk of dark blue metal, the shattered windshield gaping like a monstrous, snaggletoothed grin in the eerie moonlight.

While the police conducted their examination, Paulo and Bethany walked hand in hand around the wreckage. Bethany's stomach was knotted tight with horror at the devastation, even as she kept telling herself that Zoe was going to be all right.

One of the officers came and spoke to Paulo for a few minutes. When he left, Paulo was visibly shaken, his dark eyes mirroring Bethany's concern. "The policeman couldn't find any evidence of hazardous road conditions and thinks she may have fallen asleep at the wheel and lost control." He paused, a slight catch in his breath. "He also said that if she hadn't been wearing her seat belt she would never have survived the impact."

Blinding waves of relief washed over Bethany; it seemed the most natural thing in the world for her to seek the safe harbor of Paulo's arms. For a few time-less moments, they clung to each other, Bethany's sobs echoing the anguish Paulo was man enough to express. Their tears forged an unspoken, unconscious bond between them, singling out this moment as their very own.

Slowly they regained their composure. Bethany rested her head on Paulo's chest, enjoying the simple serenity his embrace instilled. She heard his heartbeat relax to a steady, soothing rhythm as he stroked her hair and murmured soft reassurances. Bethany looked up and saw Paulo's eyes still glistening in the moon-light; and with a will of their own, her hands slid up-ward along his chest and anchored themselves behind his neck. Her fingers toyed with Paulo's curls and, in response, he pulled her closer into his arms. When he lowered his head to kiss her, for a moment she won-dered if it was loneliness, fear or curiosity that im-pelled her to respond, but she immediately pushed aside the analytical workings of her mind and gave herself up to Paulo's heady kiss.

Bethany parted her lips beneath Paulo's as soon as the moment felt right. And it did feel so right, though in some ways almost frightening. His kisses were soft and intoxicating as his lips moved over hers with quiet insistence. Paulo's hands roamed her back hungrily, pressing her to him. Bethany, only marginally aware of her actions, rocked her body subtly against his, conscious instead of the sense of completeness in Paulo's arms.

As the flare of initial rapture dimmed, Bethany pulled away and stepped back, staggering a little.

Paulo's hands traveled the length of her arms and captured her fingers in his. "Shall we go home?" he asked in a low, husky voice.

Overwhelmed by the cascade of emotions pouring over her, Bethany merely nodded. Paulo curved his arm around her shoulders, and silently they walked past the twisted wreckage with the gaping grin and climbed into Paulo's car.

Neither of them said a word on the way home, yet the silence between them spoke volumes. Highly charged with sensitized physical awareness, Bethany felt as though her body was being stroked by the bristles of a sable brush. Every nerve, every cell, was tingling and alive. Her eyes, no matter how she tried to will them to do otherwise, kept gliding to Paulo's powerful profile. Now and again, he would turn to look at her, and when their eyes met, the air between them ignited.

Once they were home, Paulo switched on the lamp, and Bethany moved across the room to look out at the lights of Copacabana far below. She wrapped her arms around herself and shivered, though she wasn't cold. She heard him come up behind her, and she shut her eyes in blissful anticipation of his touch. His fingertips came to rest lightly on her shoulder, and he turned her around as effortlessly as if she were floating. Then he looked at her a long, long time.

"I wish things were different between us," he said in a voice thick with longing. "If only..."

There was no need for him to finish the sentence. Bethany knew what he meant as surely as if the words had come from her own mouth. They had nearly lost someone they both loved, and now there was no one else to turn to but each other. Tonight, she and Paulo were family, reaching out and drawing strength from compassionate arms. Tonight was not the time—if, in fact, there would ever be a right time—to become lovers. As long as Zoe lay in a hopsital bed and needed her family, they had no right to chart new and unexplored paths with each other, paths that could ultimately lead nowhere. For Zoe's sake, if for no other reason...

Bethany reached out and laid her palms against Paulo's bristly, tanned cheeks just long enough to assure herself she was doing the right thing. Then she stepped back.

"Good night, Paulo."

His expression of desire wrapped itself around Bethany's heart like honey-tipped briars. "Good night, *querida*. Sleep well."

DEVOID OF MAKEUP and wearing a white hospital gown, Zoe looked pale, but her smile was bright. "Morning, darlings. Oh, look at the flowers. They're lovely!"

Bethany went to the far side of the bed to place the vase of fiery lilies on the night table while Paulo greeted his stepmother. Zoe's eyes narrowed as she studied each of her visitors in turn. "I'm the one who's supposed to look bad, so why are you two carrying a full complement of baggage under your eyes?"

Paulo and Bethany exchanged glances across the bed. "Uh...we were up late worrying about you," replied Bethany none too convincingly.

"How are you feeling?" Paulo asked, hastening to pick up the slack before Zoe could comment further.

His stepmother grimaced. "I feel as though a thousand little men were building a railroad tunnel between my ears, but the doctor says that's to be expected for a few days. And it hurts when I breathe, and it hurts when I laugh, but other than that..." She trailed off with a weak smile.

"Do you remember what happened?" Paulo asked gently, taking Zoe's hand. "Do you think you fell asleep at the wheel?"

Zoe blanched, looking even paler than she already was. "Hardly, darling. I couldn't have been more wide-awake." Suddenly she began to tremble and gripped Paulo's hand. A tear escaped and trickled down her cheek. "I was forced off the road. Someone tried to kill me last night!"

Chapter Five

Uneasy anticipation filled the room, Paulo and Bethany half expecting Zoe to retract her accusation with a characteristic laugh and a wave of her hand. But there was only silence. Prickly, blood-chilling silence.

"Are you absolutely sure?" Bethany finally asked.

Zoe, her fingers still clenched around Paulo's hand, turned and looked at her niece. "Absolutely sure," she replied, her voice ominously flat.

Paulo's face turned stony, his eyes smoldering with anger. "Why don't you tell us about it?" he said.

Wincing, Zoe tried to take a deep breath, but all she could manage were short, labored intakes of air. "The first time I noticed the car following me was on the Avenida Brasil."

"What did it look like?" Paulo asked.

"Large, black, with fins—an old Chevy, I think."

"What about the driver?"

Zoe shook her head. " I couldn't see his face; it was already dusk."

"Did you try to lose him?" Bethany asked.

"I did everything I could think of to lose him. I sped up, slowed down, switched lanes—but he might as well have been chained to my bumper. I even considered pulling over, but then I realized, if he were to do the same thing..." Zoe's voice faded, and she shuddered.

"It's best that you didn't," Paulo said gently. "Please go on."

Zoe nodded. "By the time we reached the outskirts of the city, the traffic had dwindled to practically nothing, and I knew beyond a doubt I was being followed." Her voice quavered, and she rubbed weary eyes with her thumb and forefinger. "Fortunately, I had filled the car up with gas before I left, so I knew I'd be able to reach the police station in Ouro Prêto. But of course, I never got that far."

Bethany recalled how little evidence the police investigation of the accident had produced. "What did the car do to force you off the road?" she asked her aunt.

"We were on an empty stretch of highway when a huge truck approached us from the opposite direction. Just as the truck was about to pass, the black car veered into the oncoming lane and tried to pass me. He swerved abruptly in front of me, forcing me off the road toward the shoulder. The last thing I remembered seeing was a wall of solid rock." Zoe closed her eyes and fell silent. Beneath the covers, her whole body was trembling.

Bethany touched her aunt's shoulder lightly. "It's okay, Zoe. It's over, and the doctor says you're going to be just fine."

"That's right," said Paulo, "and you'll be well enough to come home in a few days."

Zoe looked up, her face frigid with fear. "What if whoever it was finds me here?"

Bethany glanced at Paulo, who, like her, seemed to be at a momentary loss for words.

"Don't worry," Paulo assured her. "I'll alert the hospital staff not to allow any visitors but us, and we'll contact the police right away. You do realize they're going to want to ask you a lot of questions about the accident."

"I know," replied Zoe. "It's all right." She gave her stepson an intense look. "Surely, now you believe me that something is very wrong."

Paulo didn't answer right away. "Zoe, there's no reason to think this incident was connected in any way with the company."

"But what other reason could there be?" she asked in a thin, frightened voice.

"There could be any number of reasons. Perhaps the driver of the car was on drugs, or wanted to commit suicide."

That struck Bethany as highly improbable, but she let Paulo continue.

"You've never been involved with Sebastian's," he pointed out, "and no one yet knows you're the beneficiary."

Zoe looked hurt. "Why won't you believe me, Paulo? I loved your father, too, but how much more proof do you need?" The painful edge in her voice silenced him, but Paulo's expression remained intractable.

Bethany, incensed by his callous attitude, stepped in. "Don't worry, Zoe. We'll start going through the books tonight. If something's wrong, we'll find it. In the meantime, the police will be on the lookout for the black car. I'm sure that everything will be straightened out in a matter of days. Isn't that right, Paulo?"

she asked, applying as much persuasiveness to her voice as if she were twisting an arm behind his back.

"Yes. Yes, I'm sure it will," he mumbled, his reluctance obvious only to Bethany, or so she hoped.

Zoe gave them a pleading look; her face was slightly puffy and shadowed with fatigue. "Would the two of you mind leaving now?" she asked. "I'm very tired."

SEVERAL HOURS LATER, when Paulo and Bethany were in the car on their way home, Bethany said, "I think I know who did it."

Paulo turned and gave her an odd look. "Oh? Who?"

"Choco."

He rolled his eyes upward and muttered something unintelligible. "What led you to that brilliant deduction?"

Bethany clenched her jaws and silently counted to ten. "Don't you remember when he threatened you the other night? He said he'd make you regret cheating him."

"Nobody has cheated Choco!" Paulo protested, indignant. "If he worked for my father and has not been paid, we would owe him at most a few thousand cruzeiros—about a hundred dollars. And if there's no record of what he's done—no invoice, no receipt— he'll get nothing. Either way, the sum is hardly enough to warrant attempted murder."

"How would you know what his services were worth? Maybe he was involved in something complex in this job he does, this *des...desp—*"

"*Despachante,*" Paulo concluded for her. "I doubt it very much. The job seldom pays well, and even if my father did have some large assignment, Choco would be the last person he'd choose to do it. The man's ineptitude is legendary."

Bethany remained unconvinced. "But you can't deny that he threatened you!"

Paulo gave a sigh of exasperation. "In this country, we live by our emotions. A butcher once threatened to come after me with a meat cleaver for accusing him of holding his thumb on the scale. That does not mean I am in actual danger of losing my life."

She slumped in her seat and glared at him. "I'd hardly call that the same thing. What happened to Zoe was very real."

"I know that, and I'm not trying to downplay the danger she was in, nor do I intend to let the matter lie unresolved. I'm only trying to point out that in the three days since you arrived, you have spoken to very few people in English, one of whom, unfortunately, was Choco. But just because he has the least appealing personality does not make him a cold-blooded murderer!"

"Does Choco drive a car?" Bethany couldn't help but ask, though it meant deflecting a particularly scathing look.

"If I had ever seen Choco get around on anything but the outside of a bus—especially if it were a large black car with fins—I think I might have made the connection!"

"Okay, okay," she relented, deciding it would be a complete waste of time to mention the niggling feeling in the pit of her stomach. "But why are you so unwilling to believe there might be something wrong with your father's company?"

Paulo reminded her of a volcano biding its time, simmering. "You have a father yourself, don't you?" he asked.

"Of course."

"Would you be willing to suspect your father of illegal activities solely on the basis of speculation and rumor?"

Bethany had to admit she wouldn't. "But it's not just anyone who's saying so. It's Zoe, and surely she must have known your father as well as anyone could."

"True, but she also has an abysmal lack of business aptitude and could easily misinterpret the confidentiality of business negotiations or the process of seeking tax loopholes as something illicit. You must also remember, Bethany, that my father's death came as a great shock to Zoe, as it did to all of us. To find herself suddenly the sole heir to a large corporation of which she understands nothing..." He shrugged. "I think it's simply a reaction to stress."

"Then why are you going along with the idea of an audit?"

Paulo parked the car in an angled space in front of the condominium. "To clear my father's name and, I hope, to put Zoe's mind at rest. We shall all feel better about it when it's over."

Bethany wasn't so sure, but since her opinion had not been solicited, she kept silent on the matter as she stepped out of the car and closed the door.

Paulo leaned over to the open passenger window. "Are you sure you're going to be all right spending the day by yourself? I can make other arrangements for the soccer meet."

She shook her head. "Don't do that. Antonio and his teammates are counting on you to lead them to victory. I'll be fine. What time do you want me to meet you tonight?"

"I finish work at eight. Why don't you wait for me at Oxala across the street? The restaurant is always crowded and well lit, so you'll be perfectly safe. Just be sure to let the maitre d' know who you're waiting for."

"I will," she assured him, smiling. "Have a good day, and wish Antonio luck for me."

"I'd be happy to," he replied, lifting his hand in a wave. "Take care now." A moment later, he backed out of the parking spot, put the car into gear and drove off in the direction of the stadium.

Bethany let herself into the condominium with a spare key, kicked off her sandals and lay down on the insidious champagne leather sofa, covering her aching eyes with her forearm. Sometime during the past few hours her emotions had come to a crossroads, and she felt uncertain which direction to take. The strain was beginning to take its toll.

First, there was Zoe, the aunt she loved, but knew so little about. Oh, she knew the facts well enough—whom she'd married, where she'd lived. But she knew nothing whatsoever about the forces that motivated Zoe to do the things she did. Bethany couldn't help but feel disappointed that they would have so little time to get better acquainted. Now Zoe was lying in a hospital bed, while the person who put her there remained nameless, faceless, his motives a mystery—to Bethany, at least. Did Zoe, perhaps, know more than she was letting on? That was a distinct possibility.

Then there was the matter of the audit. The more Bethany thought about it, the more she realized she might be getting in way over her head. Examining the records of an internationally renowned corporation was a task generally reserved for the most senior of corporate attorneys, not only because of the complexity of the task, but also because of the high degree of accountability it involved. Bethany was deluding herself if she thought she could report her findings to Zoe and Paulo, fly home, and put the matter out of her mind forever. If there was any basis to Zoe's suspicions—which Bethany was almost certain there was—it was not likely to be a simple case of sticky fingers in a petty-cash account. She was loath to speculate, but she was sure that she herself was taking one hell of a risk professionally.

Which called to mind her father's explicit warnings against coming here. None of this, she knew, would come as any surprise to him, nor would he pass up the opportunity to point out how consistently he was right. However, dealing with her father was the least immediate of all her problems, and she resolved not to dwell on it a moment sooner than necessary.

Lastly, there was one single overriding reason why Bethany did not want to walk into Sebastian's tonight—she did not want to be the person who told Paulo his father was not an honest man.

Yet, illogically, it was because of Paulo that Bethany wished to conduct the audit. That way, she could be the one to tell him that there was nothing wrong with the way his father ran the company.

Paulo was responsible for Bethany's desire to remain in Rio, but she knew she couldn't stay. In the few short days she'd been here, it seemed as though their two lives were being woven together into a tapestry of contrasting and symmetrical textures.

There was the fundamental aspect of their physical attraction to each other, an attraction Bethany had so vehemently tried to deny at first. Now it was a matter that was mutually acknowledged—a fragile, untouched symmetry.

The cultures they'd grown up in could hardly have been more divergent, but the contrasts, each in their own way, were pleasing.

Zoe's accident had, in its way, contributed to the fabric. Bethany now knew the depth of Paulo's love for his stepmother, and he knew Bethany's. She had tasted his pain as surely as she had tasted his kisses, and the flavor lingered, bittersweet.

In barely three days, she and Paulo had laughed together and cried together. They had danced like lovers and played on the beach like children. Each moment, each incident, taken on its own had very little strength; like single threads, they could be severed. But a tapestry was nearly impossible to tear apart.

BETHANY AND PAULO stood waiting in a dark, narrow lane for the security guard to open the service door to Sebastian's. To mitigate the effects of claustrophobia created by the towering walls on either side of her, Bethany tried to imagine an appropriate bumper sticker for the situation, like the ones that said, I'd Rather Be Flying, or Sailing, or Golfing. The truth was that she'd rather be doing anything than standing here feeling as if she were about to become a pressed leaf.

Finally a pair of eyes appeared through a slot high in the door. A moment later, the door swung open, and a guard let them in.

Paulo steered Bethany inside with a firm hand. "I don't mean to rush you, but these doors are on timers, and an alarm will go off if they're held open for more than a few seconds." He issued a few instructions to the guard, then led Bethany down the dimly lit hallway to the elevators. "Each section of the building is on a separate security system," he went on to explain as they rode up to the level where the general offices were located. "I've asked the guard to shut off the alarms for the accounting office and the cafeteria downstairs, so we can move around a little more freely."

"The inventory is in a safe place, I hope?" Bethany asked. "I'd hate to think I could be studying capital asset records with sacks of emeralds at my feet."

Paulo gave a low chuckle. "Don't worry. The gems are nowhere nearby. The most valuable things in here are the photocopiers."

The accounting office was large and nondescript, much like any other business office with rows of identical metal desks, filing cabinets and the usual computer hardware. It even smelled like any other office, the air recycled by the air-conditioning redolent of stale cigarette smoke, perfume and other undefinable odors.

"Where would you like to start?" Paulo asked.

"How about financial statements?" Bethany answered.

"Okay." Paulo pulled a large key ring from the pocket of his nylon Windbreaker and proceeded to open a large metal cabinet. He pulled out a sheaf of files. "You can go back as far as you like, but we might as well start with the last five years."

"That's fine," Bethany agreed, leaning against a desk and watching him. "Have you always had access to company records?"

He turned to look at her, his brows drawn together. "Why? Have I suddenly become a suspect in your investigation?"

"No, you have not become a suspect," she tossed back, growing exasperated with Paulo's defensiveness. "And I'm not conducting an investigation, either. What I meant was that there are some people who openly resent preferential treatment in the workplace, nepotism most of all. Has it ever happened to you?"

Paulo thought for a moment. "Not that I recall, but then, it's no secret that I'm not aspiring to be chief executive officer, and I've never used my position to step over anyone else. I take an interest in accounts payable and accounts receivable because I've grown up with the company, that's all. It doesn't make the job of selling any easier, I can assure you."

"But doesn't your name give you an advantage over other salesmen?" Bethany asked, recalling the brass nameplates prominently displayed on each table in the showroom.

Paulo shook his head. "Most of our clients come from other countries who only know us as Sebastian's. The name Andrade doesn't mean a thing." Paulo deposited the files on a large desk, and the corner of his mouth turned up in a wry grin. "I wouldn't be surprised if some of our local patrons made a point of avoiding me precisely because of whom I am." That possibility didn't appear to bother Paulo in the least.

"I see," Bethany said, and sat down at a desk. "I didn't mean to sound like the devil's advocate, but—"

"I know. You're just doing your job."

She looked up at him and grinned. "Something like that." She lifted a file from the top of the stack and opened it. "Now how about giving me a crash course in Portuguese? I recognize some of these words because of how they're set up on the page: assets, liabilities, capital, dividends, etcetera. But let's take this profit-and-loss statement for starters." Her eyes rode down the columns of sales figures and expenses until they came to the net-income figure at the bottom. She gave a low whistle. "Sebastian's does okay, doesn't it? I don't often deal with quite so many zeroes."

FOR THE NEXT SEVERAL HOURS, Bethany performed standard examinations of the company's financial standing. The gemstone firm, she determined, was capable of covering its current debt with cash and liquid assets. Inventory, consisting of emeralds, diamonds, amethysts, aquamarines, topazes and several other gems, was more than adequate to meet current and projected sales volumes; and the turnover of inventory was remarkably frequent. If it would be necessary to liquidate the company, it appeared that both creditors and owners were well protected. On the surface of things, at least, Sebastian's was thriving.

Bethany glanced at her watch; it was well past midnight. She sat up and, propping her hands onto her lower back, stretched the kinks from her neck, shoulders and spine. She reached over to switch off the computer and tried to revive circulation to her foggy brain by mussing up her hair with her fingers.

Paulo, who had been working at the next desk, wheeled his chair closer and combed his open hand upward through Bethany's hair, starting at the nape of her neck. The effect of his touch was both electrifying and soothing. "Have you had enough for one night?" he asked softly.

Bethany turned and gave him a tired smile. Although she was fatigued, she was also keyed up and knew if she went to bed now, it would be hours before she could fall asleep. As for whatever else Paulo had in mind...well, she wasn't ready to deal with that yet, either. "If it's okay with you, I'd like to run through the budgeted-income statement once more and do a few comparisons. But I'm absolutely parched. What are my chances of getting a Coke?"

Paulo's eyes were half closed and glazed. Obviously, computations didn't have the same exhilarating effect on him. "I never would have thought you were a workaholic," he muttered.

Bethany laughed and rubbed her temples. "I know. If I were Brazilian, I'd be from São Paulo, right?"

"Right," he said, laughing, as he pushed himself away from the desk and crossed the room to the double frosted-glass doors. Halfway there, he stopped. "Do you want to come with me? It's probably not a good idea to stay here alone."

Bethany waved him away with a ruler. "Nonsense. I don't think there are any evil accounting clerks lurking around to get me quite yet. Just bring the Coke...and don't forget the ice, please," she added, gently teasing.

When the spring-loaded doors slammed shut, Bethany smiled, touched by Paulo's concern. Then she picked up her pencil and returned her attention to the columns in front of her. By comparing budgeted statements with actual figures, she'd be able to determine whether Sebastian's was suffering from poor forecasting, a common problem for companies. So far she'd been lucky, having found nothing even remotely questionable.

Bethany heard the doors open sooner than expected. "Wasn't the cafeteria open?" she asked, and looked up, gasping when she saw the dark, wiry, menacing man leering at her. "Wh-what are you doing here?" she asked, her skin crawling at the very sight of him.

Choco's obsidian eyes glittered beneath a canopy of eyebrow. "My, my, have you *americanas* no manners? How much more pleasant it would be to commence with 'Good evening.'"

Time. That was all she needed. Time to stall the little creep until Paulo got back. "Good evening," she voiced evenly. "Ch-Choco, isn't it? I, uh, don't believe I ever caught your last name." She kept her reluctant gaze fastened upon him as her hands slid across the desk slowly to gather the financial records. She hoped the smile pinned to her face was convincingly dim.

"No last names are necessary," he replied. "Everyone knows me as simply Choco." He was moving leisurely across the room toward Bethany, his fists jammed into the pockets of his black leather jacket. "I, however, do not have the pleasure of knowing your given name," he hissed. "I had foolishly mistaken you for another of Paulo's many *garotas*, until I learned you are actually the daughter of an influential American attorney, no?"

"How do you know my father?" she asked, wishing she hadn't spread her papers quite so far apart on the desk. The sweeping motion of her arms seemed distressingly obvious to her, even though Choco hadn't appeared to notice.

He shook his oily head and clucked his tongue in mocking self-pity. "I know of Burgess Grey only by reputation. We have not had the pleasure of meeting, as I am but a lowly civil servant, unable to travel the world. Yet, even in my humble job, I have the privilege of knowing who is of importance in the international business world; and of course, Senhor Andrade always spoke most highly of his esteemed brother-in-law."

"How did you get in here?" Bethany didn't think she could bear to hear another word of Choco's smarmy praise. *What was keeping Paulo?*

In answer to her question, Choco shrugged. "It was nothing. Security systems are a mere crutch for the chronically insecure, do you not agree, Miss Grey?"

One had to give him credit. The man's command of English bordered on the lyrical—too bad he was such a slug. "Paulo's going to be back in a second," she told him. "He just stepped out to get drinks."

"Yes, I'm aware of that," Choco replied. "But I feel I must warn you the young Senhor Andrade may be—how shall I say—detained a moment or two longer than anticipated."

Panic hit Bethany like a blow to the stomach. She had to struggle to keep her voice calm. "Wh-Why? What did you do to him?"

"Oh, nothing fatal, I assure you. But you and I will have ample time to discuss business together before he returns."

"I have no business to discuss with you," she snapped. With a final, determined sweep, Bethany scooped up the last of the files and stood up shakily. Carrying the documents in her arms, she sidled toward the filing cabinet, her eyes never once leaving Choco. "I was just in here to clean up," she said, feigning bravado.

"Then, by all means, let me help." With one swift motion, he was at her side, gripping her forearm with the strength of pincers. His tobacco-colored skin was lined and leathery, giving him a decidedly reptilian appearance, and his breath reeked of stale, cheap cigarettes. He stood half a head shorter than Bethany, but there didn't seem to be a single ounce of him that wasn't mean, sinewy grit. When Bethany tried to pull away, his grip tightened, the skinny fingers inflicting as much pain as if they were steel teeth. "I'll take those," he offered, wresting the documents from her with his free hand.

"They're only financial statements, nothing of any significance," she protested, her attempt at nonchalance failing miserably.

"I'll be the judge of that," said Choco, his metallic effusiveness as repugnant as his physical appearance. Bethany hoped she wasn't going to do something foolish like faint. What experience she had dealing with high-pressure situations hadn't prepared her for this. Choco could hardly be compared to an emergency board meeting.

While he shoved the reports down the front of his jacket and continued to grip her arm, Bethany's mind was racing. "You're the one who tried to kill my aunt, aren't you?" she blurted out recklessly, unable to resist the opportunity to discover the truth.

The little man chortled, as though her accusation was the highest form of praise. "I must confess I am. The *senhora*, lovely and intelligent as she is, was unable to appreciate the depths of my sincerity when I paid her a visit two weeks ago. I believe I was more than generous in allowing her this much time to obtain the money owed to me for services rendered; but, foolishly, she chose the least-recommended course of action. She did nothing."

Bethany recoiled in horror at the thought of Zoe's ordeal, but why hadn't she told them everything? "So you tried to kill her! What good was that supposed to do?"

"It would have eliminated a superfluous link in the chain of command and proved to the remaining heir my determination to see a commitment honored."

"What exactly did you do for Sebastian's?" Bethany decided not to try to appeal to the man's conscience. He obviously had none.

"I conducted a highly confidential item of business for Senhor Andrade. I was given a deposit upon acceptance of the assignment and was to receive payment in full within forty-eight hours of delivering a completed document. Twenty-four hours after completing my part of the bargain, the good *senhor* dropped dead of a heart attack."

"Did you sign a contract?"

"No, it was a gentleman's agreement, a handshake. That is how Choco does business."

An incredibly stupid way, thought Bethany. "What do you want me to do? Find the document? If you tell me what it is, I can look for it."

Choco sneered like a cartoon villain, though the situation was pitifully bereft of humor. "That, my little butterfly, is a clever diversion, but I have no interest in what has become of my handiwork. All I require is the payment owed me." He named a sum that was so ludicrously high that Bethany wondered if there was any basis at all to his claim. "I have already spent the deposit to purchase an automobile, essential to my profession. I am sure you can appreciate the situation."

An automobile—large, black, with fins—the image lunged across Bethany's mind with frightful clarity. "If there's nothing in writing," she said carefully, "then no one is legally bound to honor the agreement. I doubt that a judge would even be willing to hear the case, but perhaps if you had proof—"

"They will listen!" he shrieked, his eyes bulging in maniacal rage. He released her arm as if it were a hot brand, but Bethany's freedom was brief. Choco's wrist leaped through the air with a flash of silver, and in that instant Bethany's whole world imploded to a single tip of steel, cold and sharp, against her throat.

The switchblade pressed her flesh as Choco leaned closer and hissed, "Let me tell you about proof. I completed the terms of an agreement. My word is proof enough. A *despachante* is a man of honor."

"What are you going to do now?" Bethany rasped, scarcely able to breath for fear of contributing to her own untimely demise.

He lifted his shoulder in a gesture of resignation. "It appears I am forced to employ other methods to exact payment."

Payment? Bethany's stomach gave a violent lurch as she realized, terror-stricken, what Choco meant. *Ransom was more like it!* "You—you'll never get away with this," she stammered, less than convinced of the claim herself. All she was certain of was that it wouldn't help to scream. The knife would be through her throat before the sound waves hit the walls. And even if Paulo came in—she prayed that he wouldn't—the sudden distraction might result in one single, deadly slip.

"We shall soon see," Choco said, "what happens when Paulo learns that his latest lover is at my mercy, and if he doesn't consider your life worth nine million cruzeiros, you had better hope that your aunt does. No doubt, her illustrious family would not care to have their name sullied with the scandal of murder, no?"

Even as he spoke, Choco was leading Bethany at knife point to the frosted-glass doors. She was forced to walk backward and, not knowing her way around, stumbled against some furniture. The knife danced a painful tune on her neck while Choco snickered.

Deep within Bethany's fog of terror shone one glimmering ray of hope. If Paulo was expected to come up with the money, then he had to be unharmed. Surely, he cared enough about her not to let anything happen. Bethany clung to that thought as they moved awkwardly out to the corridor.

As they rode down the hot, airless elevator, Bethany asked, "Where are you taking me?"

Choco's fetid breath and gamy smell were making the bile rise in her throat. "Do not trouble yourself about details. If fortune smiles, you need not stay away long. Otherwise, in time, I am sure you will grow accustomed to perpetual darkness." He laughed his evil little laugh, and icy shivers of fear skittered along Bethany's spine.

The main floor echoed like a tomb. "What did you do to the security guard?" Bethany asked, her eyes scanning the halls for some sign of life.

Choco, like most criminal types, was all too eager to relate the details of his master plan. "Xavier? Ah, he and I are old friends. I gave him a few cruzeiros and sent him out for lunch. He even showed me how to turn off the alarm so he can let himself back in. He thinks you and Paulo were expecting me."

That figured, Bethany thought, her hopes sinking fast. She turned in the direction of the front doors.

"Not that way!" Choco barked, twisting her arm and sliding the knife across her neck in a way that left little doubt as to the direction he wanted her to go. "The side door. Less people. Car is waiting."

His English, Bethany noticed, was becoming noticeably choppier as the pressure of the situation increased. *What a stupid thing to think of* was her next thought.

Then, in a sudden flash of clarity, Bethany realized she still had one slim chance to escape—a brief moment when they stepped out of the building and entered the car, during which Choco would be least able to control her movements. If only for an instant, he would have turn his attention away from her long enough to open the car door.

It meant she would have to be prepared to outrun him. Then and there, Bethany made a silent vow that if she were allowed to outrun the little weasel and escape, she'd run every day for the rest of her life and never complain again about the miseries of staying in shape!

She felt the adrenaline bubbling through her body as they made their way down cavernous halls. Fear was being transformed into a healthy instinct for survival. She had to get away from Choco, and she would! They came at last to the steel doors, the only illumination coming from an exit sign. Under the crimson glow, Choco looked eerily like Lucifer, his skin a sickly ruddy color, as he shoved Bethany a few final steps. Her back was against the door, and Choco pressed his body against hers until she thought she'd be sick. *Dear God, please, not that!*

"Now, my little *americana*," he warned, the knife at her throat, his mouth inches from hers. "When we step outside, do not entertain foolish notions of escape. My associates are waiting at both ends of the alley and are not so appreciative of beauty as I. They would not hesitate in carving a memento of this evening onto your pretty face before returning you to my care."

Choco's portentous threat nearly crushed the tender buds of Bethany's courage, and she wondered if her hammering heart had given her intentions away. Still, Paulo hadn't mentioned Choco having associates. It could be a bluff...

"I won't try anything," she lied in a voice that sounded remarkably convincing. The tone of defeat seemed to put Choco at ease. He reached over her shoulder and shoved the door outward while Bethany, leaning against it, slid outside to the cool evening air.

She took a deep breath, but gingerly, for the knife had not left her throat by so much as a single millimeter. Sure enough, there was the large black car with fins but, much to Bethany's dismay, it was parked barely an arm's length away from the building. Choco reached over effortlessly and opened the car door toward himself; Bethany, with the fire door held open behind her and the car blocking her on two sides, was boxed in as effectively as if she'd been crated for shipment. The only clear path was back into the building, which was little more than a thirty-story trap.

She glanced quickly toward either end of the alley. Not an associate in sight—Choco had been bluffing! Suddenly a pear-shaped figure appeared in silhouette at one end of the lane—but he wasn't lurking, he was strolling. Bethany didn't stop to consider whether he was friend or foe.

"He-e-elp!" she screamed, swerving and ducking for cover in the dark niche between the fire door and the car door, knocking Choco in the arm so hard his knife clattered to the ground. Bethany felt around, found the knife and waited, crouching. Choco tried to push the car door against her, uttering filthy threats, but he was too agitated to have much luck.

Then she heard the lumbering footsteps coming their way. Thank God! She'd been lucky enough to hit upon a rare Good Samaritan. Choco tried to lunge over the door to wrench his captive's hair, but Bethany poised the knife at his wrist, and he let go.

Time blurred to a frenzy of shouts, scuffles and curses. Then a sharp, piercing whistle sliced the night air. For an instant, all was deathly still.

Chapter Six

Choco reacted to his capture like a rabid jackal, snarling and hissing until the large, safari-suited man was able to muffle him with a stranglehold. As Choco dangled from the man's beefy forearm like a rag doll, a police van came squealing around the corner, followed by the security guard on foot.

From inside the building Paulo called out, "Bethany, are you all right?"

"I'm fine!" she hollered, nearly crumpling with relief. Hearing Paulo's voice was proof that the ordeal was indeed over, and she was safe.

The police wasted no time in slapping handcuffs on Choco, taking the knife from Bethany and helping her out from between the doors. She stepped into Paulo's waiting arms and, for a moment or two, clung for dear life.

Standing nearby, the man in the safari suit with the shiny gold whistle around his neck cleared his throat and said, "Lucky for you I happened to be passin' by, huh, Miss Grey?"

Bethany slipped out of Paulo's embrace, turned to the man who had just spoken and squinted, wondering why the mouthful of huge front teeth looked so familiar. "Elmer? Elmer Fletcher, is that you?"

He doffed an imaginary hat. "At your service, ma'am."

"I can't believe it!" she squealed and flung her arms around his ample neck. Then she leaped back and her hands flew to her mouth. "Oh, you must be aching all over. Did he hurt you?"

"Nah, not much."

Bethany took his hands in her own, and her eyes filled with tears. "I don't know how to thank you, Elmer. You saved my life."

The large man shrugged. "Don't mention it."

"You two know each other?" Paulo asked.

Bethany nodded, and Elmer held out his hand to Paulo. "Elmer Fletcher, Poughkeepsie. We met on the plane coming down here, she and I did."

The two men shook hands firmly. "I'm Paulo Andrade, a friend of Bethany's. Pleased to meet you. What you did tonight—saving Bethany's life—took remarkable courage. I can't thank you enough."

Elmer's eyes lingered a moment on Bethany. "She's one fine lady. Glad I could be of some help."

Bethany blushed. "What were you doing in this end of town?"

"I happened to have dinner over at that revolving restaurant down the street and thought I'd better walk off the dessert. Then just as I was passin' by this alleyway, I heard your cry for help." He grinned. "I always figured this birdcall might come in handy someday," he said, indicating the whistle around his neck.

"But the police were right behind you," Bethany said, pointing at the van.

"Yeah, I guess it was just your lucky day. They were parked nearby, havin' their coffee break."

"Would you do us the honor," Paulo asked, "of having dinner with us tomorrow evening?"

"Yes, would you?" Bethany seconded, delighted.

"Thanks all the same," Elmer replied, "but our group is leaving tomorrow morning for the Amazon." He glanced at his watch. "In fact, that's only a few hours from now. Never should have stayed so long at the samba show."

"Is there anything we can do to show our gratitude?" Paulo asked.

Elmer Fletcher studied Paulo a long time. "Yeah, there is. Promise you'll take real good care of this little lady. She's pretty special." Then he turned to Bethany and planted a kiss on her cheek. "See ya, Miss Grey. It's been a real pleasure."

SEVERAL HOURS LATER, Paulo and Bethany left the police station knowing Choco was securely behind bars and would remain there until the trial. The streets were quiet, the sky an inky black in the final stages before dawn. Paulo's car was on the other side of a park landscaped with fragrant blue jacarandas and stately *açcai* palms. They walked along a meandering path, arms linked around each other's waists. Bethany reveled in the feel of Paulo's hip moving against her as they walked. They fit so well together, she mused contentedly, the lapse of time and the reassurance of Paulo's nearness making the past evening seem like someone else's nightmare.

"Now why don't you tell me what you were doing while I was being dragged away to within an inch of my life?" asked Bethany.

Paulo looked down, his dark eyes solicitous. "I've already explained it three times."

"That was in Portuguese."

"Ah, yes, so it was." He grinned, and Bethany thought it the most dazzling smile she had ever seen. To think, only a few hours ago, she'd come so close to... No, she wouldn't let herself think about what might have happened! Without realizing it, she shuddered. Paulo drew her closer. "It's all right, *querida*. You're safe now, and I'll never let anything hurt you again. I swear it."

Bethany closed her eyes. If only there were some way to make Paulo's well-meaning promise come true. Here, tonight, anything seemed possible. But tomorrow...next week...a year from now?

He brought her to a wrought-iron bench beside a trickling, man-made brook, and they sat down. "I had just gotten our drinks from the vending machine," Paulo began, "and when I tried to leave, I discovered the door was stuck. After struggling with it awhile, I realized someone must have locked it from the other side. I tried calling for the guard, but of course, he was on his so-called break by that time. The alarm system had been shut off, so I couldn't contact anyone that way. Then I remembered there's a dumbwaiter in the kitchen that services the main boardroom. I climbed into the shaft, let myself down by the cables to the ground floor, and was on my way to the elevator when I heard a whistle from outside. I ran into Xavier at the front door just as the police van was pulling up." Paulo brought his hands to Bethany's face and touched her as though she were made of porcelain. His eyes were lustrous, fluid, cabochon black onyx as he studied her. "What a fool I was to leave you alone. I will never forgive myself."

Bethany covered the back of Paulo's hands with her own, leaning her cheek into the warm roughness of his palm. "You can't blame yourself, Paulo. There was no way of knowing Choco would try something tonight."

"But I should have realized he was up to something. I always thought he was too stupid to be dangerous, but of course, I had no idea he'd tried to hurt Zoe..." Paulo's voice wavered, and Bethany wished there were some way she could take his pain away. There had been enough suffering for one night, enough fear.

Paulo turned to her his eyes full of worry. "You must believe me, Bethany, when I tell you that I have no idea what Choco did for my father to expect such a payment."

"Of course I believe you. Choco might be inept, but your father wasn't. If he had found it necessary to employ the services of a person like Choco, he'd have been clever enough to cover his tracks well."

Paulo brought Bethany to her feet. "We'll find out what's behind it, you and I. We have to. Can you forgive me for being so stubborn?"

Bethany touched her finger to his lips, nodded, then tilted her head back for his kiss. At first, he was gentle and caressing, brushing his lips back and forth across her mouth as though applying careful strokes to a portrait. His kisses were at once apologetic, tinged with self-reproach and caring. Most of all, caring.

Painful memories were washed away as Bethany slipped her arms eagerly around Paulo's neck, drinking in the nectar of his solace. She was overwhelmed by the profound depth of his concern and her own sensations of relief and gratitude mirrored Paulo's feelings.

His mouth on hers was smooth, intoxicating. Equilibrium seemed to abandon them both as they clung tightly to each other exploring each other's faces and bodies. She had come so close to losing Paulo and perhaps everyone forever, but now she was here, wrapped in his arms, feeling safer and happier than she had ever felt in her life. Yet the juxtaposition of two such extreme emotions seemed almost too overwhelming to bear all at once.

But nothing mattered beyond the exquisite simplicity of Paulo's long, chiseled fingers in her hair; his mouth at her temple, breathing her name over and over; his moist, hot breath against her skin. *He cared!* With wild, reckless abandon, Bethany allowed herself to believe it, and the powerful realization rendered even the most incredible of fantasies believable.

"Let's go home," Paulo whispered.

"Yes, let's," she replied, but neither of them moved, their bodies refusing to be parted. They kissed again and then, reluctantly, moved apart to walk the short distance to his car.

They could hardly get home fast enough. It was as though their freshly kindled desire might somehow flicker away, dissipate with such mundane acts as driving the car, parking it and going to the condominium. And sure enough, Bethany felt a fleeting sense of awkwardness the instant she stepped inside the familiar surroundings. Too much...too fast.

"Would you like a brandy?" Paulo asked, standing a step away. His stance suggested that he felt the same hesitancy Bethany was grappling with.

"Yes, please." She went to the glass doors, slid them open and stepped outside. The stars were still out, the southern constellations wondrously new to Bethany, their brilliance rivaling the twinkling lights of Sugarloaf and the amber glow of street lamps along the Copacabana. An easterly breeze was blowing, and Bethany rubbed her arms absently.

The scene evoked the city Rio de Janeiro, and the thought of it never ceased to thrill her. Exotic, primeval, thrumming with the rhythms of life at its most elemental. Paulo, too, was an integral part of the magic—young, strong, possessed of a vigor and enthusiasm Bethany could only marvel at. She wondered suddenly when it was that she'd lost those qualities in herself; or, indeed if she'd ever really had them.

How easily he could make her laugh, how effortlessly he could invoke her enjoyment of life's simplest pleasures: dancing, eating, drinking, lying on a sundrenched beach and doing nothing at all. She had never known a man for whom the pursuit of happiness was so all-encompassing, yet he'd seemed to master the art without making it selfish or petty. For him, being happy was to share wholeheartedly—without question, regret or hesitation—all of himself. And to imagine making love with a man like that...

"After all you've been through tonight, you still look enchanting." Paulo's voice came from behind her. Bethany turned; she hadn't even heard him open the door. He handed her a snifter.

"Thank you," she said, taking the glass. "It's the moonlight; it's wonderfully deceptive."

The breeze lifted a lock of Bethany's hair and spread it across her face. Paulo reached out for the silky strands, letting them slip between his fingers. "Why do you always do that?" he asked.

"Do what?"

"Accept a compliment as though it were a lie."

Bethany lowered her eyes. "Is that what I do?"

"All the time."

Tasting the fine old brandy, she looked up. "Sorry, I don't mean to." Their eyes linked—Paulo's, dark and motionless, Bethany's as evanescent as a tide pool. Why was it, when she looked him straight in the eye without saying a word, she still felt as if she were babbling a mile a minute?

"It's amazing the way your eyes change color," he said, confirming her visual turmoil. "They're stormy and gray one minute, cool and blue the next. And when you smile...silver."

"You do have a charming way of putting things, Paulo." There. Was that any better, she wondered.

"I wasn't trying to be charming. I was trying to figure you out."

"Oh?"

"There's something about you that doesn't quite fit the external image. It's as though there's a constant storm raging inside, some inner conflict that's never allowed to touch the surface." He raised his glass in a toast, his dark eyes probing. "Here's to solving the mystery of Bethany Grey."

Her heart strangely fluttering, Bethany drank to the toast. If only he knew how simple and straightforward the source of her turmoil really was. Paulo was the conflict, the raging storm inside her that seemed to build in intensity with each passing day. No sooner did she travel safely through one emotional squall than there was another, even more daunting, to conquer.

And if her agitation was apparent even to Paulo, it was because the ultimate conflict loomed larger than all the rest: her undeniable, overpowering physical attraction to him.

What if an affair with Paulo sent her soaring straight to the stars and she never came down? Perish the thought, but what if she fell in love? How on earth was she supposed to return to Boston and pick up the pieces of her comfortable, predictable existence? Under any other circumstances, falling in love might be a very welcome experience, but not here. And not with Paulo, of all people!

"You're doing it again," he said, leaning back with one elbow over the balcony, his mouth turned up in an enigmatic smile. For all his assertions to the contrary, he seemed to be able to read her like a book.

She blinked. "Doing what?"

Paulo took a sip of his brandy. "Let me put it this way. If what happened in the park fifteen minutes ago had taken place on this balcony, you and I would be making love this very minute. But on our way over here, you started to worry; you began to regret things that hadn't even happened yet, afraid of losing control, afraid of letting your emotions rule for once in your life."

"What makes you think that?" Bethany asked, turning toward the view without seeing a thing.

"It's true, isn't it? You'd rather deny your feelings than decide once and for all whether you want to make love with me or not."

"No, it's not that," she said much too quickly.

Paulo reached out and took her glass. "Then tell me what it is," he said, bending over to kiss the side of her neck. The contact of his lips on her skin acted on her nerve endings like a siren, sending all of them on red alert. It was wonderful, marvelous, but she wished he would stop.

Oh, dear Lord, he was right! She was wavering badly, unable to take a stand, unwilling to assume responsibility for her own actions. And she was going to have to make up her mind very soon, for his kisses were now traveling along her neck, and—Ooh, how *did* he manage to find such sensitive places on her shoulder? If she didn't call a halt this very minute, she wasn't going to be able to resist Paulo when he guided her around to face him, as he was doing right now. She wouldn't be able to stop him when he bent down to reclaim her mouth, as he had just done...or utter a single objection when he gently parted her lips to engage in erotic combat with her tongue.

There had been something important she'd wanted to say, some valid explanation to make him understand why it was still too soon, but she was too frazzled from all that had happened earlier that evening. The explanation, whatever it had been, slipped away completely when she felt Paulo's hand pull her blouse up from under the waistband of her slacks. All her thoughts and senses seemed to rally suddenly to the touch of his hand gliding as it made its way up along her skin. When his thumb caressed the underside of her breast, all she could think of was how deliciously, wickedly sexy he made her feel, her eyes literally springing open at the new and alien sensation.

Could it be the night breeze? The stars, the moonlight, the pulsating cadence of the city far below that was changing her into someone she hardly recognized? Unconsciously, Bethany moved her body voluptuously against Paulo's, and his physical response was like wildfire. He gave a low and throaty groan against her mouth, and his hand moved to cover her breast, which she had left uncharacteristically bra-less. Her nipples sprang to life, aching and throbbing, as his palm moved over one and his body rubbed against the other. Something deep in the center of her jolted, like a low-voltage shock, and she weakened all over. Paulo's mouth was tasting her everywhere, her eyes, her nose, her ear, the hollow of her throat. Bethany threw back her head; she just couldn't seem to get enough of him.

Then, at some vague, undefinable point, their identities became indistinct and fuzzy. Bethany's nails dug into Paulo's back, but somehow she was no longer aware of him and herself as a nameless, frightening desperation overtook her. The sensations gnawing deep inside her body were not sensuous and beautiful; they were raw, almost painful. She became terrified by the inappropriate shift of her emotions when just a moment ago there had been magic.

Suddenly, in a brief subliminal flash, the nagging worry that had eluded her earlier came back, and Bethany knew what was wrong. All evening, her mind had suppressed the terror of what had happened with Choco, and the sheer relief of being reunited with Paulo had prevented the shock to surface. But it was apparent now, in a bizarre, primitive physical response that had nothing whatsoever to do with how she felt about the wonderful man who held her. The delicious thought of making love with Paulo wasn't what had hypersensitized her nerve endings. It was the prospect of forgetting Choco's evil leer and the feel of a cool knife point at her throat—a way to fall asleep dreaming of a strong, virile body instead of Choco's fetid breath. There was a crude word to describe what Bethany's fear-ravaged body had been craving, and now that she'd identified it, she couldn't allow it. No, she could never do that to Paulo. He was too special a person; he deserved better.

She pulled away sharply, and though she knew it was the only right thing to do, she still felt as if she were tearing out her own heart. Lingering vestiges of desire caused her to tremble as she stared, wild-eyed, at Paulo.

His hands gripped her shoulders to steady her. "Bethany, what is it? What's wrong?"

Paulo's expression of puzzlement and unselfish concern slashed at her like a pitchfork, and she had to turn her eyes away. "I'm—I'm sorry. I don't know what came over me tonight. It's just that...well, so much has happened."

He turned Bethany's chin with one finger, forcing her to meet his dark gaze, still smoldering. "Yes, so much has happened, and so much more would have happened, if only you had let it. It's no use trying to deny you wanted me, so why did you suddenly push me away? I cannot believe you are the kind of woman who plays with a man's passion." He looked at her as though he were afraid it might be so.

"No, I'm not! Please, believe me, I'm not!" Her voice was very nearly a sob, which she tried to choke back with little success. Paulo picked up her brandy and handed it to her. She took a sip, and the fiery liquid seared her throat, its punishing bouquet welcome. He had every reason in the world to call her a tease. She deserved it. She hated herself for having let things begin; she hated herself for stopping them.

"Paulo," she said, "I'm very tired. I think I'd like to go to my room now and try to get some sleep."

As Bethany was about to pass, he took hold of her arm, not roughly but emphatically. "Not before I hear the truth. You are no sixteen-year-old virgin who is unaware of what she does to a man. You felt the fire between us as strongly as I did, and you knew where it was going to lead. Why won't you let me give you pleasure, help you forget the pain and the fear you suffered tonight?"

Bethany looked up through damp lashes. His face was blurred, but she could see the torment she had caused. "I know what you wanted to do for me, Paulo, and that's why I stopped you. I am attracted to you...very much, but I don't want our lovemaking to be some kind of therapy. If something is going to happen between us, that's not how I want it to be."

Paulo's fingers loosened their grip on her arm, but only slightly. "Tell me, then, how you want things to be."

Bethany, her mind and body taxed beyond their limits, struggled to find the right words. "I don't know...intimate, relaxing, with candles and wine—not after policemen and switchblades." She looked at Paulo, hoping to find understanding in his eyes, but instead, she found a man as torn as she was, a man slipping away.

"I wish I could believe you, God knows," Paulo said in a low, strained voice. "I'd like to believe your actions are as spontaneous as you claim they are."

"But I—"

Paulo held up his hand. "No, let me finish. I, too, have been through a great deal in the past few weeks, and perhaps I am looking for release—some way to forget—in all the wrong places.''

"What are you trying to say, Paulo?" Bethany was suddenly frightened again, but this time it was not fear for her own safety. It was fear of losing something nearly as precious and twice as fragile.

"I don't know why you've come here, Bethany." Paulo's eyes were narrowed, and cold in their regard. "I don't know whether sleeping with the heir apparent was part of your original plan, but now that you've had your bit of fun and adventure, you might as well go back to where you came from. You don't belong in this part of the world. You never will."

Chapter Seven

Paulo watched through the open balcony door as Bethany withdrew calmly to her bedroom. He had to struggle against an overwhelming urge to smash the crystal snifter against the nearest wall. He had expected Bethany to fight back; he'd wanted her to deny what he had accused her of, to employ her legal training to prove him wrong. But all she'd done was stare back at him, her face blanched and devoid of emotion, except for a slight glazing over in her eyes, as if she'd retreated to some inner sanctum. Obviously, he was right about her motives. If he'd been wrong, she wouldn't have stood there and taken his abuse.

Not that he was pleased with himself for the way he'd acted. Far from it. He'd never treated anyone that way before, especially a woman. Even his former girlfriends still considered him the epitome of quintessential charm. So what was it about Bethany that turned him into an impatient, overbearing clod?

Paulo shut his eyes and recalled the gentle sway of Bethany's hips as she walked away from him. Her hair swung like draped satin, sleek and golden, at the back of her long neck, and the set of her shoulders hinted at an inner resilience that somehow didn't detract from her feminine appeal. She was fascinating, this woman whose body language told him she was quite capable of surviving on her own and wasn't about to be intimidated by anyone or anything.

But heaven help him, there were times when she infuriated him beyond reason—like the night they drove to Antonio's house and she asked all those stupid questions. He had felt an undeniable satisfaction telling her to wait with Zoe while he got help. He'd wanted to see her squirm, suffer a little, find out what life was like beyond her pampered North American existence. But when he returned, to his amazement, she'd somehow made herself a part of Antonio's family, hugging the children and sponging Zoe's face as if she'd been raised to a life of poverty. He never did find out what she had said or done during those few minutes she had stayed behind, and for the life of him, he couldn't bring himself to ask Antonio's family even though he'd known them for for years.

And tonight he'd almost lost her! Just thinking about that slimy Choco made him murderous with rage. How unbelievably dense he'd been to leave her alone in that office, as vulnerable as bait on a hook. Paulo smashed his fist against the concrete wall of the balcony and welcomed the reality of pain. First Zoe had nearly lost her life; now Bethany had been in mortal danger.

Paulo stepped inside and began to pace the length of the living room, oblivious to the rosy glow of dawn. He wouldn't have been surprised if Bethany had been packing right now to take the first flight home to Boston. She didn't need this kind of chaos in her life. She didn't need to get involved with the murky details of the lives of people who lived half a world away. Anyone else would gladly flee at the first sign of personal danger, so why didn't she?

He swallowed the last of his brandy and considered pouring himself a refill, but he stopped halfway to the bar. Alcohol wasn't going to help, and he had to coach in a few hours. He went to the sink, filled his glass with water and gulped it thirstily.

Why did he still think she was tied in with everything that had happened? Could she be that ambitious, so ruthlessly calculating that she was willing to risk her own safety to gain from Zoe's inheritance? Paulo's heart dismissed the notion, but what other reason could Bethany have? Was her love for Zoe really so strong, her promise to help so inviolable? The questions without answers circled aimlessly in Paulo's overwrought mind.

It was crazy, this obsession he had for her. She was nothing like the lithe, mahogany-skinned *carioca* women whose passion boiled in their veins. They lived their lives like too-hot stars, burning themselves out in a few years, to be replaced by younger, more nubile clones. There was always an ample supply of women between the ages of eighteen and twenty-five, eager to share the pleasures of the night with a good-looking man. So what in God's name was he doing lusting after a pale American iceberg of thirty who, in this country, would be considered well past her prime? Why did her inevitable return to Boston eat away at him like a guilty conscience, as if her departure were going to make some kind of difference in his life? He didn't want her to stay. He wanted her to get out, so he could get on with . . .

With what? Angrily, Paulo stalked off in the direction of the shower. Well, with some buxom, eager *garota*, for starters! He took hold of the cold-water tap, twisted it and turned the shower on full force. Sure, why not? Just as soon as Bethany stepped on that plane to Boston, he'd get himself a nice, compliant woman. And as far as he was concerned, that moment couldn't possibly arrive soon enough.

IT WAS A LONG, EXHAUSTING WEEK for Bethany and Paulo. They worked every night at Sebastian's, often until dawn. Bethany sat at her desk, checking and rechecking figures while Paulo dozed restlessly at the desk beside her. She often tried to make him go home and sleep in a proper bed, but he wouldn't even consider it. She was worried about him; she knew how close he was to total exhaustion. In addition to spending every night at the office with her, Paulo was still coaching soccer and also putting in forty hours and more in the firm's showroom.

The one positive note was that Zoe was well enough to leave the hospital after a few days. At her insistence, she was driven to Ouro Prêto by one of the employees of Sebastian's who was delivering stationery supplies to the mine superintendent's office. No amount of cajoling or convincing could persuade Zoe to spend another day in Rio, but at least Bethany and Paulo knew she'd be safe and happy in her own home.

Finally, eight days after they'd started, Bethany closed the last of the company ledgers. The examination was complete. Gently, she nudged Paulo from his post at a desk nearby.

"Paulo, wake up. I'm all done."

"*O quê?* What?"

"The audit. It's finished."

Paulo's head jerked up, and he rubbed his eyes with balled fists. His face was creased with the lines of the desk blotter, and Bethany's heart went out to him. He looked so young and vulnerable.

"What did you find?" he asked groggily.

"Nothing."

He looked up at her, squinting. "What do you mean, 'nothing'?"

Bethany held out her hands, palms up. "There isn't a single thing wrong with this company. Sebastian's seems to run better than a well-oiled clock."

Paulo roughed up his curls with his fingers, his expression one of befuddlement. "Are you absolutely sure we didn't miss something?"

"Not that I can think of. The journals are in order; the banking records are fine; manifests, shipping records and receipts are balanced to the penny; and letters of credit are handled just as they should be. We've even searched your father's office from top to bottom." She looked at him curiously. "I thought you'd be pleased."

Paulo pushed himself away from the desk and stood up, stretching his arms high above his head. "I guess I should be. But what about that payment owed to Choco? Something should have come up somewhere."

Bethany shrugged. "Who knows? It might have been a personal item, a gambling debt that needed clearing up or something. Whatever it was, it doesn't show up anywhere in the company records, so I don't see any reason why Zoe can't proceed immediately with the sale."

"I suppose you're right." Paulo walked to one of the windows, opened the slats of the venetian blinds and peered through the space between them. "Maybe it was all a hoax."

"What do you mean?" Bethany asked as she put away the last of the files.

He turned. "Choco's claim that he provided some kind of service for my father. He might be bluffing."

Bethany thought a moment. "Extortion, you mean. That makes sense, I guess. He took advantage of your father's sudden death—claimed the transaction was confidential when, all along, it never even took place. Hmm, you know, Paulo, the more I think about it, the more sense it makes. Choco might be incompetent in a lot of ways, but obviously he is a master opportunist."

Paulo tucked his light blue knit shirt into snug faded jeans, and his face relaxed in a satisfied smile. "He wasn't all that clever, or he wouldn't be wasting away in a jail cell right now." He held out his hand to Bethany. "Come on, let's go have some breakfast."

The omelets, made with onions, ham and potato, were delicious, but Bethany could hardly swallow a bite. She made a valiant attempt to finish the fresh fruit salad and pleaded fatigue when Paulo questioned her sudden moodiness.

There wasn't much else she could do but tell a white lie. She couldn't bring herself to tell Paulo now, of all times, that something about Sebastian's didn't ring true. He would be understandably less than receptive to her theory that his father's business was *too* perfect, as if an audit had somehow been anticipated and a massive cleanup undertaken beforehand.

It didn't make sense. Sebastian's death had been sudden, totally unexpected. She didn't know whether he had a history of heart trouble, but it did seem rather odd that everything, expecially in his office, had been left in such an impeccable state.

Then again, perhaps Sebastian was simply that kind of man, a chronic perfectionist, who always ran a tight ship and would never be caught unaware, even by death. After all, there were plenty of employers in the world like that, meticulous to a fault and absolute ogres to work for. Bethany, of all people, ought to know.

Sipping her coffee, she decided no purpose would be served by sharing her suspicions with Paulo. He had gone through enough heartache and misery in the past few weeks without her adding to it. Besides, her misgivings or suspicions, or whatever they were, had no basis in fact; and there was no way to prove or disprove them. So what was the point of dwelling on it? Zoe was going to sell the company, Bethany was going back to Boston, and that would be the end of it. As for her and Paulo, they were fairly comfortable with each other right now, and she preferred to leave things that way. There had been no more ugly confrontations about her motives since that night on the balcony, and though things were still somewhat strained between them, at least they were guardedly civil to each other.

Although, if she didn't know better, she would have sworn Paulo was being friendlier to her that morning than he'd been since her arrival in Rio. So, perhaps, now that she'd proved her good faith by providing a favorable audit, they could put the past behind them and start over.

Bethany no sooner had consoled herself with that thought than she realized how absurd it was. *Start over at what? When?* In all likelihood, after she left Rio, she would never see Paulo again. At most, all she could hope for was a night or two together without any conflicts coming between them to spoil everything. But even a short-term relationship seemed so purposeless that she'd just as soon not encourage it. Better to part on strictly casual and friendly terms, so that her memories of Paulo would always be pleasant instead of regretful.

When they left the restaurant, Bethany asked as brightly as she could, "Shall we call Zoe and tell her the good news?"

"No, I have a better idea. Why don't we tell her in person?"

Bethany drew in a long breath in hesitation; she had already decided to phone the airline to book the earliest flight home. "I don't know. Now that I've finished what I came here to do..." Paulo looked stricken. "But you haven't even had a chance to enjoy yourself yet, not to mention spend any time with your aunt."

"We-ell, that's true."

"You were going to stay two weeks anyway, so you might as well make the most of it. I can drive you to Ouro Prêto in the morning."

The prospect of a few quiet days in the country did have a certain appeal. "Will you be there with us?" Bethany asked hopefully.

"Not right away. I have to drive on to Brasilia for a soccer tournament. It'll last three days if our team doesn't get eliminated in the play-offs. But on the way back, I'll have a free day or two that you and I could spend together."

Bethany stopped in her tracks and looked up at Paulo. *A day or two.* Her mind seemed to leap out and wrap itself around those few nebulous hours in her future as if nothing else had ever existed or would exist again. "I'd like that," she said, her voice a trifle husky. "I'd like it very much."

THE ANDRADE COUNTRY HOME, a few miles outside the town of Ouro Prêto, was nestled in a secluded valley within walking distance of Sebastian's mines. The main house was a large two-story, pale rose clapboard with indigo-blue shutters and a latticed balcony that extended the full width of the house. The vast grounds were cultivated to resemble a rain forest in miniature—cool and shady, with towering palms, strangler figs and haphazard groves of mango, avocado and papaya. Despite the relative serenity of the setting, silence was unheard of, thanks to the ever-present howler monkeys screeching in the treetops and brightly beaked birds guarding their nests.

It was midafternoon when Zoe and Bethany strolled along one of the many paths that led to the forests beyond the property line. It was Zoe's habit to take a daily walk and, as it was Bethany's third day there, she was becoming familiar with her aunt's routine.

"Do you ever miss Boston?" Bethany asked, after they'd enjoyed a few minutes of private contemplation.

"Sometimes," replied Zoe, "but there are days when I miss Vienna and Paris and Monte Carlo as well."

"But Boston's your home."

Zoe stopped to pick a large leaf from a strangler fig, then, fanning her face, resumed walking. "It was at one time, but now Ouro Prêto is my home. I don't regret leaving Boston, if that's what you mean."

Bethany slid her aunt a curious glance. "You were only sixteen, weren't you, when you ran away with that poet?"

"Is that how your father puts it?" Zoe laughed. "That's not quite how it was. I was seventeen, and I went to Paris to study art. I didn't meet Henri until I was eighteen."

"So you didn't really run away."

"It depends on whose version you're hearing. I was supposed to enter a convent that fall and couldn't think of any other way to get out of it."

"A convent?" said Bethany. "You're kidding!"

"Quite true, darling. Your grandparents wanted their three sons to become respectively, a lawyer, a doctor and a priest. As fate would have it, they ended up with a lawyer and two doctors. Then I came along—poor, unsuspecting Zoe—and everyone decided that having a nun in the family was just as honorable as having a priest."

"Weren't you given any say in the matter?"

"Heavens, no. Women didn't have choices in those days. So I decided to leave home and seek my fortune, as the old saying goes."

They walked in silence for a minute or two. Bethany was the first to speak. "No one in the family ever accepted Henri, did they?"

"No, but they only met him once, before he died of tuberculosis."

"How about Vlad and Sebastian?" Bethany asked, trying to unearth what Zoe could have done to earn the Greys' collective ire. But maybe she was of the wrong generation to understand.

Zoe laughed, a sad laugh. "Now there's a lively topic for the family reunions, I'll wager: my succession of husbands. Let me tell you something, darling. Despite everyone's opinions to the contrary, I've only slept with three men in my life and I married every last one of them.'' Her gray eyes clouded over. "It's not my fault I outlived them all.''

Bethany touched her aunt's arm. "I'm sorry, Zoe. I didn't mean to be so nosy.''

"Nonsense, dear! I'm grateful for the opportunity to air my side of the story for once. And if there's one thing I refuse to harbor, it's regrets. If I had become a nun, I'd have made nobody happy, least of all the One I'd be expected to serve.'' Zoe cast a properly reverential glance heavenward, and Bethany had an idea He was probably in full agreement. "Instead,'' her aunt went on to say, "I was given a chance to make three wonderful men happy in their time, and they in turn gave me great joy.''

"You've been lucky,'' said Bethany.

"Lucky, hell! I had to fight and scratch for every bit of happiness that came to me. You have to be willing to work for it—real happiness, that is. I'm not talking about the mindless limbo most people exist in, working and paying taxes until they retire or drop dead. I know I could have returned to Boston at some point in my life, lived the life of a proper Brahmin widow with season tickets to the Boston Symphony Orchestra and no one would have questioned my right to vegetate.'' Zoe spread out her arms and looked around her. "But I'm having a grand old time out here weeding this impossible jungle and slapping lumps of clay together to make leaky vases.'' She scrunched up her face and turned to her niece. "Incidentally, I've been meaning to ask you, whatever made you decide to become a corporate attorney, of all things?''

Bethany stopped walking and folded her arms across her chest. "I happen to be a pretty good one." Zoe sniffed, unimpressed. "That's not what I asked."

"Oh. Well, I guess because Dad's a lawyer and Grandpa was a lawyer. Somebody had to keep the family firm going."

"Why didn't Theodore and Geoffrey follow in their father's footsteps?"

Bethany thought about her two older brothers, whom she rarely saw. "I don't know. I guess they weren't interested."

"There, you see?" Zoe stabbed the air with a ruby-tipped finger. "Just like me and the convent!"

"But no one forced me to go to law school." Bethany tried to think back to when she actually made the decision, but it wasn't clear to her now.

"Perhaps not," Zoe conceded, "but if I know my brother Burgess, he would have planted the subliminal message into your head the very day he learned his sons wouldn't carry on the tradition."

Bethany shrugged, deciding not to think too hard on the subject. It would be devastating to discover that her aunt was right.

"What did you really want to be when you grew up?" Zoe asked, stopping to lean against the trunk of a tree.

"You mean my ultimate fantasy?" Bethany asked, grinning.

"The *ne plus ultra,*, darling."

Wrapping her arms around her midriff, Bethany stared up at the sky, nearly hidden by riotous overgrowth. She couldn't remember the last time she'd indulged in such a good, old-fashioned, heart-to-heart talk and found herself growing even closer to her favorite aunt. "I wanted to be the captain of a cruise ship, something roomy like the QE Two and have a dozen gorgeous children of my own wreaking havoc with the passengers."

Zoe laughed delightedly. "Marvelous! Is there a mate aboard your fantasy ship to . . . sort of help bring about these dozen children?"

Bethany looked at her aunt and decided it had to be simply because she had seen him a few days ago that suddenly—alarmingly—an image of Zoe's stepson sprang into mind. "I think there might be," she admitted, hoping Zoe's sixth sense couldn't discern names.

Her aunt cocked her head judiciously. "I take it you have someone in mind?"

Bethany kicked a clump of dirt with the toe of her espadrille. "Well, not exactly. There are complications."

"Complications, horsefeathers! Does he live on Pluto? Does he howl when the moon is full? For heaven's sake, if your feelings are mutual, get them out in the open and do something about it! Period."

"That simple, huh?" Bethany looked at her aunt askance and laughed nervously.

"I didn't say it would be simple, darling. Nothing worth having ever is, but you're a fighter and if you put your mind to it, you'll find your happiness. I promise you." As Zoe gestured madly to emphasize her point, her eyes fell to her wristwatch and she gasped. "Oh, hear, I have an appointment with the mine superintendent this very minute. He says he'd rather quit than work for a woman. I must run, dear. Think about what I said."

"I will," Bethany promised, and watched with mild amusement as her aunt picked up the skirts of her gold-fringed caftan and scurried down the path in the direction of the mine office.

Bethany decided to linger awhile longer. The forest was so peaceful, with the air redolent of plant life and the afternoon sun filtering through the trees in golden threads. Strolling along the root-snarled path, she wondered whether there was a grain of wisdom in Zoe's advice. Only three days without Paulo, and already she missed him terribly. Maybe she owed it to herself to test the depths of her feelings for him, even if no reasonable solutions presented themselves right away.

Bethany came to a glade at the top of a hill, a place Zoe said had housed the slaves' quarters for the original plantation. There were still a few signs of the old foundations, but the jungle was quick to reclaim its own. Bethany sat down on a huge tree root. A lizard skittered past her foot and disappeared into the mossy undergrowth. Overhead, raucous birds protested her arrival, or maybe they were monkeys—she never could tell them apart. Stretching her legs in front of her, Bethany hooked her hands onto the root and leaned back, taking a deep breath of the rich air. Just then, her fingers hit something cool and smooth that didn't quite fit with the surroundings. Curious, she looked down and saw something made of glass half buried among the fallen leaves and brush.

She swept away the debris, shrugging with disappointment to discover it was nothing but an old mayonnaise jar sealed with paraffin. She picked it up and nearly dropped it when it jerked in her hands, as if alive. Peering inside, her stomach gave a sickening lurch when she saw an ugly black toad pathetically struggling to escape its glass prison; and a cold shiver ran through her when she realized why the creature wasn't croaking with fright. Its mouth had been sewn shut with black thread!

Horrified, she dropped the jar at her feet and immediately regretted jostling the already suffering amphibian. "Oh, I'm sorry!" she exclaimed, picking up the jar and trying to peel away the paraffin. She didn't hear the crackling twigs and the rustling leaves until Ovidia, the housekeeper, was standing almost directly over her.

"No, *por favor*, Miss Bethany, don't touch!" The rotund black maid was staring down at her, beads of perspiration trickling from her round face as her eyes darted from Bethany to the jar and back again.

Bethany's heart did a couple of frenzied flips at the unexpected appearance of the housekeeper. She looked up at her and held out the jar. "Do you know something about this, Ovidia?"

The woman staggered back half a step. "Put it back, Miss Bethany. It very bad thing! Very bad!" She swiped at her damp forehead with the back of her hand.

Bethany put the jar down, unable to decide whether she felt sorrier for the toad or the frantic maid. Ovidia let out a sigh of relief.

"Why would somebody do a horrible thing like this?" Bethany asked, directing an intense stare at the older woman.

"It has to be, Miss Bethany. There be no other way."

"No other way for what?"

"To fix things. Make them better for the *senhora*, Miss Zoe."

"To fix things?" Bethany echoed. An alarm went off in the back of her mind, and a sickening recollection came to her. She might have naively passed this off as some sick practical joke, except for the memory of an innocent-looking display of cigars, rum, popcorn and candles on a deserted Rio sidewalk. What had Paulo called it? *Umbanda!* "Ovidia," she said. "Is this a magic spell, an *umbanda* offering?"

The maid, stricken with a wave of panic, snatched up the jar and held it protectively to her ample bosom. "It's only for the *senhora*. She suffer too much. I make suffering go away for all time." She wagged her scarf-covered head. "He was no good for her—gone all the time."

"Who was no good for her?" Bethany demanded. "What are you talking about?"

Ovidia, aware she'd said too much, clamped her mouth shut.

Bethany glanced at the toad. It was lying still at the bottom of the jar. The possibility that it might be dead, suddenly, for some unfathomable reason, terrified her. "Why don't you let the toad out?" she suggested to Ovidia, keeping her voice deliberately calm.

"No! No! He must die! He be bad!"

"How can a toad be bad? There's no reason to kill it."

"Not this, Miss Bethany," Ovidia protested. "The *senhor*! He be the one who must die!"

Bethany wondered if perhaps they were laboring under a language barrier. The housekeeper wasn't making sense. "The *senhor*? You mean Sebastian Andrade?"

The woman's eyes, already saucers, widened even more in superstitious terror. "Yes!" Her voice was a harsh whisper.

Despite the heat of late afternoon, Bethany's skin began to rise in icy gooseflesh. "Sebastian is already dead, Ovidia."

The housekeeper shook her head slowly. "No, no, he lives, but this time Ovidia make sure he die." She held out the jar. "When this toad die, the *senhor* die. Exú, the devil, he make sure."

Bethany was the last person in the world to give credence to black magic, but the sudden aura of evil around them was too palpable to ignore. She reached out and grasped the woman's shoulders. "Where is Sebastian, Ovidia? You must tell me for the sake of the *senhora*."

The older woman's shoulders sagged beneath Bethany's grip. "I don't know where the *senhor* is, Miss Bethany."

"Then how do you know he's alive?"

"I know, because he make me do it, but I don't know where he go. He go far away, too far for Ovidia to find him. But Exú, he will find him and keep him from hurting the *senhora* again."

Bethany pointed at the jar with an icy finger. "With this? Is this how Exú will find the *senhor*?"

"Yes."

Bethany felt as though she were slowly losing her mind, but this was not the time to worry about her own sanity. Better to go along with things and learn all she could. "Can you reverse the spell?" she asked.

"O quê? Não comprendo." Ovidia shook her head, confused.

"Make Exú go away," explained Bethany. "Let Sebastian live. Can you do that?" While Ovidia mulled this over, Bethany was trying to ignore the distinct and eerie feeling that Sebastian or Exú himself might suddenly leap out from behind the bushes.

"Yes," the housekeeper said at last, "it is possible."

Bethany let out a deep breath. "Then would you do it, please? The *senhora* would want you to do that. She loved her husband very much. She would want you to save his life."

A tear trickled down Ovidia's cheek. Her pudgy fingers moved over the jar. "Maybe yes, maybe no. Only *Exú* can say if it be too late." With one thick fingernail, she began to scrape away the wax.

It was all Bethany could do not to smash the jar against a rock to let the toad out faster, but then the creature might be injured, or the malevolent forces might become angered. She shook her head in disbelief, reminding herself she was only doing this for the sake of the poor little toad. There weren't really any malevolent forces!

When the paraffin was off, Ovidia unscrewed the lid and tipped the jar into her palm. The toad fell out, but it didn't move.

When this toad die, the senhor *die.* The chilling words came back to Bethany, haunting her, even though she kept telling herself it was ridiculous. Sebastian was already dead and mourned, a memory, nothing more. Whether this little toad lived or not was not going to change a thing.

Ovidia held the small creature to her ear and nodded. "He live. I take him now to the *casa* and open his mouth."

"Then what?"

"I feed him milk for seven days. If the toad live, the *senhor* live.'

Bethany followed the nimble-footed Ovidia back to the large rose house at the edge of the forest. There was no time to waste.

M-X-K-U-R-W-E. The wretched combination of Scrabble tiles sat on the rack in front of Bethany taunting her. The only word that kept coming into focus was E-X-U.

"Are your letters that bad?" Zoe asked. "You've been scowling at them for ten minutes."

Bethany looked up. "Have I? They are pretty bad."

"Want me to take a look?"

"No!" Bethany pulled her tiles closer, as though Zoe might somehow decipher the same words and demand an explanation. But that was crazy! Why should she? "Would you mind if we didn't finish this game? I'm a little tired."

"Of course not, dear. You do look peaked; it's probably the heat."

Bethany got up from the game table and walked to the window. Outside, toads were croaking. "Zoe, may I ask you a personal question?"

"Certainly. We're family, aren't we?

"How did Uncle Sebastian die?"

"Why, of a heart attack. I thought you knew."

"Yes, but what I mean is, how did you find out he was dead?"

Zoe looked confused, but was courteous enough not to remark on her niece's morbid curiosity. "I, uh, found him upstairs in our bed. It was morning, and I came down here to fix coffee. When I went back upstairs to wake him . . . he was gone."

Forgive me, Zoe. "Are you sure he was dead?"

Her aunt blanched. "Of course I'm sure. What's all this about?"

"I promise I'll explain in a minute, or at least, I'll try to. Is there any possibility, do you think—even the remotest chance—that Uncle Sebastian might still be alive?"

Zoe, strong lady that she was, assumed the expression of a person who had just realized she is dealing with the feebleminded. "Come with me, Bethany." She led her niece down the hall and up the stairs to her bedroom, a lovely setting in turquoise and pale pink florals. She sat Bethany down at the edge of the bed. "There were over five hundred people at your uncle's funeral," Zoe explained with an excess of patience. "The casket was open, and it was definitely Sebastian, right down to the missing tip of his little finger." She went to the mantel and picked up an urn. "This is all that's left of my dear, departed husband."

Feeling positively ghoulish, Bethany mumbled an apology and then recounted the incident with Ovidia and the toad. When she was finished, Zoe reacted with great relief.

"Is that what all this was about, darling? You should have told me from the start."

"You already knew about it?"

"Well, not precisely, but I've known Ovidia has been having trouble coping with Sebastian's death. She's a dear woman and has been with us for years, but she is getting on, and has always been a great believer in this voodoo mumbojumbo.'' She ushered Bethany out of the bedroom and down the hall. ''Her mother was the high priestess in the nearby village. It's only natural Ovidia would take it to heart.''

A mulish look came over Bethany's face. ''So you don't think there's any truth to what Ovidia says?'

''Good heavens, no! Do you?''

Bethany stopped at the door to her own bedroom. ''No. No, of course not. Good night, Zoe.''

THE NEXT DAY, after lunch, Bethany went to the larder to check on the toad she'd named Napoleon. Looking none the worse for wear, he was squatting imperiously in a cage that had been brought down from the attic. His bowl of milk was beside him.

''How are you doing, Napoleon?'' Bethany asked, kneeling in front of the cage.

She could have fainted when a deep, familiar voice replied, ''So there you are. I've been looking everywhere for you.''

Bethany spun around on her haunches and found Paulo looking down at her, his face twitching with amusement. ''Paulo, it's you!'' she cried, half shaken with fright. She stood up, and he lifted her off the floor into his arms.

''Of course it's me. How've you been?'' her murmured, raining tiny kisses on her face. ''I've missed you.''

''I've missed you, too,'' she admitted, her fingers in his curls, loving the sensation of being swept off her feet. But then, Paulo could do that to her just by walking into a room.

"I see you got yourself a pet while I was gone," he remarked, leaning his head in the direction of the cage.

"Uh, yes. Cute, isn't he? I call him Napoleon."

Paulo let Bethany go and knelt down for a closer look. "I wouldn't go so far as to call him—" Abruptly, he stopped, his eyes moving to the bowl of milk. "A black toad," he muttered mostly to himself. He turned to look up at Bethany. "Where did you get the toad?"

Something in his eyes told her he already surmised the answer and she'd do well not to try to stretch the truth. "I, uh, found it. . .in a jar."

Paulo nodded, his eyes darkening. "Its mouth was sewn shut, wasn't it?"

"Mmm, yes, I think so."

"Ovidia?"

"Yes, but let me explain—"

"Save your breath, Bethany!" Paulo rose to his feet and stalked across the large kitchen to the backyard, where the housekeeper was hanging laundry. "This one is strictly between Ovidia and me!"

The subject did not come up again after Paulo saw the maid, but from that moment on, the mood in the house became oppressive, almost strangulating. Paulo was as high-strung as a colt, pacing the floors, barely speaking.

BETHANY WAS PACKING her bags for the airport the following day when Zoe came into her room and shut the door. "I have to talk to you about Paulo," she said.

Bethany sat on the bed beside her aunt. "Have you been able to calm him down?"

"No, I was hoping you'd be able to."

"Me? I don't think so," said Bethany. "As it is, Paulo seems to think I'm behind everything that's happened."

"That's not true, dear," Zoe chided. "I think the two of you are merely suffering from an abysmal lack of communication."

Bethany laughed mirthlessly. "On that point, at least, I agree with you."

"No, no, you have it all wrong. I know my stepson. He is battling some very strong feelings for you, whether you believe it or not, I've seen how he looks at you, and the very fact that he doesn't mention your name convinces me."

Bethany toyed with the luggage tag of her suitcase, embarrassed to feel a flush of pleasure coloring her cheeks. "Well, even if that were true, it's a little late for any of us to do anything. My flight leaves tonight."

Zoe placed her hand on her niece's. "I do wish you would reconsider."

"I can't, Zoe. Please don't ask me to. I'm not looking forward to going home, either, but it won't do any good to postpone the inevitable. If I stay any longer, Dad's going to hop a plane and come down to retrieve me himself."

"I know." Zoe stood up and crossed the room to straighten a picture. "You must go, of course, but would you mind talking to Paulo when he drives you to the airport?"

Bethany's face fell. "Aren't you coming with us?"

"No, I've told Paulo I'm not feeling well and that I won't be going to see you off. I'd like the two of you to have a few hours alone together."

"Why? What am I supposed to talk to him about?"

"His father."

"But I hardly knew the man!" Bethany protested.

"Yes, and that makes you an impartial third party, which is precisely what he needs right now. Paulo has never let go of the anger he felt over his father's death. I thought for a while that he was coming to grips with it, but after this unfortunate incident with Ovidia—poor soul—I can see he hasn't even begun to accept it."

"What do I say?" Bethany asked, wishing desperately that she and Paulo were children again. Things were so much easier then.

"Say whatever comes into you heart, darling. The right words will come. The important thing is to make him listen. Get angry if you have to; and if you can get him to shed a tear or two, so much the better. He needs that."

Bethany folded her hands in her lap and let out a long breath. What harm could it do to talk to Paulo one more time if it meant that much to Zoe? If the effort blew up in her face, it wouldn't be the first quarrel she and Paulo had ever had . . , though it would be the last, she thought sadly. What ever became of the blissful day or two she and Paulo were finally supposed to have had together? Suddenly, there were no days left.

"All right, Zoe. I'll talk to Paulo."

Her aunt rushed across the room to embrace her. "Thank you, Bethany. Thank you so much for everything. You two are all the family I have now. I don't know what I'm going to do without you."

Bethany could feel Zoe's tears spill onto her shoulder and could feel her own eyes welling. She hugged her aunt tight, then stepped back to look at her. "I'm so glad I came," she said, "despite everything. I'll never forget all of our wonderful talks—'' Then Bethany's voice broke, and the two women had a good, long cry.

FOR THE FIRST HOUR OR SO, Bethany chatted at great length about nothing in particular, but Paulo's mood did not lift, nor did his fingers loosen from the steering wheel as they drove along the winding mountain highway. Zoe was right; he was taking things badly. It suddenly occurred to Bethany that Paulo had been so busy ensuring that his stepmother would be all right that he hadn't devoted any time to his own mourning. Bethany didn't want to be the one to cleanse his wound, but she knew it had to be done.

She decided it would be best to aim straight for the heart of the matter. "Were you able to convince Ovidia that your father is gone?"

Paulo flinched, and a quick stab of pain shot through Bethany's heart as if his heart and hers were somehow strung together. "I didn't bother trying," he answered. "The woman is a superstitious fool, and totally mad."

"If that's true, then why were you so hard on her, Paulo? I thought you had a soft spot for the poor unfortunates in this world. You're the one who spends so much time in the *favelas*, helping people who can never hope to repay you. Why lash out at a poor old woman who happens to harbor a few harmless delusions?"

Paulo's eyes swiveled sharply to Bethany's, and she was chilled by their icy black depths. "You call someone who conjures spirits to control other people's lives harmless? I'd call her a witch, and in your country, I believe they used to hang witches."

Bethany folded her arms defiantly. "That was three hundred years ago. Listen to yourself, Paulo. You're not making sense. If you have to be angry at someone, be angry at your father for dying and leaving you and Zoe alone. Let the emotion out and be done with it! Sebastian Andrade is gone, he won't be coming back, and you have a long life ahead of you!"

Her indignation was wasted. Paulo's thoughts were eons away, and it didn't appear that he'd even heard her. Bethany wondered what cataclysmic forces it would take to penetrate the thick protective layers Paulo had shrouded himself in.

Suddenly, in a gentle voice, he said, "My father was a great believer in *umbanda*. Did you know that?

At least Paulo was talking about his father. It was a start. "Was he?" she asked.

"He used to make Ovidia cast spells to ensure the good fortune of the company."

Bethany nearly blurted something totally irresponsible about the spells having worked, but stopped herself in time. "That's not so hard to understand," she said, in place of her original impetuous thought. "A lot of people give credence to forces that others can't accept."

She saw the glimmer of a smile on Paulo's face, but she suspected he was barely listening to her. He was listening to his own inner thoughts, and that was good. "I remember Father would be furious with the old woman whenever the shares went down. Of course, Ovidia had no idea of what a stock market was or how it worked, no matter how much Father tried to explain it."

"Just a lot of mumbojumbo to her, right?" Bethany teased gently.

Paulo glanced at her then, and he actually chuckled. "I guess you could say that." They were driving through the northern outskirts of Rio when Paulo spoke again. "My father *is* dead, Bethany." His tone of voice was sad, but it was clearer and stronger than it had been all day. "I saw his body and I touched his hand before they closed the casket. He *is* dead."

Bethany's heart swelled with relief when she saw a tear fall from his eye. "I know, Paulo. Your father's gone."

"I WISH YOU WOULD STAY LONGER," Paulo said as they stood by the departure gate; the first boarding call had already been announced. "We hardly had a chance to get to know each other."

Bethany looked down, her hands in Paulo's. She could feel her eyes brim with tears. "I can't" she managed to reply. "I have so much work waiting for me at the office." Lord, how she hated goodbyes! Everything always came out sounding so trite.

Paulo released her hand and tilted her chin upward with his finger. He was always such a stickler for eye contact, Bethany mused, her heart shattering at the thought of all the precious little memories she'd be taking back with her. How long would it take, she wondered, before everything no longer reminded her of Paulo?

"Are there no other lawyers?" he asked, his eyes moving over Bethany's face, committing her features to memory, as she was doing to his.

"Yes, of course there are, but I can't stay, Paulo. We both have obligations."

"Have we no obligations to each other?"

Bethany tried to grin and failed miserably. "I don't know," she answered. "Have we?"

Paulo nodded slowly. "I, for one, do. From the start, I misjudged you and treated you badly. When I had time to think in Brasilia, I realized how wrong I had been. Your reasons for coming here were motivated solely by your love for Zoe; I know that now. Can you ever forgive me for being such a thickheaded idiot?"

Bethany threw her arms around his neck and choked back a sob. "Of course, I forgive you, you idiot, but don't be so hard on yourself. I'd have probably reacted the same way." she lifted her head from his chest and wiped the tears off his nylon jacket.

"Then don't run away, *querida*. I have so much to make up for. Won't you give me a chance?"

If Bethany hadn't been jarred back to reality by the final boarding call, she might have considered staying a little while longer. But then, such impulsive behavior never came easily to a person like her; for a few short, blissful weeks, she had only imagined it might. She stepped back to the cold emptiness outside Paulo's embrace.

"I'll never forget you," she murmured. "Maybe someday we can . . ." But her voice faded. She was only deluding herself if she thought there could really be any "someday" with a man as wonderful and as far away as Paulo.

His eyes never leaving her face, Paulo reached underneath the collar of his jacket and lifted the gold chain from his neck. The amulet hanging from it was a stylized fist, the thumb protruding from between the index and middle fingers. He slipped it over Bethany's head, and it nestled comfortably between her breasts under the sundress of royal-blue silk. "It's a *figa*," he explained. "Wear it, and it will bring you good luck."

Bethany smiled as she fingered the chain. She could feel the gold against her skin, still warm from Paulo's body. "I thought you didn't believe in that sort of thing," she teased gently.

"I don't," he admitted, "but I was wearing the *figa* when I met you, so it must have some kind of magic."

Paulo took her in her arms for one final kiss, and Bethany, for an instant set briefly apart from her immediate surroundings lived for nothing but the feel of Paulo's soft, intoxicating lips on hers. Then, all too soon, it was over. Bethany picked up her carry-on bag and, with some force of will beyond her own, made her way through the departure gate. She turned and lifted her hand. "Goodbye, Paulo."

He waited until she was gone from sight. Then he turned to go. "*Adeus, querida,*" he whispered, and at that very moment, in the plane, Bethany touched her *figa*.

Chapter Eight

Paulo needed a few minutes alone to think, to unwind before he could face the horde of noisy tourists milling in the showroom. No one ever asked any questions when he entered his father's office and closed the door behind him. They seemed to understand the solace he found there. The room was fraught with memories: the paneled walls, the leather-bound books, even the ashtray studded with agate chips he'd made for his father at school.

He sat down at the enormous rosewood desk and leaned back in the leather swivel chair, the way his father used to do, resting his feet carefully on top of the desk. "Good for the circulation," he remembered his father saying while he'd cross his arms over his paunch. Paulo shut his eyes and folded his arms over his lean stomach.

The sound of the buzzer tore through his thoughts like a barbed spear. Paulo jerked up, his taut nerves snapping as he slammed his fist on the intercom console.

"Yes, what is it?" he barked angrily in Portuguese.

"I'm sorry to bother you," his father's secretary said, sounding genuinely remorseful, "but there's a gentleman here who say he has a confidential matter to discuss with you.''

Paulo wished he hadn't yelled. ''What's his name?'' he asked in a much gentler tone.

''Mr. Lars Hansen.''

The name didn't mean a thing, and Paulo was in no mood for some pushy sales representative. ''Tell him to speak to the general manager.''

''I tried that, Paulo, but he says he will only speak to Sebastian Andrade's heir. He's quite insistent, and although he won't divulge the nature of his business, I suspect it's fairly urgent.''

Paulo knew his father's secretary was capable of turning away the devil himself, if necessary. So if she hadn't done so, there had to be a good reason. Perhaps it had to do with the insurance claim. Paulo let out a sigh of fatigue and depressed the intercom button. ''All right, Maria. Send Mr. Hansen in.''

Lars Hansen spent nearly half an hour with Paulo in his father's office. After the tall, sandy-haired Dane had gone, Paulo sat, unmoving, staring at the bound document left behind on the desk, feeling as though he'd been sold for thirty pieces of silver. He picked up the report, his hands trembling with rage. His eyes read the words over and over, disbelieving, yet unable to deny the evidence right there in front of him, bold and unvarnished.

He switched on the intercom to buzz his father's secretary.

''Yes, Paulo?''

''Maria, I'd like you to book a round-trip flight for me to Boston.''

''Certainly. For what day?''

"What day?" he repeated. "Let me think." Paulo turned slowly in the swivel chair and gazed through the window at the rounded summit of Sugarloaf Mountain. "Why don't we make it . . . Christmas Day?"

BETHANY WAS GLAD to be home. There was a certain solid comfort in being able to look out one's own living-room window, see the colored Christmas lights reflecting off the blanket of freshly fallen snow on Washington Street, and hear familiar carols playing softly on the stereo. Bethany thought about calling her parents and letting them know she was back, but somehow she didn't feel up to conversation; tomorrow would be soon enough. Tonight she would drop in at the office, check her messages, then come home, have a hot bath and curl up in bed with a good book.

Bethany drank the last of her tea and crossed the living room to the kitchen, placing the empty mug in the sink. The kitchen was her favorite room in the whole apartment—not that she was any great culinary whiz—but it was the one room in which she'd allowed her tastes free rein.

Her kitchen was red and white. The canisters were red, the pots and pans were red, the trivets and oven mitts on the wall were red, as was the whimsical enamel rooster that sat bobbing its head on the glossy white countertop. The walls and ceiling were white; the curtains had bold red-and-white stripes; and the soda fountain table and chairs were of white wrought iron with bright red seats. Stepping into her kitchen was like stepping into a giant candy cane—it was great!

Pleased at being back on familiar turf, Bethany went to the front closet and pulled out her winter coat, scarf, hat, mittens and boots. As she dressed, she realized she wasn't feeling quite as happy as she ought to be; there was some vague, undefinable achiness pulling at her.

She trudged through the snow to the office and tried to diagnose what ailed her; sometimes it helped to be able to put a name to it. At first, she thought it might be postvacation blues, but the trip to Rio—apart from the destination itself—could hardly be termed a vacation. Then she thought it might help her spirits to put up the Christmas tree and a few ornaments in her apartment, but just thinking about it made her feel even more tired. It could be the flu, she mused, and made a mental note to check her temperature once she got home.

As she rode the elevator up to the offices of Grey & Associates, Bethany thought of Paulo, and it was as though she'd discovered a miracle cure. Was that what it was, she thought, aghast. She stepped into the dimly lit reception area and decided that was the only thing it could be. She missed Paulo! All she had to do was think about him for the achiness to go away, to feel all warm and tingly inside. She shook her head and laughed, marveling at the awesome powers of the subconscious.

Of course, there was no reason to be concerned about her condition. Bethany felt quite certain that after a few weeks of indulging her fantasies, her memories of Paulo would grow dimmer until they were nothing more than . . . memories. Then she could get on with her life.

Bethany was about to open the door to her office when she noticed a sliver of light under the door of her father's office at the end of the hall. *That's odd,* she thought. Her father seldom worked late here; evenings he preferred to labor in the comfort of his study at home. Then again, it could be the cleaning staff; Bethany reminded herself to investigate on her way out.

She flipped on the lights in her office, took off her coat, threw it over a chair and went to the desk piled high with memos, files and telephone messages.

"Yeeh," she said without realizing it as she sat down and began to lift random pieces of paper from the myriad heaps. *This could take hours,* she said to herself.

As it turned out, the job only took twenty minutes—long enough to toss out the irrelevant stuff, scan the urgent items and divide the rest into piles of descending priority. By morning, she'd probably be ready to tackle her work with some degree of enthusiasm; and besides, it was less than a week until Christmas.

Bethany got up, slung her winter coat over one arm and closed the door, then turned in the direction of the shaft of light at the end of the hall. It never occurred to her to listen first, before she rapped on the door and pushed it open. She simply assumed that if it was her father, he'd be alone. By the time she saw the dark-haired man sitting in the wing chair with his back to her, it was too late to do anything but apologize.

"Sorry," said Bethany. "I didn't realize you had company."

Burgess looked at her as though he were seeing a ghost.

She giggled nervously. "It's me, Dad. Your daughter, remember?"

He stood up and stared at her for what seemed like ages before he stammered, "Be-Bethany, I wasn't expecting you."

The man in the wing chair turned around, showed her a mouthful of huge front teeth and said, "Hullo there, Miss Grey. Nice to see you again."

Bethany's eyes could have popped right out of her head. "Elmer Fletcher, what are you doing her?"

"You two know each other?" her father boomed out. Bethany looked at him. Wasn't that exactly what Paulo had said?

"Sorry, Burgess," Elmer said. "I figured things would go a lot smoother if your daughter and I got acquainted right from the start. That way she wouldn't get the feeling she was being tailed by some weirdo."

"What?" Bethany demanded, her mind splitting into at least five different trains of thought. This man resembled Elmer Fletcher, but he certainly didn't act like him or talk like him—and he'd called her father Burgess! Nobody ever called her father Burgess!

Elmer Fletcher was dressed in patched and faded jeans, a black leather jacket and heavy motorcycle boots. He was smoking a filterless cigarette and when he took a drag he squinted like Humphrey Bogart. He even talked tough!

Bethany turned to her father. "What is Elmer Fletcher doing in your office, Dad?"

Her father was looking rather pasty. "Uh, I hired him to keep an eye out for you."

"You hired him to spy on me?" she asked, feeling like she'd just been punched in the stomach.

"No, no! Not to spy on you," her father hastened to explain. "Just to—er, make sure you'd stay out of trouble."

Bethany nodded. "Stay out of trouble," she repeated in disbelief. She turned to Elmer. "You were spying on me!" Both men shouted vehement denials in unison, sounding like the back half of a barbershop quartet. Bethany sank into the nearest available chair and waited for one of them to begin explaining himself.

Elmer spoke up first. "I wasn't spying on you, and your father was only trying to look out for your safety."

Bethany folded her arms across her chest and slid an unsympathetic look at her father. "I went to a conference in Honolulu last year and I don't recall anyone being sent along to look out for my safety."

Her father opened his mouth to speak but Elmer stopped him. "Let me handle this, Burgess. Sometimes it's best to have a disinterested party do the explaining." He turned to Bethany. "Look, Beth, your dad was worried about your going down to Rio by yourself because of the situation with his brother-in-law's company."

Bethany held out her hands. "What situation? He died, that's all!"

Elmer lifted one ponderous black boot onto the opposite knee. Bethany wondered how he managed to walk in those boots, then chided herself for letting her mind wander. Her attention span wasn't what it used to be.

"He not only died," her father interjected, "but he left behind a vast corporation, and from what I've been able to determine, he did not name a successor to run the company. Now when something like that happens in a volatile—or shall I say, developing—nation, it can give rise to all kinds of insurrection and havoc."

Bethany suppressed a groan. She recognized the picture her father was trying to paint: embassies under siege, looting and rioting, military coups. Sebastian had only been a gem merchant, not a dictator. But there was no point in trying to explain what a civilized place Brazil really was; he wouldn't believe her anyway.

"Not only that," Elmer added, "but he was concerned that your aunt—his sister—might be in such an emotional flap that she might unwittingly place you in jeopardy while you were there. I was hired simply to make sure nothing like that happened." Bethany tossed her father a triumphant look. "See? Here I am, safe and sound—all in one piece!" No sooner had she uttered her self-applauding remark than she regretted it, recalling what had actually happened while she was in Rio. *How much did he already know?*

Elmer, bless his heart, picked up on her quandary right away. "I was just telling your father, before you came in here, about that night on the Copacabana when you got hit on by the pickpocket."

Bethany turned to him and her mouth dropped open. He was covering for her! Hastily, she closed her mouth. "Uh, yes, that's right. Lucky for me you were there, huh?" She turned to her father and manufactured a conciliatory grin. "Guess you didn't waste your money after all, right, Dad?"

She felt like jumping into Elmer Fletcher's lap and giving him a big, fat kiss. How could he have known her father would be furious if he found out that she was at Sebastian's after hours. But then again, he'd called him Burgess; obviously he knew him fairly well.

Her father appeared measurably more relaxed, giving Elmer a look that said, "Thanks for humoring my daughter." To his daughter, he said aloud, "I'm sorry if I wounded your pride by hiring a detective, but you know it's only becuase I love you that I worry." Bethany wasn't ready to forgive him yet, but she would eventually. She always did. "It's okay, Dad," she said with enough reluctance so as to make her message clear.

"So what say we all have a drink?" Burgess announced grandly as he strode to the elaborate bar at the far end of his office. Neither Bethany nor Elmer bothered to raise an objection.

"Tell me, Elmer," said Bethany, "all those things you know about Amazonian bird life. Was it just a front?"

He grinned his toothy grin and draped beefy forearms over the chair. "Nope. When I'm not being a detective, I'm a birdwatcher. Get more mileage out of my binoculars that way. I didn't get a chance to make any sightings on this trip, but maybe next time."

The three of them drank sherry amid a rather strained silence. "What about the whistle?" Bethany asked. "You know, the one you used to scare off the, uh, pickpocket. Do you always wear it?"

"Not always. It's a birdcall. See, I can't usually carry a firearm when I'm in a foreign country, so I gotta depend on other kinds of defense." He made an odd movement with his hands that suggested he was well versed in some effective form of martial arts. The birdcall was for effect. Involuntarily, Bethany shuddered.

She finished her drink and was suddenly anxious to get home to her tub. "Thanks for the drink, Dad." She said her goodbyes and was on her way out the door when she stopped and turned to Elmer. "Just

one more question. Are you really from Poughkeepsie?''

He gave her a nice smile. "Yeah, but a private eye
could starve to death there.''

Bethany returned his grin. "I daresay. Goodbye,
Elmer.''

"G'bye, Miss Grey.''

BEACON HILL SHONE AT CHRISTMAS. Every year, the
red brick town houses were festooned with lights and
holly wreaths, and Bethany always felt the same
childlike excitement when she walked alongside the
snow-covered hedges. Christmas was the one time of
year when she truly appreciated the unchanging tra-
ditions of the neighborhood she grew up in. To her,
Beacon Hill turned into the embodiment of a Dickens
novel, replete with bell ringers and carolers and people bustling home with their fatted geese and plum
puddings.

Turning the knob of her parents' front door, Bethany nearly fell in when the door was yanked open from
the other side by her five-year-old nephew, Timmy.

"Where've you been, Aunt Beth? Santa got here
ages ago, but Grandma said we had to wait for you!''
His freckled face was puckered with annoyance, while
in his fist he clutched some frightful outer-space alien.

Bethany placed the shopping bags full of parcels on
the floor and bent down to remove her boots. "I'm
sorry, Timmy. I was hoping I'd make it before Santa,
but I guess he beat me again.''

"Well, never mind. Come on!'' Timmy tugged at
his aunt's arm, nearly toppling her in the process.

"Okay, okay," she cried. "Give me a second. But first, where's my hug and kiss?" Reluctantly, Timmy delivered, but then ran off to escape further assault.

Bethany's mother, Georgina Grey, appeared from the kitchen, looking flawless, as always, in an eggshell-colored wool dress and a freshly starched apron. Her hair was a perfectly styled coif of salt-and-pepper curls, and her figure was a perfect size four. "Hello, Bethany. Merry Christmas! I'm so pleased the holiday's arrived, or heaven knows when we'd have seen you otherwise."

"Hello, Mother. Merry Christmas!" Bethany towered over the fine-boned, diminutive woman and had to bend down to kiss her cheek. She never could get used to the startling difference in their physical makeup. Not that her mother had ever done anything deliberately to promote it, but Bethany always felt awkward beside her. "I would've dropped by," she explained, "but I was away and then had so much work to catch up on . . ." Lamely, she reminded herself it had only been three weeks and let her defense trail off.

"Yes, of course," her mother replied. "Your vacation. Your father told me; how lovely. You do look so much better with a bit of color in your cheeks." She ushered her daughter smartly down the hall. "Barbados, wasn't it?"

Unseen, Bethany rolled her eyes. "Brazil, Mother."

Georgina Grey, educated in the finest of private girls' schools, was far from stupid, but she maintained a carefully cultivated indifference to those parts of the world she classified as foreign. She adored Hawaii, thought England delightfully quaint, and had been amused by the brightly dressed natives who played steel drums on their Caribbean cruise; but beyond that, she simply didn't care. And while Bethany was quite sure her mother knew that Zoe lived in Brazil, it was one of those topics she found so distasteful that it didn't merit even the briefest of comments. Zoe, to Georgina, bordered on barbaric.

Christmas was the only time of year the family was allowed to gather in the formal living room. In one corner, Timmy's eight-year-old twin sisters sat huddled in earnest conference with their twelve-year-old cousin, Kathy. Each of them appeared to have no fewer than three Barbie dolls and were discussing the relative merits of various Barbie shampoos and conditioners.

Bethany's brother Geoffrey, father of the twins, was five years older than she. He was reading the paper, or hiding behind it, and hadn't changed at all since Bethany last saw him at a summer barbecue. A high-school math teacher, he looked the part: with horn-rimmed glasses, thinning hair, rumpled tweed sports coat, and a slightly fraying white shirt. His wife, Frances, was Bethany's age, but the trials of raising three spoiled children on a teacher's income had left her looking chronically exhausted and years older.

The older of Bethany's two brothers, Theodore, was, as usual, arguing the stock market with his father. Theodore was the handome, gregarious one, a partner in one of Boston's finest accounting firms. His wife, Linda, vivacious and stunning, sold real estate exclusively for the carriage trade. Their professional success, however, had taken its toll on at least two of their four children.

Theodore, Jr., at seventeen, was slouched on a chair reading a comic book; his blond hair was standing up in two-inch sculpted spikes and an assortment of metal things were hanging from his ears. His younger sister, Debby, looked less than comfortable in skintight purple leather pants and a fake leopard-skin tunic, but she, at least, greeted Bethany with a crooked grin and a ''Hi.''

Their mother gave Bethany her finest apologetic smile, the one she always used whenever someone had just finished looking at her kids. ''They'll outgow it,'' Linda's smile seemed to say, and Bethany suffered no doubts that they would. Ted, Jr. and Debby had been outgrowing progressively worse phases all their lives.

''Where's Nathaniel?'' Bethany asked, referring to Linda and Theodore's youngest.

''In your father's study, where else? No doubt reading *The Wall Street Journal*.'' Linda's disparaging tone infuriated Bethany. At ten years of age, Nathaniel was well beyond his peers, a brilliant, sensitive child never appreciated by his parents, who would have preferred a more popular, athletic younger son.

When all the children were gathered together, and Burgess and Theodore had been coaxed away from their debate, the frantic, happy bedlam of opening gifts began. For the next half hour, the room was filled with squeals and laughter, flying bows and gift wrapping. Bethany received her usual assortment of lingerie and toiletry items, but the gifts didn't matter; it was the presence of the children and the closeness of loved ones that made the gestures of Christmas noble and memorable. She wished Zoe and Paulo could be there with them; now, more than ever, she felt as though they were part of her family.

For several years, it had been the custom for Nathaniel and Bethany to save their gifts to each other for

last. Nathaniel sat beside his aunt on the sofa, his eyes
shining with excitement. No one else paid much attention to their private little tradition; they were too
caught up in their own recently acquired treasures.

"Here's your present, Aunt Beth," the boy said
shyly, handing her a large, neatly wrapped box. "I
hope you like it." Nathaniel wore glasses that seemed
too heavy for his delicate nose; his brown hair was
thick and wavy, his blue-gray eyes luminous with curiosity. He would grow up to be a handsome man, but
if he ever became aware of it, he probably wouldn't
care. For Nathaniel, there would be too many other
fascinating aspects of life to explore.

Bethany smiled gently. "I'm sure I will. But here,
open yours first."

The child didn't wait to be asked twice. He ripped
the paper off in large swatches to reveal a black leather
box with a gold clasp. Inside was a collection of several dozen Brazilian gemstones with an accompanying full-color guide. Nathaniel was awestruck. "Oh,
Aunt Beth, this is great! All I've got in my collection
so far is the local stuff!" He gave her a look of profound gratitude. "Thanks! Okay, now it's your turn."

As Bethany opened her gift, Nathaniel suggested, "I
can help you put it together if you like."

When she saw what it was, she, too, was momen-
tarily struck dumb. It was a model of a cruise ship—
sleek, white, beautiful, accurate to the tiniest detail.
She looked at her nephew, and suddenly the cycle became clear. Bethany could remember herself at his age,
opening Aunt Zoe's gift and wondering how she always managed to find something so perfect; and Zoe
used to react the same way to whatever her niece
picked out. She and her aunt had a special kinship that

nobody else understood, much less cared about. Now, seeing Nathaniel, his features turned up at her rapturously, Bethany realized her bond to Zoe wasn't some random aberration of fate. It was a family legacy, one she could now pass from herself to her nephew. She looked at the box with the picture of the cruise ship on the cover: "This is a beautiful gift, Nathaniel. It couldn't be more perfect."

Her nephew squirmed with delight. "Know what?"

"What?"

"I'm gonna be the captain of one of those ships someday."

Bethany gazed lovingly at the boy, and her eyes filled. "That's wonderful, Nathaniel. And if you work real hard, and hold on tight to that dream of yours, it'll happen. Old Aunt Beth will be one of your first passengers."

When Bethany came home to her apartment that evening, she felt a strange mixture of loneliness and joy. Christmas at home had been as it always was: chaotic and happy, tripping over kids and presents; the resurrection of family stories and silly old sibling spats; singing carols around the piano, the words of which were engrained in one's memory as an eternal part of the holiday tapestry.

Bethany switched on the light in her kitchen and put the leftover turkey into the refrigerator. The loneliness that tinged her thoughts was part of a newer memory, but one no less precious—that of a tall, dark *carioca* with dancing brown eyes and charm that would melt an iceberg. She leaned against the counter and drew in a deep breath. She'd get over it. Christmas always made a person weepy for lost loves and distant friends. Perhaps she'd call a few people and find out what they were doing for New Year's.

Bethany was filling the kettle for tea when she heard the knock on the door. She stopped and turned, tilting her head with curiosity. Visitors always buzzed from the intercom in the foyer, unless of course, it was her neighbor, Mrs. Gates, with her annual delivery of shortbread. Smiling, Bethany went to the door and opened it.

It was Paulo!

Chapter Nine

If she'd had the tiniest notion, even the faintest glimmer of hope, that Paulo might show up unannounced at her door, Bethany would have greeted him with appropriate aplomb. She would have cried out his name, flung herself into his arms, maybe even babbled charmingly for a minute or two. Instead, all she did was stare, wide-eyed, mute as a post.

He was impeccably dressed in a three-piece ivory suit, a brown-and-cream-striped shirt, a chocolate silk tie, and a fedora with the brim snapped down jauntily over his eyes. He had a leather travel bag and a fawn suede overcoat tossed over one shoulder. Bethany had never seen him wear so many clothes all at once, the first of many irrelevancies to bounce off her mind as she stood there gawking.

"Merry Christmas, Bethany." Paulo's rumbling voice was like an undertow that pulled her tenuous mental grip right out from under her.

"M-Merry Christmas," she squeaked.

"May I come in?"

"Oh...yes—yes of course!" She stepped back and gestured him inside. Could it only have been a week since she last saw him? He seemed older, but maybe it was the refined cut of the suit or the rakish tilt of his hat that created the illusion. It seemed his tan had deepened, but she might have been comparing him to the wan, wintry faces of those around her during the past week.

Paulo was looking around her apartment with its comfortable forest-green furniture, the braided rugs, the antique bric-a-brac and arrangements of dried flowers. Fortunately, Bethany's working hours of the past week had kept the place orderly by default.

"Very nice," said Paulo, turning to her, his eyes dark and warm as toast.

She gave a light, nervous laugh. "Thanks. It's the period known as Old Slippers."

"I beg your pardon?"

"Never mind," she answered, waving her hand in dismissal. Better to abandon any further attempts at cryptic humor and concentrate instead on being minimally coherent. "So what are you doing here?" she asked, then hastened to amend her blunt but well-intentioned question with, "I mean...it's wonderful to see you, and you look great, but—"

"But you were not expecting a *carioca* for Christmas, no?" he asked, grinning. Then his expression altered, and he glanced around the room. "I am not interrupting anything, I trust?"

Bethany stared at him blankly. "Interrupting?" After a moment or two she realized what he meant, and that single glimmer of Paulo's insecurity was enough to cure the lingering symptoms of her own. Now she wished she had kissed him at the front door. "No, Paulo, you're not interrupting a thing."

"I'm glad to hear that," he said, looking noticeably relieved as he sat down in the chair nearest him.

God, he looked good! No one in the world could wear a suit like that and look so sexy. Ever since he'd shown up at the door, Bethany had been vaguely aware of recurring shivers racing along her spine. Now there was a stirring deep inside her, whipping into a small flame, and her breasts were actually prickling beneath her blue angora sweater.

"I was about to make myself some tea," Bethany said, her voice hopelessly ragged. "Would you like some?"

Paulo's sable eyes traveled over her in that leisurely manner that was exclusively his, and there was something else...an amber spark, a startling intensity in his gaze that belied his casual posture. "Yes, please. I'd like tea."

The time it took for his answer to reach Bethany's brain and the message to be forwarded to her legs was embarrassingly long, but eventually she managed to tear herself away to go in the direction of the kitchen.

It seemed to take an extraordinary long time for the kettle to boil but Bethnay welcomed the illusion of suspended time and was relieved to take refuge in the kitchen alone. If Paulo had tried to rush her, to pick up immediately where they'd left off in Rio...

But then, he wouldn't do that. He wasn't that kind of man.

She hugged her midriff and leaned against the counter with her eyes closed. She could feel a current of emotions and memories rushing toward her. Any moment now, her resistance might be washed away by the onslaught, and quite frankly, she didn't know what she was going to do if that happened.

While she was in Rio, she thought she might be falling love; and granted, there had been plenty of occasions when the chemistry between them had been strong enough to knock her over. But she'd had the gumption to withstand temptation then, if only to make her inevitable return to Boston more bearable. Paulo's appeal, Bethany had so smugly assumed, was little more than an integral part of Rio's magic, as were the palm trees, the hedonistic beaches, the heated rhythms of the music and the nightlife.

But tonight, there were no palm trees, no sandy beaches, no music—only Paulo. So if it had been nothing more than a brief Brazilian summer love, then what was she doing in the middle of this Boston winter wanting him more than she'd ever wanted anyone in her life? The still, small voice that was supposed to help out at times like these remained stubbornly uncommunicative. *Well, I'll just have to wing it, won't I?* she thought. She sliced some fruit cake and put it on a plate, lifted hot, soggy tea bags out of the pot, filled the tray with appropriate accoutrements, and carried it all with remarkable grace into the arena.

"You're looking good," Paulo said as Bethany placed the tray on the coffee table in front of him. "Maybe a little tired."

"Yes, I suppose I am a little," she said breezily, serving his tea and pouring some for herself before sitting down on the sofa. "I just got back a little while ago from Christmas at my parents' where everyone eats too much and drinks too much, and there are nieces and nephews running all over the place..." Good heavens, she was babbling! Hastily, she took a sip of tea to stem the verbal flow.

"I envy you," Paulo said wistfully. "Even though I enjoyed Christmas as a boy, I found it difficult to generate the requisite amount of noise and excitement being an only child. I often wished I could bring my friends home with me from boarding school, but of course, they had their own homes to go to."

What on earth was the matter with her? All this time, she'd been agonizing over what to say and how to act, and even worse, yakking about her own populous family, when she should have been more sensitive to Paulo. He had no brothers and sisters, his real mother was dead, and it was Paulo's first Christmas without his father. As for Christmas dinner, no doubt it had been served to him on a plastic tray, thirty thousand feet in the air.

A vicarious stab of pain shot through Bethany, and she longed to take Paulo into her arms, hold him to her breast and tell him he wasn't alone, that there were people who cared...very much. But he might mistake her response for pity, and she cared too much to let that happen.

"How's Zoe?" she asked instead, feeling hopelessly inadequate, unable to express the swelling warmth inside her.

"Fine. She sends her love." Paulo's eyes caught hers, and for a moment, there was a bond of understanding.

"That's nice," answered Bethany.

They drank their tea in silence for a while. The hot liquid, combined with Bethany's already excessive body heat, formed tiny beads of perspiration along her hairline. She liked the feeling of being with Paulo in her cozy living room with only the ticking of the antique wall clock to break the silence.

When Paulo finished his tea, he placed the cup and saucer on the coffee table and began searching in his jacket pockets, finally pulling out a small black velvet box.

"I wanted you to have this in time for Christmas," he said as he handed her the box.

Bethany sat up and nearly choked on her tea. *Wasn't he rushing things just a little?*

With icy fingers drained of blood that had raced to her cheeks, Bethany lifted the lid. The moment she saw the ring, she knew her fears had been exaggerated. The marquise-cut aquamarine simply set in eighteen-karat gold, was stunning. As if it were yesterday, she recalled their first evening in Rio, when Paulo had taken her hand and said emeralds would never do her justice. For her, he had said, he would find a very special aquamarine: silver-blue, the color of the moonlight glinting off the crest of a wave, the same color as her eyes. How magical that evening had seemed, how untouched by reality; and now she had a memento, one she would cherish forever.

She lifted her misty eyes. "Thank you, Paulo. It—it's exquisite." She smiled tremulously, overwhelmed by the way his gift made her feel, almost as if she were plummeting irrevocably in love. No, she realized now, she'd been doing that all along. The ring merely opened her eyes to it.

Paulo reached out and took her hand. "The stone was mined last week," he said. "As soon as I saw it, I knew it was yours." He slipped it on the ring finger of her left hand and, for a moment, the world disappeared. All that existed was the dazzling purity of emotions set free, the singular brilliance of a flawless gemstone, the warmth of a pair of strong hands holding hers...

Light-years later, Bethany floated back to earth and remembered it was still Christmas, and she had one more gift to give. "I have something for you, too, Paulo, but I haven't had a chance to wrap it yet."

Paulo smiled, reaching out to slide his finger along her cheek. "That's all right. Yours wasn't wrapped, either."

"True enough... Okay, you're sitting on it."

A startled expression crossed Paulo's face, and he fairly leaped off his chair to look underneath. "A cushion?" he asked.

"No, silly, the chair. It's an authentic Boston rocker. I assembled it this morning to be sure all the parts were there and was going to ship it to you, as soon as the freight office opened."

Paulo seemed genuinely surprised and touched. "It's marvelous, Bethany, and very comfortable."

"I thought it might be useful in your condo to...you know, have something that doesn't seduce you the minute you sit down in it."

Paulo assumed a convincingly aggrieved expression. "You disapprove of my leather and brazilwood?"

"Maybe if I were eighteen and a little more flexible..."

He laughed heartily. "To tell you the truth, I never cared for it myself, but a friend of mine who's an interior decorator did it, and I never had the heart to change anything. But I think now I would much prefer this...this Boston style."

"Early American," Bethany corrected gently.

"Yes," he replied, grinning. "Early American."

Suddenly it all seemed so clear. Paulo had taken the first step by flying five thousand miles to be with her on Christmas; if there was going to be a next step, it was she who was expected to take it. "Paulo, do you remember what you said the day you saw me off at the airport?"

"I accused you of running away, if I remember correctly."

"I was," she admitted softly, "but I'm not running now."

Paulo rose from his chair and came to sit beside her. Could it only have been a week? She looked even more enchanting than he'd remembered. He knew what she was offering, and he should have felt triumphant, his mission to seduce Bethany Grey virtually accomplished. But it wasn't that simple anymore.

There was a time when he'd have made love to her just to gain the psychological upper hand. Later, he had longed to protect her, shield her forever in his arms, if only she'd let him. But now, he understood his feelings so much better than before. He loved Bethany and wanted her so deeply he would have gladly torn out his heart and given it to her. But it wasn't what he'd come here to do. He'd come to find out whether the woman he adored was an angel or the lowest kind of sorceress.

Bethany read the hesitation in Paulo's eyes, and she didn't blame him. Heaven knew she'd led him along this path more than once. But now, she was certain, the time was right.

"I've missed you, Paulo." Her silver-blue gaze was shimmering like the crest of a wave by moonlight.

He took her hands in his. "I've missed you, *querida*...so much."

"Then make love to me," she whispered.

He couldn't bring himself to say a word. The moment was so perfect—and so treacherous—he could barely nod. Their fingers intertwined, and he brought her to her feet.

Bethany needed no words. As she led him to her bedroom, the feel of his arm around her waist and the fiery glint of love in his eyes were enough.

The air in the room was cool, and Bethany shivered as she drew back the handmade calico quilt, but Paulo's touch was warm. He turned her to him gently and lowered his mouth to hers. His velvet lips were a thousand times more intoxicating than she remembered. He traced her lips with his tongue, teasing the corners of her mouth, and skimmed the pearly surfaces of her teeth.

His caresses were insistent, yet languorous and heady. His hands roamed her back and his thighs shifted to link with her. The sudden flare of his arousal traveled her body like a blaze out of control.

Bethany's fingers explored the lines of his neck, the shape of his ears and the hollowed planes of his cheeks. When he grasped her below the waist and thrust his tongue seductively into her mouth, she felt a flame burst deep inside her, licking her, consuming the last shreds of hesitation.

Their kisses came to a reluctant end, and Paulo stepped back to remove his jacket and vest, tossing them to a nearby chair. The soft glow of the lamp cast patterns of light and shadow across his face, searing his image into Bethany's subconscious, so that even when he lifted the angora sweater over her head, she could still see him gazing at her, almost worshipfully.

"You are wearing the *figa*," he whispered, toying with the amulet nestled between her breasts.

"I never take it off," she whispered. "It brings me luck."

He looked up, and the glow in Bethany's eyes told him she wore it to remind her of him. Maybe it did bring luck.

When Paulo shrugged out of his shirt, Bethany caught her breath at the sight of his bare chest, the manly contours just visible beneath the thick, dark hair. She moved her hands across him, caressing the gentle slope of muscle, sliding over subtly aroused nipples to the sinewy arms that reached out to unclasp her bra.

The light undergarment slid to the floor. Then, cautiously, Paulo moved his hands to cup the undersides of her small, high breasts. He lifted them gently, and when his thumbs grazed across the taut nipples, Bethany grasped. He brought his mouth to each one in turn, nipping and teasing with quick, light motions. Then, with a firm movement, he took possession of one breast, and Bethany felt the shuddering impact deep within her womb, as if he had unleashed some latent primordial instinct.

When they had both shed the rest of their clothes, she lay down on the bed and slid across the cool white sheets to make room for Paulo. But he stood where he was for a long time, looking at her. If she'd been the least bit capable of objectivity, she might have discovered something strangely out of place, deep in his eyes. But it had only been a flicker, after all, quickly replaced by a finer, more candid emotion.

At last, he came to her and simply held her. Then, slowly, instinctively, their bodies began to move in tandem. Paulo rained tiny wet kisses along her shoulder and brought his thigh to rest between her legs.

With his shallow breathing echoing in her ear, she became aware of her own body moistening in anticipation of him. His fingers brushed against the core of her, sending a myriad of sensations spiraling upward and she could feel the taste of his mouth on her tongue.

He plied her with the lavish attendance of a courtier, not to impress or exhaust her with selfish manipulations, but to give her pleasure slowly, to ripen her body for love's ultimate union. Not until Bethany was writhing and calling out his name in frenzied gasps did he raise himself from his intimate savoring of her and enter her. And when he knew that her body could receive him fully, he began to move with sure, steady strokes.

With a hunger that reached out from the deepest part of her, Bethany wrapped her legs around Paulo and dug her nails into the taut flesh of his buttocks. Her moans grew stronger as she swiftly soared to supernatural heights, crying out when the galaxies spun and the heavens burst open, her body a tumult of sensations transcending anything she'd ever imagined. Paulo's answering cry was a universe away, yet came from Bethany's very soul. He collapsed against her, and lingering passion surged through them. Finally, there was the perfect, blissful silence of two hearts, two bodies...now one.

A DELICIOUSLY EROTIC DREAM came to an abrupt end when Bethany rolled over and collided with icy sheets. Grumbling, she opened her eyes and glanced around the coral-hued bedroom, vivid with sunlight filtering through lace curtains. She looked down at herself and frowned. What on earth had possessed her to go to bed without her flannel nightgown?

The steady pulse of the shower emanating from the bathroom, and the feeling of warm contentment deep inside her, brought the wondrous lovemaking of the night before back. It didn't matter if her toes felt like icicles; in a few minutes, Paulo would come back and warm her. Not only that, they had the whole day ahead of them, no commitments, no obligations. Just the thought of it made her curl up like a sated kitten, purring.

Paulo came out of the bathroom, a towel wrapped around his waist, his body ruddy from the heat. "Did the shower wake you?" he asked.

Bethany smiled and brought the ineffectual covers to her chin. "No, the sheets did. There is nothing in the world that torments me as much as icy sheets."

Paulo didn't smile back. In fact, he walked right past the bed, hardly looking at her and went to his suitcase for some clean socks and underwear. "You should have turned on the electric blanket," he said curtly.

"I didn't think I had to," Bethany replied, flinching at his coldness. "I thought you'd..." She let her voice trail off, realizing that it was not something she should have to explain.

Bethany propped herself up in bed and watched, incredulous, as Paulo stepped into a pair of light gray slacks and put on a blue shirt. If she didn't know any better, she'd have sworn there was a stranger in her room, though even a stranger would have acknowledged her presence and seen from her expression that he'd hurt her. A stranger would have been civil.

There was no point in pursuing the discussion until both of them were dressed and fortified with hot, steaming coffee. She swung her legs out of bed and clenched her teeth, her feet curling reflexively when they hit the hardwood floor.

How could she have been so wrong about him? She had virtually lived with Paulo day and night for two weeks and had never seen an inkling of insensitivity, let alone cruelty. Everyone loved Paulo Andrade. Zoe adored him, his coworkers thought the world of him, even his former girlfriends were thrilled when they saw him. So she could hardly blame herself for falling under the same spell. In fact, what chance had she ever had to resist him?

Bethany stood beneath the hot, stinging spray and struggled to clear her mind of extraneous emotions. Her rational, legalistic side told her it was time she woke up. She was thirty years old, and at her age, she ought to have been better prepared. It wasn't the first time she had discovered things were less idyllic and magical than they'd seemed the night before.

The premise was disturbingly straightforward. Bethany had fallen in love with Paulo and, after much deliberation, had agreed to go to bed with him. Paulo, a young, virile man unaccustomed to being refused, had finally succeeded in his latest conquest. Fortunately, in his advantaged position as Sebastian Andrade's son, he could afford the eight-karat ring and the round-trip flight from Rio necessary to achieve his purpose. And there you had it: a simple case, with precedents *ad nauseam*.

Breakfast was a strained affair, and Paulo, much to Bethany's disappointment, did not choke on his meal. In fact, he ate rather heartily. "How did you know that French toast is my favorite?'' he had the audacity to ask.

Bethany stabbed a sausage on her plate. ''Because you told me so in Rio, and I even fixed it for you while I was there.''

''Oh. Yes, I suppose you did.'' Paulo did not look up until it became necessary to tilt his head to drain the coffee mug. By this time, Bethany's perception had cleared up enough to realize there was more behind his mood than lack of respect. There was out-and-out hostility!

Bethany's knife and fork fell to her plate with a deliberate clatter. ''Okay, Paulo, if it's something I said or something I did, why don't you tell me about it? The silent treatment always makes me jumpy.''

His eyes took aim at hers for the first time that morning and, for a moment, Bethany could have sworn she caught a glimpse of remorse, a hairbreadth of hesitation; but then the scraping of his chair across the linoleum floor overpowered all such subtleties. ''You're right,'' he mumbled. ''There is no sense in prolonging things any further.''

She heard him go into the bedroom. When he came back a minute later, he was carrying a large manila envelope. He sat down, his dark eyes strangely opaque, as he pulled out a bound document and handed it to Bethany. ''Perhaps this will refresh your memory.''

She looked at the title and flipped through the neatly typed pages with the standard topographical maps, charts and diagrams. Looking up, she shrugged. ''It's a geological assessment of your father's mines in Ouro Prêto. What does it have to do with me?''

"It was given to me by a Danish geologist named Lars Hansen." Paulo's statement was issued as pointedly as the stare that followed.

"Is that supposed to be an answer to my question?"

"You deny knowing him, then?"

"Of course I deny it. Why shouldn't I?"

Paulo's resolve seemed to falter for a moment. "Hansen represents the Danish consortium that's interested in acquiring Sebastian's."

"That's good, isn't it? Zoe should be pleased to have a prospective buyer so quickly." Bethany decided to disregard Paulo's inference that she was supposed to know what he was talking about.

"The sales proceedings were initiated by my father," he replied in a dry tone.

Bethany thought for a moment. "Oh, I see. But why, when the business was doing so well?"

"Apparently not as well as we thought. In fact, it was in enough trouble that it probably brought on my father's heart attack at the end." Paulo leaned back tiredly in his chair, and Bethany saw the look of painful resignation on his face. Despite everything, she was relieved to see the reality of his father's death had truly sunk in. And there was nothing wrong with Paulo's trying to pinpoint the possible source of Sebastian's heart attack, as long as he kept within reason. Heart trouble was usually the result of a lifetime's worth of problems.

"What did you find out about the company, Paulo?"

"I learned, after much bribing and threatening, that our mine superintendent had been purchasing high-quality emeralds from small, private landholdings, because our mines haven't produced any for years."

"You had no idea the mines were running low?"

"No, but I wasn't meant to find out, nor was anyone else. The miners were still finding plenty of smaller stones, enough to keep everybody working and happy. But this purchasing venture was being conducted strictly under the table in Ouro Prêto. I'd been aware of a slight reduction in the number of high-quality stones we were receiving in the showroom, but there was no reason to be overly concerned, and certainly no way to identify where the emeralds had come from."

Sebastian Andrade's squeaky-clean records were beginning to make more sense, Bethany thought, with a pang of sympathy for Paulo. His father was a man who had reason to keep his tracks covered at all times.

"Why couldn't your father just buy more property if he knew his reserves were running low?" she asked.

"Because most of the land in the ore-bearing regions is already bought up, by us and our competitors."

"Couldn't he have bought out the small landholders?"

Paulo shook his head. "He'd never get back his investment. They'd band together and hold out for outrageous sums. No, they had a good thing going with Sebastian's. They'd never have sold." He pointed at the report. "Take a look at page sixteen."

Bethany flipped through the pages and skimmed the section Paulo referred her to. She blanched. "It says here that the mines have an estimated ten years of operating life ahead of them with a steady supply of high-quality emeralds. When was this written, Paulo?"

"A few months ago," he said in a bitter voice. "As you can see, the report is not merely an exaggeration; it's fraudulent."

"But who would have written such a—"

"Choco."

Just the sound of that vile creature's name was enough to make Bethany's skin crawl and her heart hammer, even though she knew he was safely behind bars five thousand miles away. She slapped the report onto the table. "So that's how he was able to claim such a high payment. Your father was backed right into a corner." She let out a deep breath and thought quickly. "If I were you, I'd go straight to your father's attorney and tell him everything, before you end up in a lawsuit."

"That's exactly what I intend to do." Paulo's expression was grim as he reached into the pocket of his shirt. "This is the business card that was attached to the report." He tossed it across the table, and Bethany recognized the creamy vellum and the elaborate script even before she picked it up to read the name.

Burgess Grey, Attorney-At-Law.

Chapter Ten

"There must be some mistake," Bethany said, her mind groping for some reasonable defense. "Where did you say this came from?"

"Are you sure you don't already know?" Paulo's voice was silken, the quintessence of civility, but Bethany couldn't miss the faint hint of accusation.

She looked up and, dropping the card neatly on the table, said in a voice that matched his smooth delivery, "Paulo, I have a fairly good idea what you're thinking right now. But not only have I never in my life seen this report until today, I've never heard of what's-his-name Larsen or Hansen and, as far as I'm concerned, you could just as easily have set this whole thing up yourself. So don't hold your breath waiting for a confession or an explanation because I have none to give."

Their eyes locked in a moment of silent, vitriolic challenge, neither of them wanting to be the first to display a sign of weakness. It was Paulo who backed down first, not to confess or apologize, but to pour himself another cup of coffee.

"How do you suppose one of your father's business cards ended up in Rio?" he asked, giving her a deeply probing look.

Bethany felt as though she were trying to scramble up a steep, icy precipice. It was terrifying not to have any answers and no prior warning. "I don't know...I— Wait a minute! I always carry one of my father's cards in my wallet, and I had my wallet in Brazil." She leaped up from her chair but froze when she saw that Paulo didn't share her sense of relief.

"You don't think, surely, that someone would have stolen it from you." he said, incredulous.

"I didn't mean—" Bethany threw up her hands. "Oh, for heaven's sake, Paulo, I was nearly kidnapped while I was there! Forgive me if I'm so bold as to suspect petty larceny."

At that, he relented. "Then, please, go ahead and check your wallet."

"Thank you," she said, seething. "I think I'll just do that."

Bethany always made a point of carrying exactly half a dozen of her own cards, and one of her father's. She kept his card in a separate compartment together with the cards of her business associates. She riffled through them quickly, dismayed to discover her father's card in place. For an instant, her heart leaped when she saw there were only five of her own. Someone could have taken it, had an identical one printed up with her father's name on it... No, that didn't make any sense! Why would someone go to all that expense and bother when her father's card was right there for the taking? Then she remembered handing one of her cards to the lapidarist in Sebastian's with the usual "If you ever come to Boston..."

Bethany returned to the kitchen at a slow pace and deep in thought. She glanced at Paulo as she went to pour herself some more coffee and was surprised to find his expression tinged with sympathy. Suddenly an explanation occurred to her.

"I think I have an idea where the card came from," she said, bringing her coffee to the table. "Choco claimed to know of my father's reputation from your dad. Perhaps your father had one of his cards, and Choco just took it and tacked it on the report."

"Where would my father have gotten one of Burgess Grey's business cards? We've never even had a Christmas card from him."

Bethany's eyes widened; then she turned away in sudden embarrassment. *Not even a Christmas card?* "Maybe Dad gave it to him when your family visited us in Boston."

"That was eighteen years ago. Has your father been using the same cards for eighteen years?"

Her nerves getting edgier by the second, Bethany got up and moved to the counter. "No," she admitted. "The firm moved its offices just after I started to practice." Silence hovered between them. "That means our fathers have been in contact with each other sometime in the past six years," she said with a strange, sinking feeling.

"So it would appear."

More silence.

"Wait a minute!" Bethany slammed her mug down on the counter. "If you knew all this and suspected that I might be involved, how the hell did you have the nerve to make love to me last night?"

But Paulo appeared to have anticipated her accusation. "I considered having this discussion last night, but do you think we still would have made love?"

Bethany gave a bitter laugh. "I should hardly think so."

"That's why I decided to wait until this morning." His eyes didn't so much as flicker.

"You admit it?" shrieked Bethany. "You can sit there and calmly admit you used me?"

"What do you think you were doing to me?"

At first, Bethany was confused. Then her rage rose once again. "I wasn't using you! I had nothing to do with this...this...whatever it is!"

Paulo's expression softened—inappropriately, thought Bethany. "That's what I was hoping I would hear you say, *querida*, because if you had no knowledge of this fraud, then you have nothing to regret for having slept with me."

Bethany felt her anger begin to subside, almost against her will. "But you knew about it, and you slept with me. Do you realize what that makes you?"

Paulo shrugged. "Yes, I'd say that makes me a man who acted out of love rather than common sense."

Bethany caught her breath. "What was that you said?"

"I said I'm in love with you."

"Oh, I thought that's what you said." She began to pace as if she'd been faced with another quandary, halting abruptly to face Paulo. "You thought I might be involved in fraud, and you still fell in love with me?"

Paulo's mouth turned up in a mulish grin. "I've since discovered that the two disparate situations are capable of existing at one and the same time. But I am grateful to hear that I fell in love with an honest woman."

The tension in the room exploded like a bursting bubble, and Bethany, rendered temporarily insensible, could think of nothing to do but yank an oven mitt off the wall and hurl it at Paulo. "You're unbelievable!"

The mitt plopped harmlessly on the floor and Paulo, laughing, opened his arms. "Come here, Bethany."

So what did it matter if she was walking into enemy territory, she asked herself, still stupefied, as she closed the distance between them. She happened to be crazy about this enemy.

Bethany snuggled down into his lap. Paulo locked his arms around her waist, tipped his head and kissed her long and hard. Passion rose inside her like a fountain, and Bethany vowed, there and then, that they would work this thing out. Whatever the misunderstanding, it could be fixed. Whatever mix-up had brought them together, it was not going to tear them apart. She couldn't bear the thought of losing Paulo again. No matter what happened...

"I'm sorry, *querida*," he murmured, as he cradled her face in his hands, and his dark eyes caressed her. "Perhaps we should have had this talk last night, but I couldn't bear seeing you again and not being able to make love to you. I didn't care if you were lying to me; it was a risk I had to take."

Bethany traced Paulo's gentle mouth with her finger, feeling as warm and safe as a kitten. "Did you really suspect me all along?"

Paulo shook his head. "Never in my heart, only in my mind. Even when Hansen gave me this report, and the evidence was so damning—I was furious, mind you, and probably would've strangled you if you'd been there."

"Lucky for me I was gone, but I take it you got over being furious."

"More or less. By the time a week had gone by, I had almost convinced myself you were innocent. I'd seen too much of your goodness, your decency." He brushed his long fingers through her hair. "Besides, you have these remarkable lie-detector eyes. You'd never make it in crime."

"You're right about that," she said, her face nestled in his curls, her heart swelled to bursting. "And I'm glad you trusted me," she added in a whisper. It felt so right being here with him, their lives unaccountably meshed once more. Even something as inconsequential as the scent of her shampoo in Paulo's hair gave her a comforting sense of oneness with him.

"There were a few times in Rio when you might not have trusted me," Paulo said, his head resting on her breast.

Bethany sat up. "There were? When?"

"How about the night Choco tried to kidnap you? Did it never occur to you I might have set it up?"

It hadn't; and thinking back on the incident, Bethany had to admit his suggestion was plausible. But now, she couldn't seem to conjure even the slightest doubt. "Sorry," she said, grinning. "You'll never convince me."

Paulo's smile showed how grateful he was. "Does that mean you trust me?"

Bethany nodded, looking at Paulo's face through misty eyes. "With my life," she said.

"Good, because we're going to have to rely on each other's complete trust for the next little while."

Bethany knew what he meant, but her mind steadfastly refused to acknowledge anything beyond the immediate present, so she didn't reply.

Paulo pressed on. "We must find out what's behind this report. We can't get any answers from Choco...or my father."

"I know," Bethany replied in a quiet voice. "That only leaves Dad."

Gently, he took her hand in his. "You can think about how we should handle it. You're the one who knows your father best."

All of a sudden the world didn't seem so rosy anymore—not even here on Paulo's lap, in her candy-cane kitchen, on the day after Christmas. Bethany stood up and began to clear the dishes from the table. "We might as well begin with Dad's office," she said with a deep sigh of resignation.

LATE AFTERNOON of the next day, Paulo stood at Bethany's full-length mirror and adjusted his necktie. "I still don't understand why you don't simply have a talk with your father, instead of doing all this sneaking around behind his back."

"You'd understand if you knew my father," Bethany answered as she applied mascara to her lashes at the bathroom mirror. "If it turned out he had nothing to do with this fraudulent sale, and I so much as implied that he had, he'd hit the roof—and probably fire me, too."

Paulo came into the bathroom, his eyes traveling appreciatively over Bethany's violet mohair dress. "Okay, I can appreciate your hesitation, but let's assume he does know something about this whole business. Don't you think, if you confronted him with your proof, he'd be forced to admit it?"

Bethany turned away from the mirror. "You call a business card proof? Ha! We're talking about an attorney who sends presidents of multinational corporations slinking away with their tails between their legs—and I'm only his daughter. Why do you think I put us through the bother of searching for four hours in his office yesterday? If I'm going to get him to admit anything, I'll need something irrefutable—a file, correspondence, signatures and dates." She leaned over and planted a kiss on Paulo's mouth. *"Compreende?"*

Paulo slid his arms around her waist and moved closer. *"Compreendo*, and, *querida*, you look fabulous."

"Thank you. Now do you remember what it is you have to do when we're at my parents' tonight?"

"Yes. After dinner, when your father brings out the liqueurs, you're going to excuse yourself and go upstairs. My job is not to allow your father to go to his study under any circumstances." Paulo gave her a doubtful expression. "I fail to see how you expect me to keep the man in one spot if he doesn't want to stay in one spot. Even if I were to spill a drink all over myself, it would be your mother who sops me up, and your father would probably escape to his study in utter disgust."

Bethany, despite her case of nervous jitters, burst out laughing at the thought of Paulo pulling such a stunt. "Right," she agreed. "I see your point. Just give me a minute to think." She went into her bedroom and sat down on the bed. Suddenly she leaped up. "I've got it!"

"You sound inspired. Let's hear it." Paulo was putting on the jacket of his ivory suit, and Bethany could feel her bones melt just looking at him.

"Uh...where was I?" she mumbled. "Oh, yes. Dad has been working on a pet project in the basement for years. He likes to consider himself a woodworker, but he only spends about fifteen minutes a month at it."

"What's the project?"

"A deacon's bench made out of cherrywood. The last I heard, he had the pieces cut. He loves to talk about his hobby to anyone who'll listen, especially about his tools. He has a fortune tied up in power tools."

Paulo considered this for a moment, then nodded. "You want me to ask him about the deacon's bench— I hope I'll remember what it's called; then go to the basement, and let him talk all he wants about his tools."

"You got it. Believe me, the plan is foolproof, which it has to be. *No one* is allowed in Dad's study on pain of death! I'll bet I haven't spent a total of twenty minutes in that room in my entire life, and whenever I was there it was only to be disciplined for some infraction or another."

Paulo chuckled and took her arm. "Let's go, Mata Hari. I'm starved."

While they were in the car, Bethany pointed out various places Paulo had visited as a nine-year-old, including the park in Beacon Hill where she'd tried to lose him. They had a good tension-relieving laugh about it; the park seemed so small now.

"Does your mother still shout?" he asked as they climbed the steps to the Greys' front door.

Bethany gave him a curious look. "I beg your pardon?" But she didn't get an answer; just then, her father opened the door.

"Hello, hello!" he boomed out. "Come right in. Can't have you out there freezing when you're not used to our New England winters." Burgess Grey, at a shade over six feet, had to look up to greet Paulo; he shook Paulo's hand firmly. "Well, well, I never would have recognized you, son. You've grown to be quite a man."

"It's a pleasure to see you again, Mr. Grey."

"Burgess. Call me Burgess," he insisted, much to Bethany's surprise. Her father took their coats and hung them up. "How are you, Bethany? Recovered from Christmas yet?"

She leaned over for a kiss. "I'm just fine, Dad, though I overdid it, as usual. Where's Mother?"

"Here I am," a voice said from the kitchen. Georgina, looking like a Dresden-china doll in beige crepe de chine, came out to greet her daughter and her guest. "So this is little Paulo," she claimed, nearly tipping over backward to look up at him. "How nice to see you again after all these years."

At first, Bethany thought she was imagining it, but her mother actually *was* speaking louder. Paulo, however, a paragon of courtesy, seemed not to take the slightest notice of Georgina's sudden attempt to reply mostly on monosyllabic words.

The dinner that followed was a torturous affair for Bethany, though she kept reminding herself that her pain was self-inflicted. She was the one who had called her mother yesterday morning to announce with great enthusiasm, "Guess what? Cousin Paulo is in town!" Of course her mother immediately extended the dinner invitation out of simple courtesy, which had nothing whatsoever to do with how she felt about the

Andrade branch of the family. There were times when Bethany was grateful for her mother's predictability.

After the pot roast and dishes were cleared from the table, and trays of assorted petit fours were put out to serve with coffee, Bethany excused herself. As she moved her chair away from the table, she gently nudged Paulo's leg to remind him that their operation was about to commence. All evening, he had seemed so thoroughly enthralled with everything her parents had to say that Bethany began to wonder if he remembered why they had come.

As she headed up the stairs, Bethany could hear her mother say to Paulo in a loud voice, "Be sure and say hello to Zoe when you go back to your own country!" She emphasized the final word as if fearing that it might be too difficult for him to understand.

Bethany cringed. But when she heard Paulo reply in an equally loud voice, "Thank you! I will!" she had to clap her hand over her mouth to muffle her escaping guffaw.

As soon as she entered her father's study, however, all seriousness rapidly returned. There wasn't much time, and she had a lot of ground to cover. She started at her father's desk, an antique oak rolltop with many small compartments. Searching every nook and cranny; she found only current bills, a few ledgers and some stationery supplies—but no files.

Next, she went over to the large steel filing cabinet and slid open the heavy drawers, careful not to make any noise. Most of the files in the cabinet turned out to be outdated, containing old tax returns, expired insurance policies and a few legal cases settled years ago. It was possible, of course, that her father had deliberately mislabeled the transactions dealing with Sebastian's, but somehow she doubted it. He was too punctilious, too orderly. If he'd done legal work of any kind for his brother-in-law, there would be a file somewhere, and it would be immediately recognizable.

With a sinking heart, Bethany realized that this search was going to be far more time-consuming than she'd bargained for. The clock on the mantel was ticking away noisily as she combed through the bookcases, feeling beads of perspiration break out over her as the pressure mounted. Nothing, nothing—everywhere she looked, there was nothing! She wondered if Paulo had succeeded in getting her father to the basement. If her mother walked in Bethany could always make up some excuse about retrieving a file or a law book.

She glanced at the clock. This was ridiculous, skulking around like a thief in her own home. Maybe Paulo had been right. She could have leveled with her father, endured the fireworks and been done with it. He might even have surprised her and admitted everything. But this nonsense of tearing up the floorboards for a—*Wait a minute*, she thought. Her father was meticulous, he surely would be capable of hiding something he thought shouldn't be seen. She looked down at the Persian carpet. Why not? She got down on her hands and knees. Sure enough, as her eyes scanned the carpet, she saw a bump, about the size of a legal file, a few feet away, over by the— Bethany froze when she looked up at the new piece of furniture in her father's study. The bump was right in front of a cherrywood deacon's bench. He'd finished it!

Poor Paulo! She wondered how he'd managed to stall her father this long. Bethany crawled closer and had just begun to lift up the carpet when the door opened and her father walked in.

"No, this is the first piece I've ever—" Burgess Grey stopped dead in his tracks and looked down at his daughter crouching on all fours with the carpet rolled back. "Bethany Amelia Grey!" he bellowed. "What in the hell are you doing here?"

Chapter Eleven

"Dad!" Bethany cried, feeling her face and neck turn crimson.

Paulo, looking positively woebcgone, appeared from behind her father. "Bethany, I had no idea he'd bring me up here—"

"You stay out of this!" snapped Burgess, glaring at his guest.

"It doesn't matter, Paulo," Bethany said from the floor. "Dad, don't be angry with him. This wasn't his idea."

Burgess's heavy brows came together. "What wasn't his idea?"

Thinking quickly Bethany decided to clear the matter up in one split second. "This wasn't his idea!" she announced grandly, pulling back the carpet to disclose an eleven-by-fourteen-inch...wrought-iron grate.

Everyone stared in stunned silence at the latticed wrought iron. Bethany, her mouth agape, sat back on her heels. She had succeeded in making a complete and utter fool of herself in front of Paulo and her father.

"I assume you have an explanation for your bizarre behavior, young lady?" her father uttered in his finest basso profundo.

Bethany scrambled up from the floor, brushed her knees off, and kicked the carpet rather violently into place with the toe of her black suede pump. Covered up, the grate still looked to her like a legal-sized file, she consoled herself silently.

She folded her arms and looked up. "Yes, I have, Father."

Something in the tone of her voice took him aback for an instant. But when he did speak, Burgess Grey was once again in complete mastery of the situation. "Then, pray, enlighten me." He moved across the room to a morocco recliner, sat down and waited.

Oh, no, he's doing it again, thought Bethany with a mixture of irritation and panic. Her father had assumed his most authoritarian expression. Dismally, she turned to Paulo. "Would you mind leaving us alone for a few minutes?"

"Are you sure it wouldn't be easier if I stayed here with you?" he said.

Bethany gave a resigned smile. "I'm sure it would be, but this is one I have to handle myself." She put her hand on Paulo's forearm, finding the brief contact reassuring. "Promise you'll wait for me?"

He nodded. "I'll be downstairs if you need me."

When the door was closed, Bethany took a seat across from her father. She drew in a deep breath and told herself everything would turn out well, although she felt far from convinced.

"I wasn't completely honest with you, Dad, about my reasons for going to Rio," she began.

Her father responded only by lifting one silver-tipped eyebrow in a barely perceptible gesture.

Bethany continued. "Zoe needed to...that is, she inherited Sebastian's and wanted to sell it as quickly as possible."

"Go on," her father said.

"She asked me to check the company records before she approached her own legal advisers."

"I see. Am I correct in assuming that this...search was also to include the pillaging of your father's study?"

Bethany cleared her throat, and an image of Copacabana Beach flickered through her mind. She'd much rather have been there right now. "Well, sort of," she said, and told her father the whole story, up to and including the part about the geological assessment that had his business card attached to it.

As the tale unfolded, Burgess registered no shock, no anger, no surprise—nothing; his strong features remained totally impassive. When Bethany finished speaking, her father shifted his position, an indication that he was about to present his own views on the matter.

"I take it, then, that this cloak-and-dagger business you engaged in rather clumsily this evening hinges on your finding my business card attached to some questionable report," he said.

"Yes, that's right." Bethany braced herself for the inevitable rebuttal that would tear apart her flimsy case.

"Would it alter your perception any if I were to tell you Zoe wrote to me months ago requesting a number of my business cards?"

Bethany felt her chest tighten. "She did?"

Her father nodded somberly. "I was made to understand they would be handed out to patrons of Sebastian's who come from this area—a sort of goodwill exchange—in return for which I would recommend their establishment to clients of mine who were planning to visit Brazil."

"Oh." Bethany looked down at her hands in her lap. "I had no idea." It was somewhat disconcerting to realize she'd never even considered that her aunt might be behind all this, yet she'd been quick enough to condemn her father. But why would Zoe and Paulo go to all this trouble and expense to ridicule her and her father?

Bethany raised her eyes, feeling like a recalcitrant child. "I'm sorry, Dad. I know it doesn't change what I've done..." Her words dwindled away, and she lifted her hands in a gesture of helplessness.

Incredibly, her father's face softened. "It's all right, Bethany. We've all been through times when the very foundations seem to be crumbling beneath our feet, when we don't know which way to turn, whom to trust." He leaned back in his chair. "Perhaps you wonder why you became a pawn in this rather elaborate scheme concocted by your so-called favorite aunt."

"Yes...I am a little confused."

"It goes back a long way," her father began. "Zoe was always willful, rebellious and headstrong—not unlike you, at times." He gave a hint of a smile. "You, fortunately, learned to harness many of your...shall we say...less admirable qualities; your aunt did not. When she ran away from home, not yet of age, the scandal she created was heinous, the humiliation she caused our family unforgivable. As the eldest, I made the suggestion that she be disinherited from our father's will; he complied. Zoe learned what I had done and vowed someday to take revenge. It would seem that day has arrived."

Bethany sat in silence, listening to her father's words. She saw the expression of earnestness on his face, yet wondered why it all seemed so incongruous—like a puzzle with pieces that refused to interlock. Zoe...disinheritance...revenge. Such motives simply didn't fit in with the image of the woman she'd come to know in Brazil. Zoe was already wealthy, the money having come from her second husband, Vladimir, years ago; and, no doubt, more had come from Sebastian. So why would she harbor notions of senseless revenge after all these years?

But, senseless or not, that's what Zoe had apparently done.

"I appreciate your telling me everything, Dad," said Bethany. "I only wish..." She groaned and covered her face with her hands. "Oh, God. And you even went to the trouble of hiring a detective."

Burgess waved his hand. "Don't give it another thought. We're all entitled to a mistake now and again; the important thing is, you learned your lesson about Zoe." He came over and patted his daughter on the shoulder. "I'm just pleased I can finally retired the file permanently."

Bethany looked up. "The file?"

"Oh, well...yes, of course, the file. Where else would I put the letter from Zoe and the invoice from Fletcher?" He chuckled.

Bethany relaxed a little. Her father was never one to toss out a piece of correspondence or a bill. "If you don't mind, Dad, I'd like to see the letter from Zoe sometime, just to satisfy my own curiosity."

Her father withdrew to the window. "Certainly, Bethany. But it's, er, at the office right now. I liked to keep it handy in my desk drawer while you were in Rio. Haven't thought to bring it home yet."

Her father wasn't looking at her, and suddenly she knew why. Bethany rose from her chair, feeling strangely disembodied. "I understand, Dad. I—I think I'll go down and thank Mother for dinner, then be on my way. It's been a long day."

Burgess's steel-blue eyes pivoted to his daughter's. "I'm glad we had this little talk, Bethany."

"Yes, Dad," she mumbled. "Me, too."

"I'll go downstairs with you and say good-night to that young Andrade fellow. How long did you say he was staying?"

"I don't know," replied Bethany, backing toward the door. "He didn't say. Probably no more than a day or two."

Paulo was in the kitchen loading the dishwasher, Georgina at his side, obviously smitten. Any other time, Bethany would have found the situation amusing—but not tonight.

They said their thank-yous and goodbyes hurriedly, and Bethany ushered Paulo out the door. Her car was parked a few houses away, and she didn't speak to him until they were in the car, with the doors locked.

"Now how about explaining why you dragged me out of there as if the house were about to blow up?" Paulo asked, emitting wisps of white vapor in the cold car as he spoke.

Bethany sat behind the steering wheel without moving. "Dad sat there tonight and lied to me." Even coming right out and saying it didn't make it any easier to accept.

"Are you sure?" asked Paulo.

"Very." Bethany told him everything her father had said, including the part about the file.

Paulo seemed genuinely sympathetic. "Are you sure the desk he mentioned is the one we searched?"

"There is only one desk in his office, and we searched through the whole thing. You remember, I even dug up the key to his locked center drawer. There was no file."

"Perhaps he's simply remembering wrong about where he left it."

"Are you kidding? Ask my father where to find the Katzenjammer acquisition of 1958, and he'll pinpoint it blindfolded." Bethany shook her head. "It wasn't only that, Paulo. I got off much too easily. It was as if he'd been expecting it. He should have blown up with rage, the way he always does, then cooled off later. I mean, the man spent a few thousand dollars to hire a detective and just brushed the matter off as though it was an everyday occurrence.

"So what's your next plan of action?" Paul asked.

"I don't know. I'll have to think." Bethany started the engine and let it idle for a minute, then backed out of the parking space and drove out into the quiet residential street.

During dinner Paulo had decided that, difficult as it might be, he wouldn't interfere in the way Bethany chose to deal with her father. Burgess Grey was a powerful, intimidating man—Bethany hadn't exaggerated on that score—and Paulo had watched with barely controlled scorn how Burgess wielded his authority to keep his family in line.

Georgina was a tiny, ineffectual mimic of her husband's opinions, obviously having long since forgotten how to think for herself. Paulo pitied her.

Burgess had been far less successful in subjugating his daughter, but that was probably because Bethany had inherited much of his temperament. Paulo knew she could be headstrong, stubborn and shortsighted, but she was also kind and generous and caring. It infuriated him to see how much Bethany feared her father. On several occasions during the dinner Paulo expected Bethany to challenge Burgess's arrogant pronouncements, but she simply listened to him quietly and smiled cheerfully, no doubt to preserve a pleasant atmosphere for her dinner companions.

Paulo sat in the car beside Bethany and made no comment when she turned down State Street and headed toward the waterfront, past the turnoff to her apartment. He was not going to put any pressure on her. She was the only person capable of exposing her father's deception, and now that he'd spent an evening with the man, he could understand Bethany's need to be cautious. One misstep, one hasty accusation, and Paulo had no doubt Burgess wouldn't hesitate to throw his daughter out of his life forever, and Paulo, of all people, knew how it felt to be without a father. He'd made up his mind. Bethany would have whatever time she needed, whatever space she required and, most of all, whatever love she needed to see this through.

The iron posts and chains stood like heavy iron sentinels along Lewis Wharf. There were no yachts gracing the water at that time of the year, and only a few distant lights pierced the icy blackness. Paulo studied Bethany, who was still lost in thought.

"Would it help to take a walk?" Paulo suggested. "It might clear your head."

Bethany turned to him and nodded. "That's a good idea."

They walked along the quiet cobblestoned pier. The night air was crisp and chilly, but calm.

"I assume what's bothering you is how to get your father to admit the truth," Paulo said.

"I guess that's part of it. It's not easy to learn you've been deceived by a member of your own family."

"I know, Bethany. I've been there, remember?"

She turned and her eyes met Paulo's dark, penetrating gaze. "Of course," she said. "I'm sorry."

"You don't have to pursue this anymore," Paulo told her. "You could wash your hands of the whole matter right now and tell me to go back where I came from. I wouldn't blame you if you did."

Bethany lifted her gloved hands to his shoulders. "I couldn't do that. Not after all we've been through together."

Paulo lowered his head and gave her a kiss that felt wonderfully warm against the frigid night air, a kiss that conjured up memories and took Bethany halfway around the world, if only for a moment or two. Then he slipped his arm around her waist, and they walked the way they used to—though the winter coats they wore made their embrace less intimate.

"Okay, Bethany, think hard. Where—besides the office and the study—does your father keep confidential papers?"

"That's what I've been trying to figure out," she replied.

"Your parents have a big house; the papers could be anywhere."

"Not necessarily. Dad would never leave anything the slightest bit controversial in a place where Mother might find it, and she has snooping privileges everywhere except his study."

"Then where else does he spend time? What does he do? Does he belong to a private club perhaps?"

Bethany shook her head. "He's the archetypal workaholic. He drives to work, works all day, drives home, works all night." Bethany's boots crunched on the snow when she stopped suddenly. "That's it! I've got it!"

"What?"

"His car!"

Paulo reminded himself he was here to help. "You're grasping at straws, Bethany. Why would he leave a file like that in his car?"

Her agitation stopped just short of jumping up and down. "No, no, you don't understand! To him, it's like a third office. He has a telephone, a dictating machine—even office supplies. If he has a case out of town or needs to get to the airport, he gets one of the law clerks to drive for him so he can work." Bethany began to drag a reluctant Paulo back to her own car.

"Bethany," he pleaded. "Tell me you're not considering something as stupid as breaking into your father's automobile."

She slid into her seat and unlocked the door on Paulo's side. "Okay, I'll tell you I'm not considering something so ridiculous." She drove away from the waterfront as if the devil were at their tail. "But I'd be lying," she added with a mirthless grin.

Paulo slumped back in his seat and wondered whether it was too soon to rescind his earlier promise to himself. He'd honestly thought Bethany had had enough skulduggery for one night. But then, she was Burgess Grey's daughter. Oh, what the hell...

"Isn't it still a little early in the evening to be breaking and entering?" he suggested, diverting his energies to the refinement of her strategy.

Bethany glanced at the digital clock on the dashboard. "Oh, blast. You're right." She thought for a moment. "Mother and Dad are always asleep by eleven, so...what do you say to a doughnut and hot chocolate at a great little truck stop I know of?"

Paulo lifted his hands. "Drive on. I'm at your mercy."

An hour later, Bethany and Paulo were walking down her parents' street. The sidewalks were deserted; the few Christmas lights that were still on looked oddly out of place now that the holiday was over. Or perhaps it was just that Bethany wasn't feeling particularly festive.

They cut through a narrow space between two houses to the gravel alley behind. "Dad's car is in a carport behind the house," she told Paulo. "That's our place," she pointed out when they had walked a short distance. All the windows at the back of the house were dark.

"Which is their bedroom window?" Paulo asked, his voice markedly lacking conviction.

"The far one, over there."

"Naturally," he muttered. "The one with the best view of the car. Okay, let's get started. Where did you say the spare key is hidden?"

Bethany went to the front bumper of her father's silver Lincoln and knelt down. "It's glued up here somewhere. I've never actually seen it; Dad just told me where..." She felt around, and her hand hit a small metal object. "Aha! I have it! I'll need something to dislodge it from the rubber cement."

Paulo groaned and reached into his pocket for a Swiss army knife. "Have you thought about how we are going to reattach the key, or do you propose breaking into your father's basement for the rubber cement?"

"Very funny. I'll just take the key with me, and when all is said and done, I'll give it back to him— with my apologies." She held out her hand for the pocketknife. "I'll do the official breaking in. You keep an eye on the bedroom window and the alley in case someone walks by."

Bethany unlocked the Lincoln's two front doors and opened them. The inside light came on, but it wasn't bright enough to shine outside the carport area. Someone would have had to be standing right at the window to see it. She found two worn attaché cases under the front seat and pulled them out. They contained a fair number of files of out-of-town clients, but nothing that struck Bethany as out of the ordinary. She returned the cases to their proper places and blew on her fingers, wishing it wasn't quite so cold. She couldn't wear gloves while conducting her search, and already her fingers were beginning to stiffen.

"Are you satisfied yet?" Paulo whispered loudly through the open door as he hopped from one foot to the other and shivered.

"Just about. I want to check the trunk." Bethany reached over to the driver's seat and pulled the lever, then scrambled out.

Inside the trunk were the usual emergency tools, a mackintosh and a pair of work boots. These she pushed aside until she found the spare-tire compartment. Chiding herself for ever having gotten into this mess, Bethany lifted up the tire and found what she'd half hoped she'd never find: a dossier nearly two inches thick, clearly labelled: Sebastian's.

"I've got it!" she exclaimed.

"Hide!" Paulo replied. "The lights just came on."

Bethany glanced toward the house and saw the illuminated master bedroom. She let the trunk door drop quietly, careful not to shut it tight, and crept around to the far side of the Lincoln, where a dismal Paulo was already crouching.

"Your father's probably on his way down here right now," he muttered, his nose blue from the cold.

"I don't think so," Bethany whispered back, straining to read the file. "The bathroom light came on, too. Dad's probably got heartburn." It was no use. She couldn't see a thing. "Paulo, could you move over, please? I've got to open the door and get a flashlight."

"Are you crazy? He'll see the light come on."

"I won't open it that wide." She pulled the door open enough to slide her arm in. With numb fingers, she felt around until she found the flashlight. Turning it on, she directed the beam of light at the file.

Paulo let out a low whistle. "I can't believe it. This file must go back years."

Bethany leafed through the contracts and agreements and correspondence dealing with matters of international law. Clearly, her father had been acting as legal counsel for Sebastian Andrade. She flipped to the earliest document at the bottom of the file, and gasped, "Paulo, look at this. A Shareholders Agreement between the two of them. Dad was one of your first investors."

Paulo glanced over it. "And read the date. It was drawn up eighteen years ago."

They looked at each other. Another thread seemed to draw them together—a strange bond that had existed, unseen, since they were children.

"Imagine," said Bethany. "Your father and mine, business partners all these years, and we had no idea."

The last document to be entered was the draft of a sales agreement, as yet unsigned and undated, destined to a Danish consortium called Andersberg. There was, of course, no letter from Zoe requesting business cards. Bethany had never expected there would be.

Both were silent, wrapped in their private thoughts, as they went through the file. Only the fact that they would freeze to death if they didn't start moving prevented them from lingering. Bethany was about to close the file when she noticed something penciled in on the cover near her thumb. She almost commented on it, but caught herself in time. She glanced up; Paulo hadn't noticed. Committing the item to memory, Bethany shut the file, got up and peered over the roof of the car. The bathroom light was off; the bedroom light was still on.

"Let's get out of here," she said to Paulo and hurriedly returned the file to its place in the trunk.

"What!" he whispered, wishing he could shout. "We go to all this trouble, and you just put the file away as if nothing happened? Why don't we just go knock on your parents' door right now?"

She lifted her finger to her mouth. "Shh!" Resolutely, she marched back in the direction of her own car, leaving Paulo little choice but to follow her. She could feel his irritation and sympathized with him; but he was going to have to bear with her a little while longer.

As soon as they got into the car, Bethany blew on her fingers, pulled down the notepad she kept on her visor, and scrawled a telephone number across it. Then she pulled on her gloves, gave Paulo the most non committal look she could muster and said, "Let's go home."

Paulo stared at her, incredulous. "I think the pressure is getting to you, Bethany. You're not behaving rationally anymore." He rolled his eyes. "What am I talking about? Here I am, going along with it all—I'm no saner than you."

Bethany made an evasive gesture but didn't bother to reply, concentrating instead on driving home. What Paulo thought, and what her father had done, no longer mattered. Something much more immediate required their attention. But in order to deal with it, Paulo was going to need his sleep.

When they got home, the first thing Bethany did was to turn up the thermostat; both of them were like icicles. She was dying for a hot bath, but Paulo needed one even more than she, for he was a true creature of the tropics. His complexion had turned almost blue.

"What's all this about?" Paulo asked when his lips had thawed enough to speak. "The sudden exit…and why in the name of heaven did you put the file back?"

Bethany turned her back to him and plugged the kettle in for tea. *Please, God, let me do the right thing.* "The file's not going anywhere, and keeping everyone awake all night with a confrontation isn't going to solve anything."

Paulo snorted with impatience. "We have just learned your father was my father's lawyer for eighteen years, had knowledge of the fraudulent sale, and all you're concerned with is everyone getting a good night's sleep?"

She turned around and nodded. "We'll need it."

Bethany's laconic delivery made Paulo grow silent, wary. He seemed to sense that Burgess Grey's daughter could be just as stubborn and unyielding as her father.

Paulo's teeth were still chattering. "Do you mind if I drink my tea in the bathtub?" he asked.

Bethany wrapped her arms around him and briskly rubbed his back for a few moments. "You go ahead and fill the tub. I'll bring you your tea."

He was asleep within the hour. The hot bath, the tea and the electric blanket combined forces to return his complexion to a healthy tan and still his shivers. Bethany nestled beside him under the covers until she knew he was asleep. She listened for a while to his deep and rhythmic breathing, then she carefully climbed out of bed, donned her robe and padded to the kitchen.

It was going to be a long night. There was nothing to be done before morning, but she'd be wasting her energy if she tried to sleep. Bethany was almost certain she was doing the right thing. Paulo was going to need his rest if he was to emerge from this winter foray unscathed, especially considering what he had to face in the morning. Bethany picked up the scrap of paper and looked at the number, recalling the pair of initials she'd seen above it. She wondered what Paulo was going to say when he learned his father was alive and living in New England.

Chapter Twelve

Paulo was on his fourth slice of French toast the next morning when Bethany got the telephone call she'd been waiting for. He watched her take down the information, thank the caller and hang up.

"Did you get what you were looking for?" he asked.

"I did," she said, replacing the cover on her pen. "How would you like to visit Connecticut?"

Paulo drank the last of his coffee and wiped the corners of his mouth with a napkin. "Now? Why?"

"Last night, when we were looking at the file, I noticed a telephone number scribbled on the cover that got me curious, so I phoned a contact in the police department—"

"You phoned the police?" Paulo said, alarmed.

Bethany gave an off-hand wave. "Don't worry. He's an old friend and he didn't ask any questions." Paulo's expression registered even greater disapproval, but he let her go on. "Anyway, he called back to give me the name and address for this number."

"What did you find out?"

"It belongs to Chasen's Paving and Gravel in Westview, Connecticut."

Paulo gave her a look of impatience. "This is getting ridiculous. What on earth could a paving and gravel company have to do with my father's gemstone business in Brazil?"

"I don't know," Bethany admitted, lowering herself to a stool, "but I seem to remember Chasen's as being one of Dad's clients a while back, and I think they went into receivership. That was the last I heard." She pulled back the red-and-white curtains and looked outside. "Who knows? Maybe they were silent partners in Sebastian's, too."

"Are you ever going to face your father, Bethany, or are we going to play cat and mouse forever?"

Bethany kept her gaze fixed firmly outside. The question, she knew, was legitimate, and she'd been amazed at the patience Paulo had shown her. But now, it was more important than ever for her to have his full cooperation...and trust.

She turned to face him. "I'll make a deal with you."

Paulo matched her gaze head-on. "I have already searched your father's office with you, diverted him—though with limited success—while you ransacked his study and accompanied you while you broke into his car. I'd say you're not in the best of positions to make any more deals."

Bethany lowered her eyes so he wouldn't see how desperate she felt. How could she make him understand that somewhere in Connecticut was the key that would unlock the door? She *had* to make him understand...somehow. When she finally looked up, her face was deliberately devoid of emotion, her voice without inflection.

"You're absolutely right, Paulo. I have been behaving outlandishly. Let's go to my father's house right now. I'll tell him we found the file and that we know everything. Then when I've finished talking to him, will you come to Connecticut with me...please?"

She could tell she'd caught him completely unaware, which had been precisely her intention. There was a flicker of uncertainty in his eyes as he considered her proposal, and perhaps he sensed the unspoken urgency, the marked departure from Bethany's usual emotional self.

"What's in Connecticut, Bethany?"

"The answers...all the answers."

TEN MINUTES LATER, they were speeding along the Massachusetts Turnpike, that wide anonymous band of highway indistinguishable from nearly every other stretch of the country's interstate system. Its efficiency, however, was indisputable, and Bethany was anxious to get the journey over with.

Paulo watched the passing scenery in silence. The snow had settled like dazzling blobs of marshmallow cream over fence posts, mailboxes and juniper shrubs, while ice had transformed the majestic pinewoods to silver. Nestled in the valleys were towns with frame houses of colonial blue and steepled white churches, the very essence of Currier & Ives lithographs.

When they reached Auburn, they turned south to the Connecticut Turnpike, and Bethany felt her apprehension grow. What if her hunch was wrong, and the initials "S.A." had meant something else entirely? Looking at the entire matter logically a telephone number and a Brazilian toad were not much to go on.

Soon after they crossed the state line, they took the exit to the village of Westview. The road was an old, two-lane highway that snaked its way through dense woods past the occasional gas station and cluster of buildings. Tiny, sleepy Westview itself turned out to be little more than a few wooden structures. Chasen's had a rural route address, and Bethany knew she'd never find it on her own, so she pulled up to the variety store that doubled as a post office.

"I'm going in to get directions," she told Paulo.

"Go ahead," he said. He watched her enter the tiny store and decided he hadn't seen this side of Bethany before. Or perhaps he had, in milder forms, seen the stubborn set of her jaw, the gritty determination that gave her eyes the look of immutable granite—but nothing that compared to the tenacity she showed that morning. He knew now what it was that made her a good match for her father professionally. She was a younger, feminine—and therefore even more formidable—replica of Burgess Grey; and emotionally she was leagues ahead of him. Paulo suspected that when she was finally ready to put the case before her father, he wouldn't stand a chance. Suddenly, irrationally, Paulo felt a pang of sympathy for the man. He was relieved when Bethany returned, so he could push that unpleasant matter firmly to the back of his mind.

"Chasen's went out of business a few months ago," she said, "but the postmaster thinks there's still a caretaker on the property."

"You don't think it'll do any good to talk to him, do you?"

"Why not? I'm sure he'll be able to tell us something, and we've come this far."

"Yes, we have," Paulo muttered and turned on the radio.

Following the directions the postmaster had given, they drove onto Westview's only street until they came to a narrow dirt road. It was still unplowed but the snow had been stamped down by tire tracks. Pine trees rose on either side to form a lofty green arch above them, dappling the morning sunlight. They continued on that course for about a mile, but at their snail-like pace it seemed longer. At the end of the road, they turned onto an even narrower street that was also rougher, with potholes and boulders beneath the snow, which caused them to lurch from side to side and created all sorts of ominous scraping noises under the car. Bethany ignored Paulo's looks of distress. If all turned out as planned, it would be well worth the cost of a new muffler or tail pipe.

The postmaster had told Bethany not to worry if it seemed as if the road were disappearing altogether, for that would mean she was getting close. She couldn't help thinking Chasen's might have fared better with their business if it had picked a more conspicuous location. Finally, when the road dwindled to little more than a pair of deep ruts, Paulo noticed the mailbox for Chasen's, the "Paving and Gravel" segment of its original name crudely covered with black paint.

"Nice place," he remarked dryly as Bethany turned the wheels sharply to climb the steep drive.

The property was large and cleared of trees: there was a gravel quarry on one side and an assortment of dilapidated pickup trucks and cars on the other. The driveway had not been cleared since the last snowfall, and Bethany could barely inch along in first gear.

"We had better stop here and walk the rest of the way," Paulo warned.

Bethany was glad to oblige.

At the top of the clearing they found a ramshackle garage-cum-office with the name of the business painted sloppily across one side. Some distance beyond that was a light blue mobile home mounted on a concrete block foundation. The place looked deserted.

They inspected the garage first. Between the cracks in the wood, they could see a fairly new pickup truck, but there was no other evidence of habitation. The windows of the attached office were broken, and the desk and shelves were covered with dust and old cobwebs.

Suddenly, the stillness was shattered by the sound from some uncertain source, of an ax splitting wood, the noise bouncing at them in sharp staccato bursts from the surrounding pines, as if a sprite were playing tricks on the uninvited guests.

"That's probably the caretaker," Paulo said. "I'll go check behind the trailer." He began to climb the sloping expanse of ground, his shoes crunching through the crusty snow as he walked.

"Paulo, wait!" Bethany called out, her courage sapped, at once afraid of what he might find.

Paulo stopped and turned to give her a quizzical look. "What's the matter?"

The ax fell silent, and they heard slow, tired footsteps coming from behind the trailer. Bethany was first to see the haggard, bearded man in the woolen toque and plaid lumber jacket, and the first to realize she'd been mistaken. This sad ghost of a man couldn't possibly be Sebastian Andrade.

Paulo turned to greet him. In the slice of an instant, he tensed and his eyes narrowed to chips of flint. "Dear Mother of God," he said, his voice tight with anguish, "it's my father."

The two men—one stooped and weary, the other young and strong—were, despite their differences, like mirror images of each other. Their expressions reflected love torn by confusion and shock tempered by stark reality—altogether too much to cope with, too much to accept in the space of a long gaze. An eternity seemed to pass before either of them could single out one emotion and act on it.

Sebastian, perhaps because of his age or experience, or because of the indestructible, overpowering love a father holds for his son, was the first to stumble the short distance to Paulo. He uttered his son's name in a strangled sob and pulled him to his chest, not caring or noticing that Paulo did not immediately return the embrace. Then Bethany saw the tears spring from Paulo's eyes. He shuddered, and it was as if a lock in his heart had released, a door had sprung open. Father and son clung to each other—for the moment not bothering to analyze what had severed them or brought them together again, responding only to the unfathomable bonds of love and kinship.

Bethany felt her eyes well up with tears and knew, at that moment, that all the risks had been worth it, that despite whatever anger or retribution might arise, she'd done the right thing in reuniting Sebastian and Paulo Andrade. She stood some distance away, a clenced hand to her mouth, not wishing to intrude on the poignant scene, but grateful to be witness to it.

"My son...my dear son," Sebastian said over and over in a voice remarkably like Paulo's, except for the tired thread of defeat running through it. "How did you ever find me?"

Their arms, at last, slipped away from each other, though Sebastian's eyes never left his son. Paulo turned to Bethany and held out his hand for her to join him, the gesture an unspoken reply to his father's question.

"You knew all along, didn't you?" Paulo asked her, as though she had performed an incredible feat of magic.

Bethany went to him and slipped her gloved hand in his, her blue eyes shimmering with tender reflection. "I was only working on a hunch," she answered. "I'm glad you trusted me."

"We agreed that we would trust each other," he replied, bringing her to his side in a loving gesture. "Father, you remember your niece, Bethany Grey."

Sebastian rested his tired eyes on her, his smile etched with remorse and gratitude. "Bethany, of course I remember you. You've grown so lovely, and I have heard many fine things about you from your father," he said, holding out his hand.

It should have been an extremely awkward moment, greeting this shell of a man returned from the dead, his deception blatantly exposed; but there was love in the air as well, and love made it bearable.

Bethany shook his hand. "Thank you, and I've heard the same about you from your son and wife."

Then came the strained silence. So much needed to be said, with everyone tacitly aware that truth could destroy the tenuous joy of this reunion.

Sebastian motioned them toward the trailer. "Come in, both of you, and I'll fix us some lunch."

Bethany and Paulo glanced at each other, hesitant. The situation was too bizarre to know precisely how to behave. Yet, strangely enough, what made it easier was the fact that they'd already experienced some facet of this complex deception: Paulo, with the fraudulent report; Bethany, with her father's lies.

"We'd love to stay for lunch," Bethany said at last, relieving Paulo of the need to answer. They followed Sebastian up the stairs of concrete blocks into the trailer. The tiny room they entered was cozy and neat, a marked contrast to the dilapidation outside. Much of the furniture was built in, including settees upholstered in blue-and-green plaid and a Formica table that folded out to form a counter area for the galley-sized kitchen. At the far end of the room, a wood-burning stove emitted warmth, and on it sat a stew pot, its contents simmering. The curtains were crisp and cheery; the walls and cupboards were made of knotty pine.

Sebastian bade them sit down and went to the kitchen to take bowls from the cupboard. "I made stew," he said, his eyes directed at his tasks, as if embarrassed by his altered station in life. "I make enough to last me several days.... It saves me having to cook so often."

His guests murmured polite replies. Within minutes, they were eating, and Bethany could see out of the corner of her eye that Paulo was doing his best to force down his food.

Finally, Paulo could tolerate the tension no longer. His soup spoon clattered into the half-empty bowl, and he looked up. "Why, Father? Why did you have to reduce yourself to this?" He made a sweeping arc of the room with his arm.

Sebastian Andrade was a paler, older version of his son, though shorter and of a slighter build. His skin hung slack as if he'd recently lost a great deal of weight. He looked thirty years older than Bethany had remembered him, though his voice was still melodious, his accent fluid and soft. His eyes, however, drooped with weariness, and his mouth had thinned. Little remained to remind Bethany of the great international gem merchant she had swooned over as a child.

"How can I explain to you, my son, in a way that would make you understand? You've grown up in such a different world than I. You can't know what it's like to start with nothing and build an empire with one's bare hands."

"Can't I?" Paulo countered. "I might have been a child, but I was witness to the price you had to pay to accomplish your dream. I might not have understood what is meant by ambition and determination, but I remember how difficult it was for you to leave Mother and me alone for weeks at a time while you were setting up the offices in Rio. I remember sneaking out of my room in the middle of the night and finding you working at your desk, so exhausted you had to hold your head up with one hand, the ashtray filled to overflowing beside you. I remember the first time we entertained royalty in our home, the descendants of the emperor's family, and you were so worried that I'd do or say something to humiliate you."

"You...you remember all those things, Paulo? What am I saying? Of course you would; you were always such a clever boy. Unlike your father, who failed at everything...even in death." Sebastian covered his face with his hands. "You never should have come here. Burgess should never have told you."

"Dad didn't tell us," said Bethany. "We found you ourselves. But you still haven't explained what drove you to...this. You have a fine, strong son and a wife in Brazil who adores you and misses you every minute of the day. How can you possibly imagine they'd rather have you dead?" She only needed to look at Paulo to know that, despite everything, he was happy to find his father alive. He could hardly take his eyes off the man.

Sebastian's hands trembled as he spoke. "At least this way my wife was left with her name and reputation intact, and my son had the insurance money to...pursue his own dreams. Better to be dead and respected than alive and a disgrace."

Paulo slammed his fist on the table. "That's right, Father! At the moment, you are neither!"

Bethany reached out and held his arm. "Paulo, please—"

"No, he's right. I am in the worst possible position—a living purgatory of my own creation."

Paulo rubbed his hand over his face, wishing he hadn't displayed his temper, but there were so many emotions churning inside him it was hard to know how to react. "We know about the report you paid Choco to prepare. But surely that wasn't reason enough to...do what you did."

"No, it was more than that. I knew it was only a matter of time before Sebastian's had no more fine emeralds to sell, and I realized the risk involved in purchasing them confidentially from other sources, but I thought...if we could just hang on long enough for our exploration teams to develop new sources, no one would ever have to know. We were doing so well, our name was one of the most respected in the business. But as you know, no new finds have been made in years, and the mine superintendent who was arranging the transactions knew that. He became greedy and threatened to expose our operations. I told him I'd sooner sell than be blackmailed, but he called my bluff. Fortunately, I soon found an eager buyer who knew next to nothing about the emerald business."

"So you decided to gild the lily, as they say, Father?" Paulo asked, his jaw pulsing.

"A tragic error, I know. The superintendent learned of this as well and planned to tell them everything. I couldn't let everything I'd built up be destroyed; so many lives would be ruined."

Paulo leaned forward, fists clenched. "Instead, you chose to deprive Zoe of a husband and me of a father. I'd like to get my hands on that super—"

"No, Paulo," Sebastian said with a sudden display of authority, "you mustn't judge him. Each of us is driven by a different spirit."

"Why couldn't you have simply gone public with your situation, told the entire truth? It would have crippled your enemies, and you'd have had your re-spect intact. The company could have altered its mar-keting strategies, emphasized other gems—"

"How easy it is for you, son, to alter the course of your life, but you are young. An old man like me does not take risks easily. I built my name on emeralds. Can you imagine how it would be if DeBeers were to an-nounce it would no longer sell diamonds but opals in-stead? The public would soon go elsewhere." He took a deep, ragged breath and coughed. Then he reached over to the counter for a bag of tobacco and papers to roll a cigarette. No one spoke; they were watching how Sebastian's hands shook. "You and my Zoe," he said with a quiet laugh of reminiscence, "you always ex-pected too much of me...everyone did. I was sup-posed to be the great Sebastian Andrade, capable of miracles. But as you can see, I'm not. I'm a weak, fearful man who once entertained delusions of gran-deur. If it had not been for your stepmother, I'd have failed years ago, but even Zoe could do no more than postpone my failure by a few years."

Bethany could feel Sebastian's anguish like razor blades through her heart. She looked at Paulo whose features, though taut, were still strong, perhaps be-cause having a father like Sebastian had forced him to be. She was afraid to ask, but knew she had to. "How much did my father have to do with...everything?"

Sebastian turned to her. "Not as much as you probably fear, my child. He invested heavily in the company years ago, when we came to see you in Bos-ton. He also agreed to act as my international counsel as a way for him to keep abreast of his investment.

When I told him the mines were running low, he advised me to sell immediately."

"And the report?" Bethany asked.

"My idea, entirely. I had hoped to squeeze a few more million for all of us, and chances were we might have gotten away with it, but too many people were aware of what I had done. One of the principals happened to contact your father and mentioned the section referring to the mines' potential output. He was understandably upset, but by then it was too late to cancel the sale proceedings. My only way out was by pretending to die."

"Good God, Father, you coerced Burgess into perpetrating this...this sham? You were so desperate that you would even risk his reputation as well as your own?"

Sebastian shook his head. "The risk was not so great for him. Our partnership was always kept a matter of utmost secrecy, and it seemed better this way than to risk scandal later with a fraudulent sale. He's been very kind to furnish me with this place to stay, and he promised to keep me informed of how you were getting along."

"But how could you conceive of spending your life here, with nothing, no one, after all you've had?" his son asked.

"I have had a good life, Paulo, but now I am tired, tired to the very marrow of my bones. All I wish to do is spend what time is left to me in peace, perhaps to atone for my errors. I am not so young anymore."

"Nonsense," Bethany interjected. "You have years ahead of you. You're no older than my father!" Both men turned to look at her, surprised by her sudden outburst, but she'd had quite enough of Sebastian's self-pity. What he needed was to get back into the world of the living. She stood up and went to get their coats. "Paulo, perhaps your father would like to come back with us to Boston?"

At first, Paulo's eyes were questioning, but then, with the tacit understanding that comes with the sharing of experiences, he nodded. Turning to his father, he said, "That's a good idea. Why don't you pack a few things, and we can go?"

A ghost of a smile played on Sebastian's lips. "Young people, these days. Always in a hurry. No, my son, not now, not today. I am not so naive as to think I can stay here now that you know. I would not expect you to share this lie. But I need a few days to...collect my thoughts."

Bethany glanced at Paulo and read the same look of alarm that she was feeling herself. "I don't think..." she began.

"It's all right, Bethany," Sebastian said. "I won't do anything foolish. I was too cowardly when I thought I had reason to die; it would hardly seem rational to kill myself when I have been given a second chance at life."

The two young people hesitated, unwilling to press the matter, yet worried about the effect of solitude and loneliness on a man with so much to fear.

"Let me make a suggestion," he said to allay their concerns. "When you get home, call Zoe. Tell her I love her, and call me tomorrow and tell me what she says." He looked at his son. "You know how I feel about her. Do you think I would willingly leave this earth if there's a chance she'll take me back?"

Paulo got up from the table and went around to embrace his father. "No, I honestly don't think you would."

BETHANY AND PAULO were on the highway before either of them spoke, so wrapped up were they with all they had seen and heard. Bethany was first to break the silence.

"How did he do it, Paulo?"

"Do what?"

"Stage his own death."

"Oh, that." There was a trace of disgust in his voice, but not as much as there might have been had he not seen and spoken to his father. "It was as Ovidia said. She helped him."

"An *umbanda* spell?"

"Nothing quite so magical. It's a mixture of herbs and poisons that can simulate cardiac arrest. I've never actually known of it being done, but obviously it works."

"But you saw his body, and the casket being closed…and the ashes!"

Paulo chuckled at the rising hysteria in Bethany's voice. "Don't worry. It's not quite that effective that a person can be reduced to ashes and then brought back. I would imagine my father had everything well planned. The attending physician would have had to be in on it, and the undertaker—as for the ashes, they might have belonged to some unclaimed beggar they found dead on the street."

Bethany grimaced. "That's disgusting."

Paulo gave her a knowing look. "I agree. Perhaps now you can understand why some of us are repelled by ritualistic practices. But look at it this way. Whoever it is in the urn that sits on Zoe's mantel has managed to provide her with some small comfort, and that's not such a bad thing.''

They fell silent once more, and Bethany found herself almost envying his newfound peace of mind. So much had happened to Paulo in the past few weeks that reconciling with his father had to have been an upswing. She wished she felt that way herself, instead of feeling leaden, dragged down.

When she turned the car down her street, Paulo motioned for her to pull over. ''Don't bother going into the parking garage. I'll walk from here.''

''Why do you want to do that?''

Brooking no more excuses, he stared at her fixedly. ''Because you have another item of unfinished business, and I don't want to hold you up a minute longer.''

Her stomach was already compressing into a hard, painful knot. ''Will you come with me?''

Paulo leaned over and kissed her. ''Not this time, *querida*, but after all you've been able to accomplish in the past few days, you'll do just fine.

''COME IN.''

Instinctively, Bethany's knees began to knock at the sound of her father's voice. He made an invitation to his study sound like an order. *This is it*, she thought, turning the knob and stepping into the room. *This is my one chance to say everything that needs to be said. If I back down now, I'll be backing down forever.*

''Hello, Father.'' She walked to the chair in front of his desk and sat down before she was asked.

"Bethany, this is a surprise." Burgess's tone was pleasant, but oh, so wary.

"I can't imagine why," she said in remarkably even tones. "After finding me on all fours last night, you should have realized I'd stop at nothing to find the truth."

Burgess lay down his fountain pen and folded his hands carefully. "And what truth might that be?"

"Paulo and I spoke with Uncle Sebastian today."

A ripple of insecurity, a new phenomenon, could be seen briefly on her father's face. "Ah, yes, he is in a somewhat...pathetic situation, I'd say."

Bethany slid forward in her chair, her anger flaring. "Yes, he is, and he has you to thank for it!"

"Oh, no," he protested, rallying quickly, "Sebastian Andrade is a grown man. I did not force him to do anything he wasn't already prepared to do on his own."

"Come now, Father, I've seen you in a courtroom. I've seen you reduce men with ten times his emotional stamina to tears. You knew Uncle Sebastian was a weak man, but you let him go on believing all these years that you were his friend and ally. You used him, and you hurt his son and his wife deeply in the process. Doesn't that prick your conscience at all?"

Burgess leaned back and viewed his daughter through hooded eyes. He was stalling. "He can't be as weak as you claim; he's obviously managed to sway your opinion dramatically in the course of a day."

"You're evading the issue," she tossed back. "You could have found ways around that sales agreement—ways that wouldn't drive the man to stage his own death—"

"Now wait a minute, young lady. I was not the one who counseled him to exaggerate the value of his holdings. He sank that ship all by himself."

"But you've helped people out of self-inflicted situations before! If you were the partner you claimed to be on that shareholder's agreement, you'd have been aware of his desperation. Even I knew how proud he was, how hard he'd worked to build his company. You could have convinced him to invest in other gems, or helped him clear up the blackmail situation. Anything would have been preferable to forcing him to sell. And then...sending him into permanent exile— God, the man is actually grateful to you." Bethany had to push herself to continue. "Why? What benefit or satisfaction could you possibly have derived by making Sebastian give up the one thing he'd struggled so hard to achieve?"

Burgess didn't answer right away, but in the space of an instant, he seemed to have aged. His eyes grew rheumy, his jaw slackened and the color drained from his face. "I needed the money."

"The money?" Bethany gasped. "Why did you need the money?"

"Because if I didn't sell my shares in Sebastian's for a hefty profit, there was a good chance Grey & Associates would be out of business within the year."

With a heavy, relentless thud, the last piece—the ultimate motive—fell into place. "Did Uncle Sebastian know that?"

"Yes. So, in a way, I suppose I was indirectly responsible for his obtaining that fraudulent report. He regretted that I had invested so heavily in the business and thought he might be able to squeeze out a few more dollars for both of us.''

What was the expression she found herself grasping for? ''Thick as thieves.'' Everyone had become so inextricably knotted together, it was becoming impossible to untangle the threads. And who were the thieves when one came right down to it? Was it Sebastian, who had hired Choco to do his dirty work? The mine superintendent who had taken advantage of a profitable situation? Was it her father? Or was it she, herself, who'd spent the past twenty-four hours skulking around trying to establish her father's guilt? Should she be angry with him that she was nearly kidnapped, or grateful that he'd hired Elmer Fletcher? She honestly didn't know. All she knew was that the reprehension she'd intended to heap on him was stuck in her throat, refusing to come out.

''How long have you had financial problems?'' she finally aked.

''Several years. We've had no lack of clients, but there are so many young attorneys out there now, offering cut-rate services and with fancy advertising gimmicks... And many of our corporate clients are having trouble paying their legal bills.'' Burgess shook his head sadly. ''The legal profession does not have the dignity it once had.''

For the first time since Bethany could remember, her father was speaking to her like an equal, a colleague; and for once, he wasn't striving for maximum effect. He was simply unburdening himself. Suddenly, of her own accord, Bethany felt like an ungrateful and irresponsible child. She had never taken any interest in the firm, had never wondered whether the bills were being paid or thought to ask if they should be soliciting for new clients. She had always been content to let her father handle things while she blithely played at lady lawyer.

"I'm sorry," she said, feeling hopelessly inept.

Burgess raised his hands, palms up. "You have nothing to be sorry for. You can't stop times from changing."

"What are you going to do now?"

"I don't know. I have a great deal of thinking to do. But I do have a favor to ask of you."

Bethany smiled, amazed to feel the leaden weight begin to lift. "What is it, Dad?"

"Don't leave me just yet."

Her heart gave a strange flutter. "What makes you think I would?"

Burgess's steel-gray eyes gave in to a sparkle of paternal pride. "You're a fine attorney, but I've always known you didn't love the work as I do. But do you think you could stay long enough for me to get things sorted out? I need you."

She'd never heard her father say those words before, and she felt as though a band around her heart had burst. "I'll stay for as long as you need me."

"How do I look? Don't tell me, I've gotten fat, haven't I? Oh, dear, I never should have gone with purple." Zoe was fluttering around Bethany's apartment like a nervous bride, and looking every bit as radiant in her lavender suit and deep violet silk blouse.

"You have not gotten fat, Zoe!" Bethany laughed and tried to latch on to her aunt before she had a chance to swoop by again. "Sit down, will you? You're making *me* nervous."

Zoe glanced at her wrist, not even noticing that she wasn't wearing a watch. "What's keeping them? They should have been here by now."

"Relax. It's an hour-and-a-half drive, and Paulo left over three hours ago. They should be here any min—"

The door opened, and Sebastian stepped in, followed by his son. The air positively crackled with nervous excitement as the reunited couple's eyes met.

Sebastian stood rooted to his spot as if his boots had been nailed down, every bit the nervous suitor. Paulo had to give him a nudge from behind to get him moving.

Zoe's hands went first to her mouth, and then they flung outward. "Sebastian, you crazy, impossible, exasperating fool!" In the next moment, they were in each other's arms, clinging, laughing and crying.

"My Zoe, my dear, beautiful Zoe. How could I think of leaving you? Will you ever forgive me?"

Zoe stepped back but still clung to her husband's shoulders. "No, as a matter of fact, I will never forgive you, and you shall have to spend the rest of your long life making it up to me. Do you know what it's like to become a widow for the third time? People were calling me Lucrezia Borgia; they were saying it was my passion that did it!"

At this, Sebastian threw his head back and laughed heartily, and Bethany had a glimpse of the great international gem merchant once again. "I, of all men, should know that's entirely possible, my dear."

"I think this calls for a celebration," Bethany announced when she'd finished dabbing at her eyes.

"I couldn't agree more," Paulo echoed coming to her side.

Zoe turned and wrapped her husband's arm around her waist. "Uh...thank you, darlings, that's really very sweet of you, but I—I've taken the liberty of booking a suite at the Copley for, well, just the two of us. I hope you won't be offended."

"Not at all," Bethany said. "Don't worry about us. The champagne will keep." She was delighted to see Sebastian turning a tawny red.

"Don't count on it," Paulo muttered in an aside. And then in a louder voice meant for his parents, "Go ahead, you two. Have a wonderful time."

After the goodbyes had been said and the door had closed, Paulo took Bethany into his arms. His eyes caressed her slowly, sweetly. "At last we're alone. Do you realize how long I have been waiting for this moment?"

Bethany wrapped one of his curls around his finger. "All your life?"

"It seems that way. Now, I meant to talk to you about that champagne. It won't keep..."

Moments later, nestled on the sofa, the two of them enjoyed their first real taste of total relaxation. There were still matters that needed attending to, but nothing that couldn't wait. For now, being together was all that mattered.

"Marry me, *querida*." Paulo's voice was soft and seductive.

She closed her eyes and smiled. There hadn't been time to deal with her feelings for Paulo. She'd set them aside, secure in the knowledge that one day there'd come a time when she could devote serious thought to how she felt about him. Now, to her eternal amazement, the answer was there, ready and waiting—somehow it had blossomed unawares.

Paulo cleared his throat. "People are generally expected to answer such a question," he said, lifting a lock of her hair and kissing the skin underneath. "They aren't supposed to grin from ear to ear."

She looked up through a veil of lashes. "Is that what I'm doing?"

Paulo nodded, then dipped his finger into the champagne and held it out for Bethany to taste. She licked it and brought his finger to her mouth. She could feel the electric thrill passing through his body into hers. "Tell you what," she said. "I'll give you my answer in the morning, but right now I'd like to work on becoming a full-fledged *carioca*."

Paulo's mouth turned up with a knowing, reminiscent grin. "You want to play soccer?"

Bethany shook her head slowly and wrapped her arms around his neck. "I want to make love...all night long."

Chapter Thirteen

Bethany finished making entries in the ledger and closed the heavy book with a sigh. She arched back and pressed her hands to her lower back, easing out the kinks in her spine and shoulders. Working with figures never failed to stimulate her mind, but it always wreaked havoc on her joints and her muscles. Too bad there wasn't some way to exercise while bookkeeping, she thought with a wry smile as she pushed herself away from the desk and stood up.

She padded barefoot across the quarry-tiled living-room floor to the French doors that opened onto the terrace. Stepping outside, she breathed in deeply and gazed at the lush green mountainside sloping down from the promontory and the land thrusting sharply up on either side of the house, a wild amalgam of granite and greenery. From where Bethany stood, Rio de Janeiro looked like a toy model of a city, capped by a diaphanous cloud of smog. The cable car leading to Sugarloaf Mountain looked no bigger than a beetle hanging from a slender thread. Beyond the city, the ocean stretched for miles until it faded into an azure horizon. Clouds were beginning to gather over the mountains as they did every afternoon, but it was so warm that Bethany didn't even need a shawl to cover her bare shoulders.

It was hard to believe that in a few days it would be January, she mused, leaning against the wrought-iron balustrade. More than a year had passed since that fateful call from her Aunt Zoe asking her to come to Rio. Bethany's mind drifted back to the later developments that, at the time, had seemed so catastrophic...

The scandal of Sebastian Andrade's resurrection and Burgess Grey's collusion had rocked the very bastions of the business world, from Wall Street to Geneva. But as time passed and other crises followed, the world soon forgot what two men had been driven to do out of self-perceived desperation. Perhaps such incidents created headlines simply because they were so universally understanble.

The astute group who had formed the Danish consortium chose not to press charges regarding the faudulent geological assessment and, instead, took economic advantage of the situation. They bought Sebastian's—including the mines—at a fair market price, launching immediately into full-scale exploration of other gemstones and shifting their marketing strategy.

Bethany's father sold his practice to an aggressive junior partner with numerous contacts in Boston's up-and-coming entrepreneurial class. It wasn't long before the stuffed-shirt image of Grey & Associates gave way to a more modern look as the young lawyer took on a brash young clientele with condominium investments on the waterfront and glitzy galleries in the Back Bay—even a rock bank or two retained the firm as counsel. Burgess adjusted to retirement by lecturing at Harvard and writing a law text in his study at home.

Sebastian earned enough from the proceeds of the sale to retire comfortably with Zoe at their country home in Ouro Prêto, even departing from tradition enough to allow his wife to pay for periodic cruises and European vacations with the money left her by Vladimir.

It never ceased to astound Bethany that people could not only endure such thoroughly monumental shake-ups in their lives but even end up being better persons for having weathered their misfortunes, like rough gemstones made perfect by grinding and polishing.

In a few months, Burgess and Georgina would be coming down to Brazil to join Sebastian and Zoe on a cruise down the Amazon. Paulo, with his legendary charm, had affected the reconciliation. He'd chosen the one occasion when grudges are hardest to maintain—his and Bethany's wedding—and simply persuaded everyone to sit down and talk.

The story of Zoe's being disinherited was simply an excuse Burgess had learned to rely on when it suited his convenience to explain his estrangement from his sister. Their father had, in fact, written her back into the will soon after her first husband died. Georgina, too, changed her opinion of Zoe as soon as Burgess decided it was time for the families to be reconciled. Besides, Paulo wanted his stepmother and mother-in-law to get along, and Georgina found it hard to refuse her son-in-law anything.

Bethany and Paulo wouldn't be accompanying them on the cruise this time. They were too busy with their new business: a small but thriving gem shop in Copacabana called The Crimson Butterfly.

Bethany, her face now a golden tan, smiled. Paulo would be coming home for dinner soon, and she had a few last-minute ingredients to add to the shrimp salad marinating in the refrigerator. Paulo had turned out to be even more successful with his own customers than he'd been at Sebastian's. People were drawn at first to The Crimson Butterfly's intriguing decor. Red-and-white-striped awnings shaded the entrance, and the interior of the shop was embellished by whimsical displays of Brazilian butterflies created in mosaics of garnet, citrine and chrysoberyl; Bethany had done all the decorating herself. Her principal job was to take care of the books; the rest was Paulo's domain. He was a natural with people. Once the customers stepped inside, they were treated like royalty, even if they'd only come in to ask for directions. The store already enjoyed a sizable local following, and word of the attractive shop and its charming owners was spreading fast among major hotels and tour operators.

In what turned out to be a very wise move, Paulo had sold his beachfront condominium, which enabled them not only to purchase the shop but also to make a down payment on a three-bedroom house in the mountains. A simple but comfortable home, it had whitewashed walls, a red-tiled roof and arched doorways. Bethany had used her savings to purchase furniture, every piece of which she and Paulo chose together. Most of it was rattan, upholstered in fiery florals. The Boston rocker, of course, occupied a very important place in the living room, which offered a spectacular view through the picture window.

"Daydreaming again, are we?" a low seductive voice came from behind. "How's a man supposed to get a decent dinner around here?"

Bethany whirled around, the long skirt of her white lace Fortaleza dress billowing out as she turned. "Paulo!" she cried, reaching out to him, "you're home early!"

"I asked Maria to lock up for me tonight," he answered, his dark eyes dancing over the low bodice of her dress hungrily and lovingly for an instant. Then he swept her into his arms and kissed her. "Mmm, I couldn't wait any longer to get home to you, *querida*." He stepped back, and his fingers toyed with the scarlet satin ribbon laced through her dress and tied in a bow between her breasts.

"Paulo!" Bethany chided with fierce joy. "You know what happens when you untie the bow."

His face split in a devilish grin. "Your dress falls off; that's why it's my favorite."

Bethany whacked him playfully across the hand. "You beast! This is the one dress that doesn't make me look like a beached whale. It's the only reason I wear it." On a billow of lace, she floated past him toward the kitchen, loving every word of their carefree banter, amazed at how radiant and feminine she felt with the new life growing inside her.

Paulo, far from being awkward or inattentive during his wife's pregnancy, seemed to cherish her even more as her condition progressed. Evenings they would spend hours lounging on the terrace, holding each other. He'd massage her back and her legs, and concoct incredible—and at times, undrinkable—vitamin-enriched shakes for her from cashews and papayas and coconut milk. Most of all, he loved to talk about their prospective parenthood and to feel the baby kick against Bethany's abdomen. His love must somehow have communicated itself to the unborn child, for each time he uttered some endearment to it in his deep voice, Bethany would feel such kicking and churning iñ response that she laughingly likened it to a soccer match. The experience, however delightful in principle, was becoming distinctly uncomfortable. Although she was only five and a half months along, she had grown quite large.

Paulo set the table while Bethany arranged the salad on a platter with garnishes of fresh tomatoes and lettuce. In the background, the radio was playing a soft samba rhythm.

She waited until they were seated before she spoke. "Paulo, you know how you're always talking about forming your very own soccer team?"

Chewing a forkful of shrimp salad, Paulo creased his cheeks in a grin. "Yes, I remember—composed entirely of little Andrades—but I also said I'd settle for a volleyball team if you weren't up to having eleven children."

His wife rested her elbows on the table, laced her fingers together and propped them under her chin. "That issue is still up for debate, but what would you say to one-third of a volleyball team?"

Paulo lowered his brows and regarded her closely. "Six on a team...and one-third makes two—" His dark eyes widened, and when Bethany answered his questioning look wtih a nod, he nearly knocked over the table in his effort to reach her. "Twins? We're going to have twins?"

Bethany heaved a great sigh of relief. "You are happy?"

He brought her to her feet and pulled her to him. With one hand cupping her chin and his other arm around her shoulders, he said, *"Querida*, every day I thank my lucky stars that you came into my life and were willing to leave your home and your family to share a life with me. Now you're about to bless me with not one child but two—me, who never had the pleasure of knowing a brother or sister." Paulo tilted his head to kiss her deeply. "Yes, Bethany, I'm happy we're having twins; and it's always nicer to play ball with two children than with one."

Bethany laughed delightedly. "I love you so much, Paulo."

His arms dropped to his sides, and he gave her a stern look. "I love you, too, Senhora Andrade, but you are going to have to sit down and finish your dinner. For dessert, I'll make you a cashew-and-artichoke milkshake."

She gave her best rendition of an obedient smile, recalling the many shakes that had fertilized the jacaranda tree near the terrace. "It sounds delicious, dear," Bethany replied sweetly. "I think I'll have it outdoors."

What romance fans say about Harlequin…

"…scintillating, heartwarming…
a very important, integral part of mass-
market literature."

"…it is a pleasure to escape behind a
Harlequin and go on a trip to a faraway
country."

"Their wonderfully depicted settings make
each and every one a joy to read."

*Names available on request.

EYE OF THE STORM

MAURA SEGER

A powerful
portrayal of
the events of
World War II in the
Pacific, *Eye of the Storm* is a riveting story of how love
triumphs over hatred. In this, the first of a three-book
chronicle, Army nurse Maggie Lawrence meets Marine
Sgt. Anthony Gargano. Despite military regulations
against fraternization, they resolve to face together
whatever lies ahead.... Author Maura Seger, also known
to her fans as Laurel Winslow, Sara Jennings, Anne
MacNeil and Jenny Bates, was named 1984's
Most Versatile Romance Author by *The Romantic Times*.

You're invited to accept 4 books and a surprise gift Free!

Acceptance Card

Mail to: **Harlequin Reader Service**®

In the U.S.
2504 West Southern Ave.
Tempe, AZ 85282

In Canada
P.O. Box 2800, Postal Station A
5170 Yonge Street
Willowdale, Ontario M2N 6J3

YES! Please send me 4 free Harlequin Superromance® novels and my free surprise gift. Then send me 4 brand new novels every month as they come off the presses. Bill me at the low price of $2.50 each—a 10% saving off the retail price. There are no shipping, handling or other hidden costs. There is no minimum number of books I must purchase. I can always return a shipment and cancel at any time. Even if I never buy another book from Harlequin, the 4 free novels and the surprise gift are mine to keep forever.

134 BPS-BPGE

Name _____ (PLEASE PRINT)

Address _____ Apt. No. _____

City _____ State/Prov. _____ Zip/Postal Code _____